THE SELFISH SERIES | BOOK THREE

sel*fl*ess

SHANTEL TESSIER

Copyright © 2017 by Shantel Tessier
All rights reserved.

No part of this book may be reproduced or transmitted in any form or by any means, electronic or mechanical, including photocopying, recording, or by any information storage and retrieval system without the written permission of the author, except for the use of brief quotations in a book review.

This book is a work of fiction. Names, characters, places, and incidents either are products of the author's imagination or are used fictitiously. Any resemblance to actual persons, living or dead, events, or locales is entirely coincidental.

For more information about the author and her books, visit her website- www.shanteltessierauthor.com. You can sign up for her newsletter on her website, or you can click on the link below. The newsletter is the only place to get exclusive teasers, first to know about current projects and release dates. And also have chances to win some amazing giveaways- http://goo.gl/4wd9CV

Cover Designer Dark Waters Covers
Editor Jenny Sims
Formatter CP Smith

DEDICATION

I want to dedicate this book to my husband, Jason. Happy Birthday, baby. Thank you for always believing in me even when I don't. You are my inspiration for Ryder. All the sweet and romantic things he says and does for Ashlyn, you always say and do for me. You truly do treat me like a queen. I love the hell out of you. And don't know what I would do without you. Our love story is not like any other. We are the exception to the rule. Here's to a love that will never fade or bend. We are stronger than the heaviest winds.

Love is a smoke made with the fume of sighs. William Shakespeare

THE SELFISH SERIES | BOOK THREE
selfless

CHAPTER ONE

RYDER

I pull my phone out of my pocket and send a quick text to Milton to tell him to come back and pick me up when I hear the door to her apartment open.

"Ryder." Ashlyn calls out as the elevator doors start to close.

I look up at her from my phone and hate how sorry those beautiful blue eyes look. Like she knows she just broke my heart. She stands there, that overly large shirt still on, but she added a pair of sweatpants and flip-flops.

With everything I have in me, I manage to pull my eyes away from her and look back down to my phone.

"Wait." I hear her call out but I make no attempt to stop the doors from closing.

She jumps inside just in time, trying to catch her breath before begging. "Ryder, please. Let me explain,"

"What's there to explain?" I ask flatly as I place my phone in my pocket and look up to see how many more floors I have to endure with her. The space is closing in on me. The smell of her sweet perfume is enough to knock me off my feet.

She sucks in a deep breath. "I didn't—"

"You know; it doesn't matter what you have to say." I interrupt her. "I get it." I don't get it, though. I want to turn to her and ask her why? What had I done wrong? What did Bradley do that he deserves her?

But I close my lips.

"You don't," she says defensively.

I can't listen to her voice anymore. "Save it," I say, still refusing to look at her. I can't look into those blue eyes or at those soft lips. I can't look at the face I've come to dream about. Saw a future with. All of that is gone now. "I get it, Ashlyn. He's your best friend. That you fuck."

"He's my best friend, but ..."

"You guys are different," I say, interrupting her. There's nothing she can tell me that she hasn't already informed me of. "You've said that." I nod once still unable to look at her. I may break. I have to be strong. I'm not some pussy who needs a woman to love them. I fuck them! I'm the male version of her! I'm not gonna beg and plead for her to want me.

I feel her hand reach out to me, and my entire body tenses. Just the thought of her touching him and then me ... it's too much.

The elevator dings, and the mirrored doors slide open and I all but run out of it and through the lobby of the Q's. I'm not far from the glass front doors when I feel her hand grab my upper arm, and she yanks me to a stop. My muscles tense, but I can't hold it back anymore. I spin around and harden my eyes as I look down into her blue ones. They're full of unshed tears, and they piss me off. "Why are you down here, Ashlyn?" I snap, my voice echoing through the large lobby.

She cringes and speaks softly. "I want to apologize."

I yank my arm free of her hold. "No need to apologize for who you are."

Her eyes widen in shock at my words, and she wraps her arms around herself. "What does that mean?" she whispers as her eyes search mine as if she's looking for some kind of sympathy. She won't find it!

"Just a fuck!" I state carelessly then, without wasting another second, I turn around and walk out the front doors, leaving her standing there holding herself.

I can feel her stare on me, and it just makes me even more pissed! She practically chased me out of her apartment and for what? To tell me that she loves him? That after all this time, she finally realizes Bradley is the guy for her? That she's sorry she couldn't love me? No thanks.

I don't need her to explain that I've lost the war. I figured that out all on my own.

"Mr. O'Kane ..." Milton greets me. Guess he got my text. "Something wrong?"

"Shut it, Milton!" I snap, making my way to my Cadillac that he has parked curbside.

I get into the back and pull the door shut before he can do it. I keep my face straight ahead even though she wouldn't be able to see me with the blacked-out windows anyway. I refuse to do it!

I can see Milton out of the corner of my eye as he pauses by my window. I close my eyes and take a deep breath, and I wish I could erase the past three weeks of my life.

I open them when I hear the front driver's side door open. Milton looks at me through the rearview mirror. His dark eyes look at me as if waiting for me to say something. "Something wrong?" I snap.

His brows pull together and his eyes look away from me to focus on the entrance of the Q's— she must still be standing there. "What are we waiting on?" I demand.

His eyes come back to mine in the rearview. "Nothing, sir." He places the SUV in gear and pulls into traffic as lightning lights up the night.

I lay my head against the headrest and let out a sigh. Fuck, she left my life just like she came into it—fast and unexpected!

I sit straight up, the nightmare finally over, when I hear a sound of a door hitting a wall. "Shit!" I hiss, and my hands come to my pounding head.

"Mr. O'Kane?"

"What?" I snap, looking up at my assistant, Kelly, as she walks toward me.

What the hell? I look around and realize I'm lying on my office floor. Did I sleep here?

She frowns as she looks down at me. "Here. I got you some coffee." Kelly hands me a mug, and I bring it to my lips, taking a small sip.

"Thank you," I say and notice that my voice is scratchy. I set the mug between my legs and let my head fall into my hands. Fuck, what did I do last night?

"Here's some Advil," she says.

"Do you happen to know how I ended up like this?" *God, I hope I didn't fuck her!*

She shakes her head. "I came in an hour ago and found you on the floor."

Phew! My father already fired his assistant for sleeping with me. I'd hate to have to fire mine. "An hour ago …?" I grab my phone from the floor beside me. Hitting a button, I wait as it lights up. "Shit!" It's almost nine o'clock.

"I tried to wake you …"

"You should have tried harder," I growl, running a hand through my hair. She reaches out her hand to help me stand, and I shove it away. I manage to get up by myself, but once I'm upright, the room sways a bit. Looking down at my clothes, I close my eyes and sigh. "I need to change."

"I'll go to your apartment and get you a suit."

That would make her useful. "Thanks," I say with a head nod, and she turns around, leaving me alone.

Sitting in my chair, I place my elbows on my desk and let my head fall into my hands. "What the hell did I do last night?" I remember walking into Ashlyn's apartment to find her standing half-dressed with Bradley. Then I stormed out. I thought I came up to the office, but I don't remember drinking up here.

I take a quick look around and don't see any empty bottles on the floor or on my desk. I open my phone to see if I spoke to anyone. I had received a text from Vicki last night around midnight.

Vicki: *I need to talk to you. It's important.*

Thankfully, I hadn't responded. I go to my recent call list and see that I had a phone call from Ashlyn that lasted thirty-one seconds.

I drop the phone onto my desk as if it went up in flames. "Fuck!" This day just keeps getting better.

What did I say to her?

Why did I even fucking answer it?

What had she called to tell me? Sorry? Would she have been that stupid? To think I needed an apology? To think I cared that fucking much?

That's the shitty part ... I do care that much. Or I wouldn't have woken up on my office floor feeling like a truck ran over me. I've never had that happen before. Not until her.

I throw my almost dead phone across my office, and it hits the wall with a thud before falling to the floor.

Minutes later, I remain behind my desk with my head in my hands. It's still pounding. And as if on cue, my office phone starts to ring. It's gonna be a typical Monday.

"Yes, Mr. Lowe. I can get it signed and back to you today," I say into my phone with my head still down.

The door to my office bangs open, and I jump to my feet, letting out a long breath when I see it's my sister. "I'll have to call you back," I say then hang up as I hear him protesting. "Becca? What are you doing here?" My head pounds harder from the sudden movement, and I feel a little dizzy.

"How long?" she demands.

I run a hand through my hair because I know it's standing every other way from sleeping on my floor. I don't want her to go back and tell Ashlyn just how awful I look. I run my hands down my wrinkled t-shirt that I wore to the bar last night. Kelly still hasn't had the chance to leave yet to pick me up a suit. Shit just keeps coming up. "I'm not doing this with you," I say, knowing whatever she is asking has to do with Ashlyn.

"How long, Ryder?" she demands again.

"It's over." I growl. Does she think I'm playing some game with Ashlyn? I'm not like her. I either want all of her or none at all. I'm not playing hard to get. It's over, and it hurts like fucking hell.

She stomps up to my desk, letting me know she's not giving up on this, and I hold in a sigh. "How long before you buy Talia's?"

My eyes widen at her words. "How do you know about the Anderson file...?"

"How could you do this to Ashlyn?" she asks, interrupting me. "You know what this job means to her."

I sigh. "It's business." I decide to say, but I've been thinking the same thing since I found out where Ashlyn had her job interview.

"Business?" she asks with a huff. "God, you sound just like Dad," she growls.

"I have a job to do."

"And Ashlyn is going to lose hers," she snaps. "When do you plan to tell her?"

I look away from her, and my eyes narrow on where I slept on the floor last night. I can't talk to her. I just can't. Call me a pussy. A dick. Either one would be true. "That's none of your business." I decide on.

She slams her hands down on my desk and I look back up at her. "I thought you were a good guy, Ryder. I thought you loved her. But now I see you're not capable of that."

My jaw tightens at her words. If only she knew just how much …

"You're a lot like Mom in that way. All you care about is money." My nostrils flare. I'm nothing like our mother. I would never do to Ashlyn, what she has done to our father. "So just so you know, if you do this, you'll never get her back."

Get her back? Doesn't she understand that is not an option? Did she not see what happened in their kitchen? Is she honestly going to pretend that Bradley didn't stay the night again last night at their place? "She was never mine to begin with," I respond flatly.

"You're right," she says and then swallows. "She wasn't." Then she turns around and storms out just as quickly as she entered.

• • •

My day hasn't gotten any better. In fact, it has gotten worse, if that's even possible. My headache is still pounding, and the words my sister said before she walked out of my office keep repeating in my head. *You're right. She never was!*

How did I not fucking see it? And why can't I seem to let it go? I just continue to torture myself.

"Ryder, are you there?"

"Yes, Mr. Clevens," I say into my phone, nodding my head as I try to hold it to my ear with my shoulder. My eyes scan over the papers that scatter my desk. I don't even know what he said to me. "What was it you …?"

"I asked how much longer you think it will be," he snaps, irritated with me.

"Maybe a week or two …"

"What?" he huffs. "You said it would be two days last Friday. It's now Monday!"

Fuck! "I know, but things came up …" My eyes catch sight of a document with his name on it.

"What the hell has come up that it's gonna take another two weeks?" he demands. He doesn't let me answer. "Ryder, you know this deal is very important to me and my company. It needs to be done. Now!"

"Yes. I agree, but …" My life is no longer my own. I wish I could focus on what is important, but I can't seem to focus on anything but the gorgeous blonde who somehow managed to make me fall in love with her just to break my heart.

"This is not acceptable," he huffs.

"I know," I growl, mad at myself. "I made the call. Now, I'm just waiting to hear back …" I look up as something catches my eyes to see Jaycent in my office. *When did he come in?*

"Ryder?" Mr. Clevens snaps in my ear. "Fix it or I will go somewhere else," he all but shouts.

"I'll take care of it," I say, but he's already hung up. I lift my head, and my phone drops from my shoulder and hits my desk with a thud. I don't bother to put it on the receiver.

"Bad day?" Jaycent asks.

Letting out a frustrated sigh, I snap, "Fuck this day."

He plops down in front of my desk as if he's here to stay. "Drank a little too much last night," he observes, looking me over.

"Not sure how much I had," I say honestly, still having no memory of last night. Kelly was finally able to go to my apartment and pick me up a suit, but I haven't had the chance to put it on yet.

"Enough to want to fuck a woman in the bathroom," he says flatly.

My head snaps up, and I look at him wide-eyed "I did what?" God, I hope it wasn't Vicki. She did send me a text …

He holds up his hand. "You didn't do it. Just tried." I fall into my chair and let out a long breath. "You really remember nothing?" he asks, leaning forward and placing his elbows on his knees.

I shake my head. "I woke up this morning on my office floor with a pounding headache and smelling like booze,"

He sniffs the air and pulls his lips back. "You do stink."

I snort. "That's the least of my worries."

He sits back and stares at me as if I've fallen off the deep end. So I continue to fill him in on my day. "Then my sister shows up yelling at me about how I should do business." I huff. "Like she knows what she's talking about."

"Did she make sense?" he asks.

I shake my head. "No. She doesn't know what's going on here, and I don't have time to explain that to her." She has a point. I've known all along that Ashlyn would lose her job. I didn't tell her 'cause I didn't want her to hate me. Now she's gonna think I did it for revenge. I'm fucked either way.

He nods as if he understands what kind of hole I have dug myself, but he can't possibly know how deep I'm in. "And Ashlyn? How is that going?"

"It's over." I'm so tired of people talking to me about her.

"You didn't seem that way last night. You were checking your phone every two minutes." I snort, hoping I didn't look like the little bitch I am. "Then you were willing to go to the bathroom with that woman like you were a man trying to forget another."

"I've already forgotten," I say flatly. Lies. All lies.

"You told me that you loved her." My body stiffens where I sit. My eyes drill into his with my shoulders pulled back and body rigid. "Pretty sure you've felt that way long before last night. Remember that?" he goes on, shoving the knife deeper into my chest. He sighs when I say nothing. "Ryder, she …"

"I don't wanna talk about Ashlyn," I snap, and he stops. "It's over. I have shit to do. Shouldn't you be at work as well?"

He stands from the chair. "Yep," he says and walks out, leaving me alone.

My head falls on my desk, and I take a deep breath. I should be ashamed of how pathetic I am. How I let myself get to this point over a woman. But instead, I just want to crawl into a hole. This morning, waking up here and hungover, I realize I can't go home. I can't chance seeing her on the elevator. In the lobby. Or out on the sidewalk. I have to move. Or possibly just live in my office. That's when I realized I was at an all-time low. The fact that I'd rather live in my office than go home to my million-dollar apartment made me realize that no matter what, my life will never be the same without Ashlyn.

"What are you doing?" I hear a familiar voice ask.

I lift my head to see my father standing in my office, his hands in the pockets of his black slacks and dark brows pulled together in confusion.

I clear my throat and sit up straight. "Trying to get some privacy," I tell him truthfully. "But people just keep walking in like they own the place."

"I do own the place," he says matter-of-factly.

I hold in a sigh. "What do you want, Dad?" I ask, rubbing my temples. They won't quit pounding. Why isn't this Advil working?

"So you broke up with your girlfriend and now your work is going to go to shit." he states.

I narrow my eyes up at him. "Who told you I broke up with …?" My words trail off. I tilt my head to the side, and he raises a brow. "How did you know I was seeing someone?" I demand.

"I knew you were seeing Ashlyn," he declares, and my jaw tightens. "I also know that she broke up with you."

"I broke up with her," I snap.

He rolls his eyes as if I sounded like a child, and I hate to admit I did.

I square my shoulders. "Who told you?"

"Doesn't matter." I go to argue, but he continues. "But I know that you look like shit." His eyes look me up and down with disgust. "And I know you've kept yourself locked in this office all day." He takes a quick look around and sees my suit that Kelly brought me earlier still lying on the back of my couch as if it cost a hundred dollars and not three grand. "And I know that you need a shower," he adds.

"Are you done?" I growl.

"Not yet." He removes his hands from his pockets and comes to sit down in front of my desk. "I also know that Ashlyn works at Talia's."

Now it's my turn to roll my eyes and mumble. "Here we go …"

"How many times have I told you not to mix business with

pleasure?" he demands.

I throw my hands up. "I didn't know she had an interview with them until after I slept with her," I declare, and he shakes his head. "And why the hell were they even hiring anyway? What was I supposed to do? She was so excited when they called her and told her she had the job. I didn't feel like *oh, yeah they're going out of business. I'm gonna buy it and tear the place down and build another hotel. 'Cause that's what this town fucking needs* was a good thing to say at the time." My jaw is tight and so is my chest. So much is building up inside that I want to scream. I fist my hands down on my desk.

He places his elbows on his knees and leans forward. "Ryder ..."

"Save it, Dad," I snap. "I've had a shit day, and it's not over yet. Becca's come in here and jumped down my throat, and then Jaycent came in here giving his two cents on my problems and how I should handle them. If you don't mind, I want to be alone. I have work to do." I gesture to the stacks of papers scattered on my desk. "I may smell and look like shit, but I'm still here."

He sits back in his seat and crosses his arms over his chest. "Is Talia's going to be a problem?" he finally asks.

This is my dad. Business first. Out of everyone I know, he is the only one who will understand that part of my life. No matter what, you do whatever you have to do to make that dollar. That's why things would have never worked out with Ashlyn. No matter how much I wanted it to, she would never understand that part of my life. That you do whatever it takes to make a buck. That you don't get where I am by being nice and making friends. It's cutthroat and bloody. And I will never change that part of my life. Not even for her.

I shake my head. "No." The only answer I have. And that alone would have torn us apart eventually.

He stares at me for a long second before finally rising from his chair. "Okay then." And with that, he turns and walks out, shutting my door behind him.

ASHLYN

I called in sick to work today. I couldn't sleep last night. I laid in my bed, eyes wide open as tears spilled down the side of my face as I cried in silence. So many emotions ran through me that I felt as if I was being torn in a hundred different ways. I would go from angry to sad then to feeling sorry for myself. It was pathetic, but I couldn't stop it. This morning, when it was finally time to go to work, I just laid there. I couldn't get my body to move. I felt nauseous, and my puffy eyes were finally getting heavy, so I picked up my phone and called in.

I stayed home locked away in my room. I only got up once to get a bottle of water 'cause I was tired of tasting my own tears when Jaycent knocked on the door. I let him in and then went straight back to my room. That was about an hour ago. Now I find myself back on my bed holding my phone, waiting for it to ring. Hoping that Ryder would have called me sometime today. But nothing. I think calling him last night was the biggest mistake I have ever made.

I take another drink of the wine, and my throat tightens. Every girl wants to be the exception. We all want that one guy to make us feel like we're worth it all. I feel that way about him. And that thought makes me want to jump. Makes me want to tell him how I feel. How much I need him. I have to do it for me.

Taking a deep breath, I pick up my phone and dial his number before I change my mind. The first ring has my heart beating faster. The second one has me taking another gulp of the wine. By the fourth ring, I'm pacing again.

"This was a terrible idea ..."

The ringing stops and so does my pacing. He's silent on the other end, but he picked up. That's a start ... "Ryder," I say, trying to swallow the lump that instantly forms in my throat. "I'm sorry." I sniff, and I hate that admitting that makes me feel worse. "I know I messed up, but it wasn't what you think. I swear I didn't sleep with him." Once I start talking, I can't stop. Tears run down my face as I cling to the cold wine bottle, and my eyes are fixated on the Romeo and Juliet *book. All I can think is that I have to get this off my chest. Becca was right. I have to do it for myself. I have to clear my conscience. What he chooses to do next is up to him.*

"I ... I love you, Ryder." My throat tightens, and my hands gets

clammy, admitting that to him. "Please know that I wouldn't do anything to hurt you." The words pour out like a dam needing to free all the extra water.

And then I start to panic over what I just said. I hang up, and my phone drops to my floor, landing by my feet

I poured out my heart last night and got nothing in return! I never knew loving someone could be so painful. Now I know why I've never done it before!

A knock comes on my door, and I find myself saying, "Come in."

"Hey, are you busy?" Becca asks, peeking her head in.

I shake mine. "Come on in."

She walks in and shuts it behind her. She sits down on the end of the bed, and Harry jumps up and crawls into her lap. "Who are you talking to?" she asks when she sees my screen light up.

"Bradley." I sigh and push the button on the side to hide my screen from her.

He, on the other hand, keeps messaging me. But I don't have anything to say to him. "He is still in New York," I tell her.

Her eyes widen. "What does he want?"

"He's staying at a hotel and wants me to come and see him." Why won't he give up like Ryder did? It would be easier if he did. I hate to hurt him twice.

"Are you going to go?"

I shake my head. "I don't think that's a good idea."

"I need to talk to you," she says, and I can hear the turmoil in her voice.

I turn to face her. "Okay. What is it?"

"I spoke with Ryder toda—"

"Please tell me you didn't do it for me," I interrupt her. "Honestly, I'm fine, Becca," I lie. I should have never called him last night. It was another mistake. I can't seem not to make one.

She runs a hand through her hair. "It wasn't for you," she says softly. "I had heard something and needed to find out for myself."

"What was it?" I ask, wondering what could make her this upset.

She takes a deep breath. "O'Kane's Enterprises is buying Talia's."

I frown, not really understanding what she is saying. "What do you mean buying Talia's?"

"I don't know the specifics; I just know they are buying it."

Ryder is buying the company I work for? What does that mean? Why would they want a gallery? And then it clicks, stinging like salt to a wound.

I look down at the wood floors and ask, "When?"

"I'm not sure. I'm sorry I don't know much. Ryder wouldn't give me much information about it. He said it wasn't any of my business. But I guess it's been in the works for a while."

I nod, still not looking up at her. Complete and utter failure is what I'm feeling right now, and it burns like a bitch. "Thank you for telling me."

She reaches out and grabs my hand. "I know this is hard to hear, but it's going to be okay."

I nod again and then remove my hand from hers. "Maybe it's just better if I go back home." Those words are hard to say, but the truth is never easy to hear.

She stands quickly. "No. That's not why I told you. That's not the answer."

"Then what is the answer?" I look up at her. Tears start to burn my eyes.

"You're not a quitter," she says. "I know you, and the Ashlyn I know wouldn't let a man dictate her life." I sigh. "Ashlyn, you are tough. You are the woman I've always wanted to be."

The first tear falls down my cheek. "We have time. I will help you find another job. I know you left your family in Seattle, but I'm your family here. And I'm not going anywhere. Please tell me you'll stay. Tell me that you will not let Ryder get the best of you. Because he doesn't deserve that."

I look around my fancy bedroom. The four-post bed up against the far wall. The white down comforter that feels like a cloud is rumpled and hanging half off the bed from all my tossing and turning last night. The floor-to-ceiling windows have my handprints on them from looking down over the city last night, and the clothes and throw pillows cover the floor. And the truth hits me like a bag of bricks. "I never belonged here," I say truthfully. It was all a big fairy tale from the beginning. Being with Ryder. Coming to New York. I should have never left what I knew just to start over.

"Please don't do this," she begs as a tear runs down her cheek as well. "If you leave, I leave."

I give her a soft smile as another tear rolls down my face. "I won't let you give up on what you have." She's crazy if she thinks I'll let her pick me over all this that she has here in New York. She's finally away from Conner and happy with Jaycent. I don't wanna be responsible for someone else's happiness.

"And you think I'll let you give up on what you have?" she asks with a sniff.

"What is it that I have?" I ask with a careless shrug. Everything I own can fit in three suitcases.

New York was a mistake. But it's one that I can fix.

"You have me," she says with another sniff.

I reach my arms out wide. "You have a life here. A man who loves you and your family."

"You're my family," she all but shouts. "Please let me prove it to you."

I look away from her because I've already made up my mind. I'm moving back to Seattle. But I tell her, "Okay."

She leans down and hugs me tightly. She knows I'm lying, and I hate that I'm going to have to hurt her. Because she truly is my sister. My best friend. Now that I've lost Bradley, she's my only friend.

She walks out of my room with her head down and sniffing. And before I can sit on the end of my bed, I find myself running to my bathroom feeling that nausea again.

• • •

Tuesday morning went about as good as Monday did. But I managed to drag myself into work after another night of no sleep. I stared at my phone for hours. Just waiting for a text or call from Ryder. And just like yesterday, it never came. But unlike yesterday, I have to go to work today.

"Wow, honey!" Thomas says as I walk past him and fall into my chair. "You look like crap."

"Thanks," I mumble.

I haven't washed my hair since Sunday, and no amount of makeup could cover the dark circles under my eyes.

"What's going on?" he asks, leaning over my desk with a look of worry on his face. "I know you called in sick yesterday, but it looks like more than a cold."

I sigh. Of course, I can't go a day without him wanting to know what is really wrong.

"Oh, no." He comes around the desk quickly and plops down beside me. "I know that tune. You're having boy trouble." I remain silent. "Is that why you were pissy yesterday when I called you?" He had called me last night to check on me. I wasn't up to chatting, to say the least.

"I'm fine," I say, refusing to look him in the eye.

"You are a little liar," he says, giving my shoulder a little shove.

"Sweetheart, believe me, men come and go. You need to get out there and get some booty."

"That's the reason I'm in this position in the first place," I say dryly, and he laughs as if I'm funny. I turn my body and face him in my chair. "O'Kane's is buying Talia's," I tell him, expecting him to stop laughing, but he doesn't.

"Oh, hun, that's been a rumor for years." He waves me off.

I frown. "A rumor?"

He nods. "Well, not O'Kane's specifically. But the fact that Talia's is going to be bought out."

My eyes widen. "And what do you plan on doing when that happens?"

"I'm not worried," he says with confidence that I don't have.

He reaches out and places his hand on my shoulder. "It will all be okay. You're stressing too much."

"You sound like Becca," I tell him.

He gives me a big smile. "Then you should listen to us. We can't both be wrong," he says, removing his hand from my shoulder and then shrugging.

And I hate to tell him that he can.

"Good morning, everyone!" I look up to see our boss, Mrs. Mills, walking down the winding staircase. She smiles brightly at us as she hits the last step. "We have a private showing in two weeks," she informs us. "I will need you both to stay late every day next week."

Thomas nods as I tell her no problem. "Good," she says, placing her purse over her shoulder and walking to the door.

I get up from my chair and all but run over to her. "Mrs. Mills, may I have a second of your time?" I ask nervously.

She looks at me, and her brows pull together. "Is everything okay, Ashlyn?" she asks, noticing the change in my tone.

I nod. "It will only take a moment," I assure her.

"Of course," she says. "Let's talk in my office."

CHAPTER TWO

RYDER

It's been four days since I saw Ashlyn and Bradley in her apartment, and I have to say the pain is starting to ease up. Now, I'm just pissed! At her. I'm pissed she invades my thoughts! That she came into my life. Then just left me hanging. She was everything I didn't know I wanted!

The worst part is that I'm not able to drown myself in booze. I've refused to stay at my apartment; that one I'm not budging on. I don't want to see her or Bradley. Who knows if he is still here visiting her. I mean, for all I know, she went back to Seattle with him. I don't know. I'm not speaking to my sister or Jaycent, so I am out of the Ashlyn loop. And that's how I plan on keeping it.

The shitty part is that I actually have to work. My father walked into my office this morning and threw a file on my desk before ordering me to get my ass up 'cause our plane was leaving in twenty.

Now I stand in a Philadelphia high rise, talking to a group of men who want to partner with me and my dad. And the sad part is I couldn't care how much money they offer us. I'd much rather be at a local Hooters getting drunk off cheap beer and eating wings while getting a good show. My father was right—my work is going to shit.

My father's phone rings, and he answers it. "What is it, Kelly?" he asks.

I look up at him and frown. *Why is my assistant calling him?*

"Did she say what was wrong?" he asks.

"Ryder …?" I turn to face the man who said my name. "Are you listening?" he asks, holding his hands out wide.

I hold up my finger. "Give me one second, gentlemen," I say to the others as I take a step toward my dad.

"Okay. I'll call her. Thank you, Kelly," he says and hangs up.

"What's going on?" I ask him, but he ignores me as he scrolls through his phone and pulls up a new number and then places his phone back to his ear. It has to be my sister. He wouldn't care this much about our mother.

I stay close to him to see what all I can hear.

"Becca, is everything okay?" he asks into his phone, confirming I was right. "Ryder's assistant just called me and told me that you showed up at the office crying."

I frown. Crying? What could possibly be going on with her? I haven't spoken to Becca since she stormed into my office, and now I feel bad for ignoring her. What is she going through that would make her cry?

"What's wrong?" he asks her again after a long pause. "Are you okay? Did he hurt you?" he demands, and I pull my shoulders back. Who could possibly hurt her … Conner! Is he back? I pulled security off their apartment because the girls wanted me to. What if her hurt her? What if he hurt Ashlyn? I fist my hands.

"Dad …?"

"Mr. O'Kane?" James, the man who called this meeting, interrupts me looking at both of us with a cold expression. "I only have an hour," he reminds us.

"It'll only be a second," I lie, not knowing what to tell him. I want to know what the fuck is going on!

"What? No, Becca," my father says.

"Mr. O'Kane!" James snaps at me. I turn to tell him to fuck off when my father speaks.

"Excuse me, gentlemen." Then he exits the conference room.

I turn around, narrowing my eyes at him. He just ruined what little chance I had to hear what was going on.

He looks down at his watch. "I have a plane to catch in …"

"An hour. I know!" I say, interrupting him with a nod. I gesture to the chairs. "Then let's get down to it," I growl and plop down.

I took over the meeting while my father stood outside the conference room and talked to my sister. I watched him as I spoke to the men. I saw him eventually hang up, and then he made another phone call. He seemed more pissed when he returned than when he walked out to talk to my sister.

The fact that I closed the deal should have made him happier, but it didn't help.

An hour later, I'm sitting on my father's private jet on our way back to Manhattan for him to drop me off. Once we land, he has to go on to Houston. I finally decide to just come out and ask. "What is wrong with Becca?"

He sits across from me in the cream and tan leather seat, his head down and eyes on his phone as he types away. I'm guessing he's dealing with business. "Nothing."

I huff. "Lying to me? Really, Dad? What is going on with Becca?"

He looks up from his phone, eyes narrowed and jaw tight. "Why don't you text your sister and ask her." He made it sound like a question, but the arch of his brow tells me it's a challenge. Somehow, he knows I've cut everyone off, and I can't do that.

So I go a different direction. "Who was the other person you called?"

He lowers his eyes back down to his phone and answers. "Jaycent."

I frown. That doesn't make any sense. Becca calls him crying, and he then calls Jaycent. I mean, the two could be unrelated. Jaycent does a lot of work with us.

I open my mouth to speak to him when my phone goes off. I look down to see it's my mother. I press ignore and look out the window of his Gulfstream G6.

"Still ignoring Ashlyn?" he asks.

"Nope," I state and then close my mouth. He doesn't need to know my personal life. I've never been one to fill him in before, so why start now? And whatever we said to one another in those thirty seconds that night she called must have been enough. 'Cause she hasn't tried since.

"Then who else are you ignoring?" he asks.

I look over at him. "Mother," I say flatly.

"Ah, I see." He nods once. "Still avoiding her after what happened on your boat."

"What the fuck?" I snap. "How do you know everything that is going on in my life all of a sudden?" I demand.

"Come on, Ryder? You think you can embarrass Vicki on your boat and not expect your mother to call me afterward?"

I roll my eyes. "I liked it better when you all stayed out of my personal life."

"And I liked it better when you didn't have one," he responds flatly, his eyes still on his phone.

"What is that supposed to mean?" I growl.

He sets his phone down on his lap and gives me his full attention. "It means when you started working for me, your personal life became my problem." I snort. "Seriously, Ryder. You run around New York like a kid on a sugar high. You sleep with woman after woman. And that reflects badly on *my* company."

"Yeah? Well, I'm sorry I'm not more like you." I scoff.

"And what is that supposed to mean?"

"It means that I don't prefer to be alone with my work all the time. It means that I don't plan on settling and marrying a woman who I can't stand to be around." I look away and take a deep breath. My life is fucking falling apart, and I'm being a dick to the man for no reason. It's true he was never really there for me and Becca, but I'm not one of those kids who looks down on him. I look up to the man who works hard for his family. I know the life he chose came with sacrifices. And we were that offering.

I look back at him, and he too is looking away from me. He takes in a long breath and then lets it out, looking back at me. "I didn't always hate your mother," he says softly.

I hold up my hand. "You don't have to explain yourself to me, Dad. I under—"

"You don't," he interrupts me. "There's so much you don't know. That you didn't see." He pauses and swallows. "But you need to know one thing. Becca already knows, and I need you to be ready for whatever she throws at you."

"Who? Mom?" He nods. "What could she possibly *throw* at me?" I ask. "So what if I threw Vicki off the boat? She knows I don't give two shits about her. All she cares about is her reputation in this town."

"We're getting a divorce."

My eyes widen, and my mouth opens slightly. "A divorce?" I manage to say the words. He nods. "When did you …?" I tilt my head to the side in confusion. Honestly, I'm not all that surprised about the divorce. I'm only surprised he has finally decided to do it.

I should feel pain at his words. You hear kids all the time discussing how their parents' divorce ruined their lives and all that. But instead, I feel nothing. "When did this come about?" I find myself asking.

"I filed last week," he states. "Becca overheard me talking to your mother about it on the phone up at O'Kane's."

I frown. "Is that why she came into my office so pissy?"

He nods. "She overheard me and your mom talking, and your mom brought up Talia's."

"That's how Becca found out …." I wonder out loud.

He nods again. "I didn't know she had overheard me until Jaycent came and saw me and filled me in."

It all makes sense now. Why Kelly called my father earlier and told him she showed up crying. She's upset about my parents divorcing. Of course, she is. Becca takes everything to heart. She cares too much.

"Did Ashlyn know you are buying Talia's?" he asks.

"No." I never had the balls to tell her.

"Well, she probably does now. If your mother didn't tell her, I bet Becca did."

"Not like it matters," I say truthfully.

"It should," he says.

"And why is that? Her knowing isn't going to change the plan," I growl. I would have lost her anyway. If she hadn't pushed me away from the beginning, she would have hated me the moment she found out I was buying it.

He frowns. "I thought you loved her."

I shrug. "You taught me never to mix business with my personal life."

He looks away from me and sighs as if my words disappoint him, and I snort. "Now what?" I ask. He looks back at me but says nothing. "Please tell me what I can do to make you happy," I say sarcastically. "God knows I can't make anyone else happy these days," I snap.

He frowns. "What about you?"

"What about me?" I demand, getting irritated at how my life has taken a turn that I never saw coming.

"Are you happy?" he asks as his eyes look into mine.

I stare back, unable to answer that question. He's never asked me that before, but we both know I'm not. I look back out the window and lean my head against the seat as his phone rings. He answers, and the subject is dropped for now. Because I have a feeling he's gonna come back to that question someday soon, and the answer is gonna be the same. I'll never be happy because I lost the only woman I've ever loved.

My phone dings, and I look down to see I have a message from my mother.

Mom: *We need to talk.*

I ignore it like the last.

ASHLYN

Sitting on my bed, I'm talking to my mother and telling her about my day when I hear the front door open and slam shut. Then I hear Becca walk past my room and into hers.

"Hey Mom, I gotta call you back," I say and hang up, not waiting for her to say goodbye.

I make my way to her room and knock on her door before I open it. "Becca?"

She's lying on her bed but rolls over and wipes her wet cheeks. She doesn't say anything, so I go in and sit beside her. "Do you want to talk?"

She sits up and sighs. "I ran into Conner today, and he told me to tell my dad to stay away from him. So I went up to his work, but he is out of town. Ryder's assistant called my dad, and then he called me, and he told me that Jaycent had told him last week that Conner was being paid to date me."

My eyes widen, hoping I heard her wrong. "He was what?" I snap. "Your dad was paying him?" I demand.

She shakes her head. "I forgot you didn't know."

"Who the fuck was paying him?"

"My mother."

"What the fuck, Becca? For how long?" I all but shout.

"Four years," she whispers. I gasp and go to speak, but she lifts her hand. "Please let me finish." I close my mouth. "Well, Jaycent had found out I guess back in Panama when he beat Conner up in the bathroom. And then after Conner laid hands on you here, Jaycent went to my dad and asked him to take care of it. Well, I still hadn't known."

"When did you find out?" I ask through gritted teeth.

"The night on Ryder's boat. Vicki told me."

"That bitch knew about it?" I snap. "Who the fuck told her?"

"My mom." I let out a long breath. "I guess my mom wasn't secretive about it."

"Have you spoken to her about it?" She nods. "And did she deny it?"

She shakes her head. "She said that Conner was what I needed."

"Such a bitch," I growl. "So then what happened?"

"I broke up with Jaycent," she says matter-of-factly.

"Why would you do that?" I ask wide-eyed. "You love him."

"And I thought I loved Conner but look at how horrible that decision was." She sighs.

"Yeah, but they're not the same," I say, taking her hand. "I don't agree with what Jaycent did, but he was just trying to protect you." I give her a soft smile. "And Conner was only about himself."

"Maybe," she says and hangs her head.

"Hey." I grab her hands. "How about we heat some leftovers and watch *Top Gun*. Girls' night?" I suggest. I had planned on sitting in my room crying my eyes out over how my life has fallen apart, but my best friend needs me. I had no idea what she had been going through these past few days. I've been too busy wallowing in self-pity to open my damn eyes and see that she was hurting as well.

She finally nods, and my fake smile fades. "I'm so sorry, Becca."

"For what?" she asks.

"For everything you're going through. I should have been there for you and not so wrapped up in Ryder. I had no idea—"

"No, don't do that to yourself," she interrupts me. "You're a great friend. Don't think you're not. You've always been there for me."

I nod, but I'm not convinced. "What were you going to say to me on the boat that night before Ryder came in and interrupted you?" She asks.

I let go of her hand and sit back. "When Vicki realized who I was, she said that your mother had mentioned me. She said that I pulled you down. And that I was beneath all of you. And I wanted to apologize if you felt that way," I say softly.

"What?" She grabs my hand again. "No, Ashlyn. That's not even close to the truth. You are the best friend I've ever had. You have always been there for me. More than anyone else ever has. I just told you that my mother was paying my boyfriend to be with me. So don't believe anything she says."

I nod. "I just ... Ryder got mad at me because I told him that she was right. I don't fit into your guys' world. And what she said made some sense."

"Ashlyn, you are the best thing about my world," she says, and my eyes fill with tears. "You and your parents have taught me so much that I could never repay you."

"You don't owe me anything," I whisper.

"That's not how I see it," she adds with a smile. "I was in a new place scared to death with a man who at the time didn't give two shits about me. You took me in, and you all showed me what life was supposed to be about. To me, that means everything."

• • •

The following night, we sit on the couch watching *Top Gun* once again when we hear a knock on the door just as my phone rings in the bedroom.

I get up and run to my room to answer it. A part of me hopes it's Ryder. I sigh when I see it's Bradley. *He just won't stop.*

"Hello?" I ask, answering the damn thing.

"Hey," he says softly.

"Hey," I say, sitting down on the side of the bed.

"I, uh ..." He pauses, and I say nothing. "I need to see you."

"I don't think that's a good idea ..." I say honestly, not wanting to lead him on.

"Please. I'm begging you. Just come and see me."

I run a hand through my hair. "We shouldn't …"

"I'm not leaving New York until you see me," he says, changing his approach.

I fall onto my back and sigh. "Fine."

"Tonight?" he asks, pushing it as if I don't already have plans on this Friday night.

"Okay." Might as well get this over with.

He hangs up, and I sit. "We need a bottle of wine," I say, walking to the kitchen but stop when I see Mr. O'Kane standing in our apartment. I had thought Jaycent was at the door. "Oh, Mr. O'Kane," I say in surprise.

"Hello, Ashlyn," he says.

"Hello, sir," I say, looking back and forth between them. "I'll give you guys some space …"

"No need. I'm here to see you too." My brows lift. "May we?" He gestures to the living room.

Becca and I both nod and turn to make our way back to the living room. I sit beside her, and he sits on the couch across from us. "What are you doing here, Dad?" she asks.

He undoes the bottom button of his suit jacket and sits back on the couch. "I just wanted to let you know that you won't be having problems with Conner anymore."

"What did you do to him?" she asks.

"Nothing short of killing him will do," I say, hating that man.

Mr. O'Kane laughs at my statement, and she just looks at me wide-eyed. "The less you know, the better," he says, and I give them a genuine smile. "Honey, I think you should call Jaycent." He changes the subject.

She snorts. "Now all of a sudden you're on his side?"

He sighs. "I didn't realize how unhappy you were. And that's my fault." He looks around the apartment and frowns as if he too doesn't like it. "I never thought you would hate this apartment. I bought it thinking you would be safe. That you would be near my office and close to your brother in case you needed anything. If you want to sell it, then I'll help you do just that. But now I see that you have someone else to help take care of you, and that person is Jaycent. Becca, don't be mad at him for telling me about Conner."

Sell her apartment? This is news to me.

"He should have told me," she argues.

"I'm not saying he shouldn't have, but I'm also saying that he realized the situation was bigger than him. And all I want is for you to be safe. And that's exactly what he did. I just want what is best for you, and Jaycent coming to me showed that he is it."

"So you condone him keeping secrets from me?"

He shakes his head. "I condone a man willing to do whatever it takes to keep the woman he loves safe." She sighs, and I wonder why I am needed for this conversation. "Give him a chance," he urges.

"A chance to what? Prove he's not like Conner?"

"You know he's not like Conner," he responds flatly.

She lifts her hand and rubs her forehead. "I did but—"

"But nothing," I say, interrupting her. She looks at me, and I give her a smile. "He's the one you've always wanted. Don't allow Conner to take something else away from you, Becca. He doesn't deserve that much credit."

She bites her bottom lip before smiling. "Okay. I'll call him."

"He's outside your door," he says. "I made the call for you."

I stand. "I'll let you guys be alone …"

"Actually"—he stands as well—"I would like to talk to you, Ashlyn. If you don't mind?"

I nod and sit down slowly. He looks at Becca. "Alone."

I swallow as she nods and walks to the front door before exiting the apartment.

I cross my legs and look anywhere but at Mr. O'Kane. He looks so much like Ryder it's scary. And it's just another reminder of what I fucked up on. "I'm assuming that Becca told you about Talia's," he says, getting to the point.

I nod. "She told me that O'Kane Enterprises is buying them."

"I know the manager very well …" He lets his sentence hang in the air, and I swallow nervously. "I must say I wasn't surprised when she called me a few days ago," he says, eyeing me.

I shift in my seat.

"She informed me that you put your two weeks' notice in."

My heart rate picks up. I didn't want anyone to know. Can she legally do that? Not like it matters. Anyone who has the last name

O'Kane owns this town. I'm just a fish in their ocean. "I did." I own up to it. I've never been a coward.

He shakes his head as if he's disappointed in me. "I told her to disregard your request."

My brows rise. "You can't—"

"I did!" he interrupts me sharply.

I sigh, feeling defeated. Can't I choose how to live my life? "With all due respect, sir, you can't control what I do."

He actually smiles at me. "I'm trying to protect you."

I snort. "You are just prolonging the inevitable. You think I'm going to work for a company that my ex owns?" I shake my head. "I'll pass. And I doubt you guys keep it a gallery."

He stands as if we're done and buttons his suit jacket. "Give me a month."

I stand as well and eye him skeptically. "A month to what?"

"To give you something better than what you have now," he says with confidence. As if putting my future in his hands would be a smart move.

"I don't know …"

"I'm a man with many connections," he adds.

I square my shoulders. "I don't need your connections," I say sternly. "I was taught that you get what you work for."

He nods. "And I respect that. You've worked hard to get where you are now. And believe me when I say that Lauren was impressed beyond words with your interview, and that you have major potential. So I'm asking you to give me one month."

I run a hand through my hair and let out a long sigh. One more month in this town that just continues to swallow me up and spit me out? Another month with the man I love living above me and wishing I didn't exist? To someone else, four weeks is nothing. To me, it's thirty days in hell. But he's right. He has connections, and no one tells him no. Finally, I nod. "One month." I agree as if I had a choice when, in all honesty, we both know I didn't.

I turn and walk back to my room to change my clothes. I have somewhere to be.

• • •

I take a deep breath as I approach the door of Bradley's hotel room in Brooklyn. The long cab ride made me nauseous. I really regret selling my car. I'm pretty sure I won't survive another month of these cab rides.

Closing my eyes, I let it out and lift my hand to knock on the white door. My eyes spring open when it's opened before I even get the chance. My hand falls to my side when I see him standing there wearing a pitiful look on his handsome face. His brown hair is disheveled, and he has dark circles under his eyes.

He moves to the side and gestures for me to enter. "Please?" He says the single word softly, and it just reminds me that this isn't going to end well.

I step into his hotel room and turn to face him as he shuts the door. I wanna get this over with and then go home, drink a bottle of wine, and pass the fuck out! "What was so important that I needed to come see you?" He opens his mouth, but I continue. "Or better yet, why are you still here, Bradley?" I'm mad at him. For doing this to me. To us. For ruining our friendship when he didn't have to.

"I ... uh, well ... I needed ..." He stops blabbering and just stares at me.

The silence in the small room makes me nervous and uncomfortable. "Spit it out, Bradley," I growl.

I watch his Adam's apple bob as he swallows and then he falls to one knee while pulling a small white box out of his jeans pocket.

I stumble back a step. "What the hell ...?"

"Please marry me, Ash ..."

"You can't be serious!" I gasp.

"You can't be this surprised, baby," he says with a smile forming on his face.

The way he calls me *baby* makes my stomach turn. I open my mouth but then shut it—unable to form a word.

He slowly stands as his eyes drop to my stomach then meet mine. "After I left your apartment, I came back."

"What? When?" I ask, trying to process everything.

He looks down at the open box sitting in his hand. "I couldn't do it. I couldn't walk away from you. Jaycent answered the door and wouldn't let me in."

I shake my head. He has to be lying, right? Jaycent never told me this. "He actually took up for Ryder. Said he just needed time."

I wish that would have been the case.

"I've thought about it, and maybe he was right in a way. It's you who just needed time." I start shaking my head. "I told Jaycent I would propose." *What?* "I told him that Ryder doesn't deserve you. That I would never walk away from you like he did, and I'm a man of my word, Ash. Here I am, still fighting for you. Please, give me a chance."

"A chance to what?" I can't help but ask.

"To show you that I'm the one for you. And that I'm the one you love," he says simply.

"All this time …" I can't finish the words.

He gives me a big smile and takes a step toward me. "I've loved you all along, Ashlyn. How did you not see it?"

My stomach knots at how wrong I have been all this time. "I … I love …" His smile widens, and I hate that what I'm about to say will destroy him once again. "I love Ryder," I whisper.

The smile falls off his face, and he looks away from me, licking his lips. Then very slowly shuts the box. He gives me his back and runs a hand through his hair.

I take a step toward him as I say, "I'm sorry …"

"Sorry?" he snaps, spinning back around to face me.

I let out a sigh. "I am, Brad. I'm sorry I can't love you like you love me," I say truthfully. My throat tightening. "You were my best friend—"

He throws his head back and lets out a dry laugh, interrupting me. "You're not even trying!" He growls. "Three years you've known me, Ash. You've known him for three weeks. And you choose him over me? Why? 'Cause he has money?"

My lips thin. "It's not about money!" I snap. "You know I don't care about that shit!"

He holds his hands out wide to his side. "Apparently, I don't know you at all," he shouts. "I mean, I've stood by while you've whored around …" I gasp. "But to fall for one of the bastards …"

"Fuck you!" I shout and then ask him "What about the girl you were seeing when I got back from Panama City?" I had asked him this before he stormed out of my apartment, but he never answered.

"I made her up," he says.

"What?" How many other things has he lied to me about?

"I did it to make you jealous, but it obviously didn't work," he snaps.

"I can't believe you," I say and start to storm toward the door.

He grabs the back of my arm and yanks me to a stop. "Let go, Brad!" I growl, looking up at him.

His dark brown eyes are narrowed and his jaw tight. "Where is he at, Ash?" he demands.

"That's none of your business!" I snap, trying to remove my arm from his grip. No luck.

He gives another rough laugh. "He never came back to you, did he?" I refuse to answer that. "Let me guess. He hasn't even called or text you." I close my lips tightly. His other hand comes up and grabs my other arm, holding me in place. "Men like him don't fall in love with women like you." His voice has softened, but he might as well have screamed it at the top of his lungs and slapped me across the face.

My shoulders slump, and my chest tightens at the truth in his words.

He lets go of my arms and cups my face. "Women like you are a dime a dozen to him." He just twisted the knife in my chest. "But to me …" He sighs. "To me, you're everything."

CHAPTER THREE

RYDER

"I need you to send these over to Mr. Rollin," I tell Kelly, handing her papers while standing in front of her desk.

"Yes, sir." He takes them from me, nodding.

"And I need ..."

"Mr. O'Kane?"

I turn to see my father's new assistant, Jackie, approaching us. "Yes?" I ask, looking her up and down. She wears a white dress with a high neck and black belt that sits high on her waist. She's the typical girl I would fuck. Her brown hair is up in a tight bun, and her plump lips are colored a pretty pink. It's crazy that as I look at her right now, I feel nothing. All I think about is Ashlyn and how much I miss her.

She comes to a stop and bites her bottom lip nervously. "I needed to speak to your father, but he is out at the moment. May I speak to you please?" She looks over at Kelly for a quick second and then back at me. "Privately?"

"Of course."

She enters my office, and I shut the door after her. "What is it that you need, Jackie?" I ask, going to sit behind my desk.

"I was going over Jessica's monthly billing ..." She opens the folder sitting in her lap. "And I have found a few things that don't add up."

I frown. "What doesn't add up?"

"Mr. O'Kane ... er, your father had me write out checks to ship off payments, and I can't find one company in particular in the system." She leans over my desk, handing me a few pieces of paper.

I take them, and my eyes scan over them. One of them is regarding Q's, another is Hahn's. Another one is a place called O'Kane Industries. I frown as I look over the payout. "This place doesn't exist," I say out loud.

"Not that I could find, sir."

"I know it doesn't," I tell her. "Is there an account number?"

"No, sir. All I could find is a name."

I nod, not bothering to look up at her. "Thank you, Jackie," I say, dismissing her. *What was Jessica up to?*

ASHLYN

Saturday morning I was up early to go to work. The fact we had a private showing in two weeks meant we were all hands on deck. Even today.

I am regretting every decision I have ever made in life. Once again, I got no sleep last night. I stayed up staring at my ceiling while Harry lay on my chest, purring loudly. I couldn't get the look of Bradley's face out of my mind. He literally looked broken when I walked out on him after he told me how he felt. I couldn't return the feelings, and there was no reason to egg him on.

I laid in bed all night and thought about the words he said about Ryder, and he was right. He would never love me like I could love him. But that didn't mean I would settle for Bradley. I've never loved Bradley like that. I've never seen a future with the two of us that involved marriage and kids. And that wouldn't be fair to him if I told him yes. He deserves someone who loves him just as much as he would them.

I stand in the kitchen of our apartment, trying to make breakfast but failing. Like everything else in my life.

I pour the pancake batter onto the burner as my phone dings. I pick it up in hopes that it's Ryder. Even though I know he's not gonna call.

"Son of a bitch." I hiss when I see that my pancakes are burned along with my bacon. I peel them off the burner and place them on a plate. And I cringe at the burning smell.

"Everything okay?" I hear Jaycent ask, entering the kitchen.

I toss the spatula onto the countertop and place my hands on either side of the counter, hanging my head. "Yeah," I say, lying. "I'm sorry if I woke you."

"I needed to get up anyway," he tells me. "Can I help you with something?"

I lift my head up and look back at him. And I hate that there are tears in my eyes. Why do I keep crying? This isn't me. I look away from him and shake my head.

"I, uh, will leave you alone …" He trails off.

"Thank you," I say, turning around to look at him.

"For what?" he asks, frowning.

I look down at the floor. "I went and saw Bradley last night."

He closes his eyes and sighs. "I guess it went badly?" he asks, looking back up at me.

"As well as I had expected." I lick my lips. "He proposed."

His brows shoot up, and he looks down at my ring finger. "And?"

"I said no." I sigh. "He told me that he had knocked on the door to talk to me again, and you answered and wouldn't let him in." I'm not mad at him for not telling me. I understand why he kept it a secret. He's on Ryder's side.

"He wanted to see you. But I wouldn't let him. I'm sorry for stepping in, but you were so upset—"

"Thank you," I say, interrupting him. "He said you took up for Ryder. That you told him to leave, and that Ryder just needed time." He nods. "And he said that after he thought about what you had said, that maybe I just needed time as well." I shake my head. "I didn't. Ryder and I may have broken up, but I never loved Bradley the way he loved me. And marrying him isn't the answer to my problems."

"Have you spoken to Ryder?" he asks.

I look down at my hands. "I did. Once. But he never said a word or called me back."

"What are you guys doing?" Becca asks as she enters the kitchen dressed in her robe.

"I'm burning shit," I answer and then laugh at myself 'cause at this point, what else is there for me to do? I pick up the pan of bacon and place it in the sink.

"I'm running late to work. I'll just grab something on the way," I say.

Becca runs a hand through her tangled brown hair. "What do you wanna do tonight after you get off work?"

I pause on my way to the door. I look from Jaycent to Becca. "No offense, but I really just wanna be alone." She frowns at me. "I just need some time to figure out …" I pause and sigh heavily. "I just wanna be alone," I repeat, hoping I could just go back to bed and then turn and walk out the front door.

CHAPTER FOUR

RYDER

The beautiful blond I just met hours ago on the beach moans as I roll her onto her back, and my hands tangle in her blond hair. "Hope you don't mind. I like to be in charge," I say roughly.

Her wet lips part, swollen from our kiss moments ago. Her eyes heavy from her recent orgasm. She arches a dark brow and gives me a weak smile. Her hands come up to my chest, and she tries to push me over onto my back, but she is unsuccessful. "Then take charge." There's a challenge in her beautiful blue eyes, and I like it.

She bites her bottom lip while scraping her nails down my chest, and my muscles tighten as I let out a moan of pain. I let go of her hair, grab her hands, and pin them down on the sides of her head. "Hope you're not fragile." My hard cock rests against her wet pussy. I can feel the heat as her legs wrap around my hips.

She smiles as her eyes light up. She lifts her chin while her hips meet mine ready for more than my mouth. I haven't fucked her yet. Not with my cock anyway but her sweet taste is still on my tongue. "Try to break me. I dare you," she taunts.

Challenge accepted.

My body jerks, and I snap my head up in surprise. A piece of paper falls from my face, and I look down at it to see the fax paper is wet. I shake my head as I reach up and wipe the drool from my chin.

I blink a few times and then rub my heavy eyes. My shoulders fall when I realize I'm sitting in my dark office and not lying in bed with Ashlyn. *It was just a memory. One of our first memories together*. Running a hand down my unshaven face, I sigh. She keeps playing in my mind. I'm unable to escape her, no matter what I do. She's there. Like a ghost haunting me. It's not only disturbing but also painful.

I catch sight of the Knicks tickets she got me for next season lying on the corner of my desk, and I toss them into my desk drawer. I didn't have the heart to tell her I have a fucking suite. But I would have much rather gone with her and sat in these seats.

I place my elbows on my desk, and my head falls to my hands. A knock sounds on my door, and I ignore it. I just wanna be left alone. In silence and in darkness. I've officially become a hermit. Thankfully, I have a full bath in my office. Otherwise, I'd have to have Kelly hose me down out in the alley behind the building.

My unlucky streak continues as I hear the knob twist followed by the door opening. *I should have locked it.* "Ryder."

I groan as I hear my father's voice. "I'm busy, Dad," I tell him, refusing to pull my hands from my face. Why won't people just leave me alone?

I hear him flip the light switch, and I finally lift my head and squint at the harsh light as I try to look at him. He stands in my office, the door now shutting behind him. He unbuttons his black Armani suit jacket and pushes it back as he places his hands on his hips. His green eyes look over the place I've been calling home for the past week now. A black blanket lies wadded on my leather couch. Some of my most expensive suit jackets cover the floor, and my slacks are thrown over my chairs.

"You're living here," he states. I don't respond, and his eyes finally land on mine. "Why are you living here?"

"There's work that needs to be done," I say, placing my hands out as if I'm actually getting shit done. Trying to convince him that I'm not throwing my life away because of a woman.

"In the dark?" he questions, eyeing me skeptically.

He huffs when I don't respond and then walks past my desk to the thick black curtains behind me. He yanks them open, and I blink as the morning sun lights up my office. I've kept them closed because, as fate would have it, a *Romeo and Juliet* billboard for the play that is showcasing here in a week is right across the street from my office. It's about the size of a semi-truck. I think the universe is trying to kill me. "Dad, I had those closed for a reason," I growl.

He comes to walk around my desk and picks up my slacks hanging over my chair. He tosses them on the floor beside my button up shirts before he sits down. "You have to go home." I shake my head in refusal. "You're avoiding her."

I slam my hand down on the desk. "Of course, I'm avoiding her." My heart starts pounding in my chest. "How can I go back there when I could run into her?" I ask in defeat as I hang my head again. "I've gotta move."

"Wow," he says dryly.

I look up at him through my lashes and snap, "Wow what?"

"I thought I'd never see the day." He shakes his head in disappointment.

"And which day would that be?" I growl. My jaw tightens. As if I really wanna hear what he has to say.

He leans forward in his seat, his elbows resting on his knees. "The day that Ryder O'Kane gave up on something." "Don't give me that shit. It's too early, Dad." I snort, trying to avoid this conversation.

He laughs as if he's enjoying this while sitting back in his seat. I close my eyes and hang my head, trying to prepare myself for another day at work, another day of endless meetings and phone calls, but all I hear and see is Ashlyn. It's really as pathetic as my father makes it sound.

My door opens, and Kelly walks in. Her usual red lipstick gone, she is wearing a pair of denim shorts and a black t-shirt with flip-flops. I go to ask her what the hell she is wearing when she speaks. "Good morning, Mr. O'Kane." She looks over at my father who has turned around in his chair to look at her. "Mr. O'Kane." She nods to him.

"Kelly," I say, refusing to say good morning. Nothing about my days are good.

"What are you doing here, Kelly?" my father asks, and I frown at his question. *Why wouldn't she be here?*

"I'm here to pick up Mr. O'Kane's laundry," she states before she bends down and grabs a pair of gray slacks. She then walks over to my couch and picks up a suit jacket. "I will drop these off at the dry cleaners for you, sir," she assures me. "And then I will run by your apartment while I'm out and grab you clothes for …"

"No," my father says, standing.

She comes to a quick stop, and her eyes shoot from my father to me. "Excuse me?" I ask.

He turns to face me, narrowing his green eyes down at me. "You are going home today."

I shake my head. "I have work—"

"You need sleep and preferably in your bed," he snaps, interrupting me before turning to face Kelly. "You may go, Ms. Blake."

She bites her bottom lip nervously as she tries to decide what to do, but when my father refuses to look away from her, she cracks under his pressure and rushes out. He turns back to face me.

I stand. "You had no right …"

"Do you even know what day it is?" he asks.

"Uh, Thursday," I say with a snort. Of course, I know what day it is.

"It's Saturday, Ryder. You have your assistant coming in to do your bitch work on a Saturday." He runs a hand through his hair. "I am not running a bed and breakfast here. I'm running a billion-dollar company. I'm giving you one chance to take your ass home. I don't care if you spend your weekend drowning in a bottle or in the fetal position, but you are not staying here," he states.

"Dad …"

"Get your shit together. And when I see you here on Monday, your ass had better be ready to work!" With that, he turns around, yanks my door open, and then slams it shut.

ASHLYN

I sit on the counter with an untouched box of pizza next to me; today was long at the gallery. And considering it was a Saturday made it seem to go by slower than usual. I look over at the front door of the apartment when I hear the doorknob jiggle. After a few long seconds, it turns and slams open.

I watch as Becca and Jaycent come barging in with their lips locked until they hit a wall. He yanks her head to the side by her hair, and she moans into his mouth. She starts untucking his shirt, and his hands leave her hair only to grab her ass. He picks her up, and her legs wrap around his waist.

I start to cough, letting them know they are not alone. She pulls away from him and jumps down. "Oh, God." She looks at me. "I'm so sorry, Ash. I didn't think you were home," she says in a rush.

Jaycent starts tucking his shirt back in and clears his throat. "We didn't mean for you to see all that," he says unable to meet my eyes.

"Don't apologize. At least one of us is getting laid," I say. I don't care what they do. I just didn't want to see them go all that way.

Becca gives an awkward laugh and then stops when Jaycent looks down at her. "So," she says, rocking back on her heels, "what are your plans for tonight?"

"Nothing," I respond and take a drink of my beer.

She frowns. "It's Saturday."

"And?" I ask. I thought we had established this this morning when she asked me what I wanted to do tonight, and I said nothing.

"You know what?" Jaycent says, clapping his hands. "You girls should go out tonight. A girls' night."

"No thanks," I say and pick up a small piece of pizza.

"Come on." Becca sticks her bottom lip out, giving me that cute little puppy dog face she has. "It'll be fun. I haven't had the chance to take you out on the town. You'll love it."

"Okay," I say, sighing to myself. Going out is the last thing I want to do tonight, but I know she is trying to cheer me up. I hate to tell her smoke and alcohol aren't going to help.

Becca jumps up and down excitedly. "Yay. You're gonna have so much fun." I give her a fake smile and a head nod.

She turns to look over at Jaycent, and I see that look in her eye return that she had a moment ago when they barged into the apartment.

"For Christ's sake, just go do it," I tell them, hiding a smile.

Jaycent laughs and Becca's cheeks turn red with embarrassment. "Give me five minutes," she tells him, kissing him on the cheek and taking off down the hall. "Be ready in an hour," she hollers at me.

"Can I talk to you for a second?"

My brows lift in surprise. "Sure." I put down the pizza and beer and then rub my hands on my sweatpants.

He enters the kitchen and comes to stand across from me. His eyes meet mine, and I immediately look away. Jaycent and I aren't that close, but anyone who looks close enough can see that I'm still hurting over losing Ryder. "I just wanna say I'm sorry."

"You didn't do anything," I tell him.

"That's exactly it. I didn't do anything!" he growls. "I should have stopped Ryder. I should have told him that when Bradley came over, we all had a late lunch then took a nap before watching a movie in the living room. But instead, I stayed back in Becca's bedroom when I heard Becca call out his name in surprise."

"You did what was right," I assure him. It wasn't anything that he needed to get involved in.

He shakes his head. "I've never been known as a coward, Ashlyn. But that night I was."

"No, you weren't. If you had done something, he would have been mad at all of us."

He runs a hand down his face and sighs, looking down at the floor.

"Do you love her?" I ask.

He looks up at me. "Do you love him?"

"I'm not sure I know what love is," I decide to say. I lost two men. Only an idiot can manage that.

His shoulders slump, and he runs a hand through his hair again. "You can't compare what Becca and I have to what you and Ryder have," he argues.

"We have nothing," I say softly.

"That's bullshit!" he growls.

I straighten my back. "Jaycent—"

"I don't wanna hear your excuses, Ashlyn," he interrupts me. "I know what I saw. I may not know you, but I know my best friend. He's been in my life since we were four. I've never seen him look at a woman like he does you. I've never seen him be so ... attentive to anyone as he is with you. Trust me; I'll be the first one to admit that Ryder can be a fucking dick. But he also has a lot to give. And I know he was willing to give it to you."

I shake my head. He's wrong. He doesn't know Ryder as well as he thinks he does. Just like I didn't know Bradley as well as I thought I did. "I don't understand how I got here," I tell him.

He places his hand on my knee. "People never see love coming."

I look at him. "No offense, but I don't see you as a hopeless romantic."

He laughs at that statement. "No one ever does." And then he smiles. "I thought I was in love with a woman for a long time." I frown at his words. "Becca," he clarifies. "Then one day. She gave me the chance to show her just how much I've loved her. And I was wrong." His smile widens. "I realized that I loved her from afar. Out of reach. When I was able to hold her. Touch her. Kiss her. What I felt for her didn't even compare to what lengths my love for her will go." Then his face goes serious. "I've known Becca all her life, Ashlyn. And I've loved her for a long time. But I was seven years older than she was. When I finally had my chance, she went off to college. Far away from me. But I believed in fate. And I've always been the guy who believes in love."

My head drops, and I stare down at my hands in my lap. "Love can't happen in three weeks, Jaycent."

"Says who?"

I look back up at him with an "are you kidding me" look. "Everyone."

"Well, everyone is wrong," he says simply, and I snort. "Every day, Becca does something new, and I fall in love with it." He smiles. "You're holding yourself back because you're afraid of what? That he won't love you the same?"

"I don't love him," I say, lying.

"Just because you say it out loud doesn't make it true." Then he turns and walks off to go have some quality time with Becca before we go.

I sit on the countertop still contemplating what Jaycent said to me when my phone rings next to me. I answer when I see it's Thomas.

"Hello?"

"Hey, girl," he says with a huff.

"What's wrong?" I ask him. Jumping off the countertop, I know I need to start getting ready if I want to look presentable.

"Are you free tonight?" he asks. "It's Saturday night, and I need to get out of the house."

"Becca and I are going out. You are more than welcome to join us," I tell him as I walk into my room.

"A girls' night?" he asks excitedly. His mood instantly changing. "I could use one of those."

I pass by Harry as he sleeps on my bed and head to the bathroom. "Okay. Can you meet us at our apartment in about an hour?"

"Absolutely!"

• • •

"Where are we headed?" I ask Becca as I sit between her and Thomas in the back of a black Escalade. The same one I used to ride in with Ryder. It's crazy, but I swear I can smell him. A sweet and spicy package that not only makes my panties wet but my chest ache.

I washed my hair and slapped on some makeup before putting a dress on, and I don't feel any better than I did earlier. It didn't give me any newfound confidence. Or make me feel empowered.

"Ryder and Dad sold some property last year to a man, and he opened a club on it."

"Great," I say dryly. Just when I thought I could get out and not think about him. He's following me around like a black cloud.

"Tonight's its grand opening," she says excitedly.

"Oh, I love grand openings." Thomas claps his hands just as excited as she is.

I roll my eyes. Thirty minutes later, we pull up to a curb, and we all pile out. It's sitting in the middle of an industrial site in New Jersey. I can stand at the front door and see a Hudson River behind it. "I wonder how many drunks will walk right off the street and into the water?" I say with laughter. They both look at me as if I'm crazy.

"That would be terrible," Becca says with wide eyes.

"They need to put a rail up," Thomas adds.

I sigh. "I was just kidding," I lie. I was hoping I would be the unlucky drunk.

They both look at one another, and Thomas places his hand on her arm. "It was nice of you to get her out tonight. She needs to get out more," he says softly as if I can't hear him.

I refrain from rolling my eyes, but I do blow some wild strands from my face and out of my eyes. "Let's get inside. I need a drink," I say, turning to the door.

We walk up to the front door, no line yet. We came early, and a man stands at the entrance. His arms over his large chest and legs wide. He has an earpiece in his ear. But instead of wearing a security shirt, he has on a black button-down, sleeves rolled up exposing his muscular forearms. Black slacks with Chucks. "Hello," he says to all of us.

"Hello," Becca says, handing him her ID excitedly.

"Well, hello there," Thomas says with a wink.

He chuckles as he looks down at her ID, using a small flashlight in his left hand. He frowns down at her. "Is there a problem?" she asks with worry in her voice.

"O'Kane?" he questions, handing her back her ID. "Are you any relation to Ryder O'Kane?"

Please Lord, drop the sky on me now.

"Oh, yes," she says, releasing a long breath. "He's my brother."

He smiles, and even his smile is threatening. I don't think he means it to be, but it comes off as don't fuck with me. He reaches out this right hand. "I am Jet Waters. Welcome to Seven Deadly Sins."

"Thank you," she says happily. I stand back, regretting this night for the hundredth time since she asked me to come out. "This is my friend, Ashlyn, and our other friend Thomas."

He shakes hands with Thomas, and I reach mine out of respect and shake it. "Miller," he says into his ear piece. "Come to the front. I have a group I need you to show to the balcony suite."

"Oh no, you don't have to do that," Becca says.

"I do," he says and then another guy appears. Guessing it's Miller. He slaps him on his back. "Their tab is on me tonight."

"No really …"

"I insist," he urges, placing his hand on his chest.

She gives him a weak smile and nods. "Thank you."

"It's my pleasure."

I open my purse and start to dig for my ID. "No need," he says to me. "You guys have fun, and if you have any problems, let me or

Miller know."

"Thank you," Thomas says excitedly."

I wrap my arm around Becca's shoulders, and she's tense. "What's wrong?" I ask her.

She shakes her head, but I think I have an idea. She has told me before that she doesn't like this kind of treatment. The kind where others give her special advantages due to her last name.

The man who went by Miller walks up a set of stairs covered in black carpet. We make it to the top and walk around a black railing. Two black couches with white throw pillows sits on either side of a black coffee table. "Here you go."

We sit down, and he raises his hand. Seconds later, a woman with black hair comes running over. He bends down and speaks into her ear. We can't hear much over the music. When she pulls away, she's nodding and smiling. He walks away.

"Hello everyone," she calls out. "What can I get you?"

"Tequila shots all around," Becca answers.

Thomas leans back in his couch and places his arms on the back, smiling. Then he looks at me and frowns. "What's wrong with you?"

"She's had a shit week," Becca says.

I snort. "You've had a shit week."

Thomas crosses one leg over the other and smiles. "Well, sister, we got all night, so start filling me in."

"It's nothing," Becca tells him.

"Nothing?" I snort and look at Thomas. "She found out her mother was paying her boyfriend to be with her."

"She what?" Thomas asks wide-eyed, looking at her.

"She and Ryder broke up, and Bradley proposed to her," she says, pointing over at me.

His head snaps to me. "You broke up with the king? And who the hell is Bradley?" He knows that my sex life is shitty at the moment, but I never filled him in on all the details. I doubted that he wanted to hear all my problems.

"The king?" Becca asks, pulling her lips back in disgust. "He's no king."

Thomas nods his head. "Oh, he is, honey." He removes his arm from the couch and leans forward, putting them on his knees, and puts his chin in his hand. "Spill. Who is this other guy?"

I sigh heavily. "It doesn't matter. They're both gone, and I would rather not discuss it." I look back and forth between them. Thomas opens his mouth, and I add, "Please?"

He closes his mouth and gives me a curt nod. The waitress returns and sets our first round of shots on the table.

They both lift theirs in toast, but before they can say anything, I pick mine up and slam it back. Then, without saying a word, Becca slides me hers, and I take it without question. Then Thomas does the same. Next time the waitress comes by, Becca orders two rounds.

CHAPTER FIVE

RYDER

I sit behind my desk. I never left as my father told me to. Thankfully, he stayed in his office all day making phone calls and avoided going home like always. Not sure why it's okay for him to do it but not me. The sun has finally gone down, and I have my lights off as I did earlier. I heard my father leave an hour ago without even saying bye. So maybe he has realized I'm a lost cause.

I hear my door open, and I guess I was wrong. "Go away," I growl, hugging a bottle of whiskey. My father had said he didn't care if I spent my entire weekend drowning in a bottle of booze, and that thought sounded appealing.

The light flips on, and I groan as I close my eyes. "Your father said I needed to come pick you up."

I look up and peel one eye open to see Milton standing there. "Go away," I repeat.

He shakes his head. "I'm not leaving unless you come with me."

I sigh but manage to get up, bringing the bottle with me. We make our way downstairs, and I crawl into the back of my Escalade. "I saw your sister tonight," he tells me.

"Oh, yeah?" I ask. "What's she up to?" Not really caring but the normal, non-brokenhearted Ryder would care.

"She and Ashlyn needed a ride."

At the sound of her name, I take another drink from the bottle. "To where?" I ask, already regretting it. I shouldn't care where she was going.

"They were going to Seven Deadly Sins."

I know that place. Well, I've never been there, but I sold the property to the guy who owns the bar. It's not in the best part of town. "Just the two of them?" I ask, wondering if they went alone. Maybe Jaycent went with them.

"No," he answers as he switches lanes. "They had a man with them ..." He pauses. "I think his name was—"

"I know who he was." *Bradley.* He's still in town? God, did he just move in with them? I take another drink.

"Nice man ..."

"Milton!" I snap, running a hand over my unshaven face. "Can we please just not discuss the girls and their *date*?"

"Sure thing, boss," he says, sounding unaffected by my short fuse.

I sit back in the seat and think about calling Jet to ask him to keep an eye on them, but then I talk myself out of it. It's none of my business. But Becca is my sister. I can check up on her any time I want, and I won't sound like a stalker. More of an older brother.

I get out of the Escalade before Milton can even open my back door and crawl out, the bottle still tightly in my grip.

"Will you need anything tomorrow, sir?" Milton asks, coming around the front of the car.

I shake my head because I don't plan to leave my place for the rest of the weekend. "I'll see you Monday."

He nods and shuts my door before getting back in the Escalade and pulling away from the curb.

I make my way up the stairs and through the glass doors. Thoughts of the last time I stood here, heavy on my mind. Not sure how long it will take to get her out of my mind, but it won't be fast enough.

I enter my apartment and walk in, not even bothering to turn my lights on. The Manhattan skyline lights my apartment enough from the floor-to-ceiling windows. Yet it suddenly feels empty. Too big. Strange, I've never had that problem before.

I slowly head toward my room and shut the door and then fall onto the bed. The liquor bottle still in my hand. I let out a sigh as I imagine her being here with me. Or there with him. I just want to scream at the thoughts I can't help but stop.

Conner stands before me. He smiles, and his once white teeth are now stained with red from my punch to his face a moment ago. "So still fucking the whore, are you?" He looks at me and laughs. "You know"—he reaches up and wipes the blood from his chin—"I used to share a room with Becca right beside Ashlyn." He leans in closer and whispers, "I used to lie awake and listen to her scream out Bradley's name." My heart beats so hard in my chest, my ears are pounding. "Then you had to go and fuck her." He looks me up and down with disgust. "How does it feel to know that no matter what you do, she'll always go back to him?"

I grind my teeth at that memory. Even that fucking bastard Conner knew that she was never going to give me more than just her body. Bradley was always gonna get the girl. I'm not sure why I ever tried.

Even after all that, I still can't help what I do next.

I pull out my phone and dial up Jet's number, deciding to do it after all.

He picks up after the third ring.

"Hey, Ryder? What's up, man?" he asks.

I hear the pounding of music in the background. "Not much," I tell him. "I was just calling to see how opening night is going," I lie.

"Great. You gonna make it out?"

Make it out? Not sure I wanna go there and see Ashlyn with Bradley. They'd be dancing or, worse, kissing. "No, I can't make it," I say and tip the bottle back. "But my sister is there."

"Yeah, she came in with a couple of friends earlier. I'm taking care of them."

Great! He's getting them drunk. I'm sure their drinks just keep coming. "Can you keep an eye on her for me, please?" I don't think he has a clue that I mean Ashlyn.

"Absolutely!" I open my mouth to say thanks when he speaks again. "Hey, man, I gotta go take care of something."

"Okay …" *Click.*

He hung up. I throw my phone to the end of the bed. It bounces off and hits the floor with a thud.

I sit up and take another swig. Then another. And then another. I drink until I've finished the bottle and my vision blurs. My father was right—come Monday, I'm going to get my ass back in the game and put Ashlyn behind me. No matter how hard it is to do.

ASHLYN

Two hours later, I'm drunk. And doing something I thought I'd never do again—laughing.

I stand at the bar of Seven Deadly Sins, holding a glass in my hand with dark liquid. I'm not sure what is in it, but a nice man bought it for me, and it is delicious. It's like my fourth one. On top of all the tequila shots I've had. And whatever drinks our waitress keeps bringing to our table, thanks to the hot owner himself.

"Where did your friends go?" the man yells over the music as he leans into me.

I spin around, the straw between my lips. I scan the busy club and dance floor. This place is packed with wall to wall people. The man who let us in stands over in the far corner talking to another man who has a security shirt on, but it's not Miller. He nods his head and points over at a hallway where I know the bathrooms are. I've visited them often; breaking the seal was a bad idea.

"I don't know," I respond with when I don't see them. But they could be standing a foot from me, and I'd probably have a hard time seeing them over the neon flashing lights and my somewhat blurry vision.

"Do I need to give you a ride home?" he asks, making sure to yell over the music as he leans into me.

I start shaking my head quickly, and it makes the room spin. He places his hands on my shoulders to steady me when I sway. I giggle. "They wouldn't leave me," I manage to say but then tilt my head to the side. *Would they?*

"Would you like me to help you look for them?" he asks, lifting the beer to his lips and taking a good size drink.

Should I find them? I mean, I'm not all that worried about them. Should I be? "Yeah," I tell him, setting my drink down on the bar.

He takes one last drink of his beer to finish it off and places it on the bar before picking mine up. "I'll carry it for you."

"Thank you," I say and go to take a step forward but trip over my own feet.

He wraps his arm around my waist, and I laugh that I need the assistance. "Come on, Bambi," he calls out over the music.

He walks me around the dance floor and down a long hallway toward the bathrooms. He comes to a stop, and I stumble forward. If not for his arm around my waist, I'm sure I would have fallen. "There they are," he says.

I look ahead just in time to see Becca running toward us. She barrels into me, pushing me backward, and then another set of arms wrap around me, and I know it's Thomas. "Where were you guys?" I yell over the music.

"We had to use the ladies' room," Thomas tells me and then looks at the man I have been talking to for the last hour. "What have you been up to?" He looks back at me and winks.

The nice man just laughs. "Whaattts your name?" Becca slurs.

"Nick," he says, reaching out his hand to shake hers. And then Thomas.

"Well, aren't you just adorable," Thomas says with a wink, and Nick shifts uncomfortably.

"You're scaring him," I tell him, and we all laugh but Nick.

"Don't worry, honey. I'm taken," he says, but the smile he is giving him looks like he's available.

"This place is awesome," Becca says, grabbing both my hands. "They have these rooms that have each sin on them." She rambles on, not making much sense, but I nod as if I understand.

"It's freaking packed," I say loudly. "Glad we got here when we did," I add.

Thomas nods his head as he eyes a man who squeezes between us. "I'll be back ..."

"Thought you were taken," Becca calls out to him.

"I ain't blind," he says, waving a hand at her.

We laugh again, and Nick offers me my drink. I take a long sip from the straw and then offer a sip to Becca. She takes it and then licks her lips excitedly. "Can I buy you a drink, Becca?" Nick asks her, and she nods her head quickly.

"Like you need another." I snort.

"That's why we're here," she screams over the music. "To get waaaasted."

"By the looks of us, we're already there," I say, making Nick laugh.

He places his hand on my lower back, and my body immediately leans into him. I know I shouldn't give him false hope because I don't plan on doing anything with him. The lights dance off the walls and floor, and my eyes have a hard time keeping up with them. My skin tingles from the alcohol, and my body is humming from the pounding of the music. "There's nothing wrong with having a little fun," he says, leaning to talk into my ear, causing a shiver to run through me. I close my eyes and imagine I'm with Ryder—that he is the one touching me—but when I open my eyes and see blue eyes instead of green staring at me, my heart shatters all over again.

I take a step back from him and pull my cell out of my purse and check to see if he has called or text me. I have one message, and it's from Bradley.

Bradley: *I'm still here. I can't leave without you, Ash. Please come see me. Let me make this right.*

I exit out of it and turn off my cell. Drunk Ashlyn doesn't need to be talking to anyone tonight. Then I turn to Nick and Becca. "How about some more tequila?"

• • •

Monday morning, I stand in the kitchen with Becca while Jaycent takes a shower. She hands me a coffee mug, and I smile at her. "Thank you."

She only nods. I can tell something is wrong. I've been trying to be in a better mood for her, but it doesn't seem to be working. We went out Saturday night and had an amazing time at Seven Deadly Sins, but things went back to normal yesterday. I wasn't happy or laughing, and she wasn't smiling anymore. "What's wrong, Becca?"

She sighs and shakes her head. "Nothing," she finally says after a long second.

I place my hand on her shoulder. "Well, I am here when you're ready to discuss it."

"Good morning, ladies," Jaycent says, entering the kitchen. He kisses her on the cheek and then nods at me.

"Morning, babe," she says cheerfully, and I know she's faking.

"Well, I am off to work, guys," I say, wanting to give them time alone. Maybe it's just me she doesn't want to talk to about what is bothering her. My phone rings, and I pull it out of my purse to see it's my mother. I smile.

"Tell her I said hello," Becca calls out.

I give her a nod and exit the apartment. "Hey, Mom," I say.

"Hey, sweetie, something wrong?" she asks. "I haven't heard much from you."

I've been avoiding our family Facebook chat ever since Ryder and I broke up. My cousin has been posting pictures of him that she finds on the internet every freaking day. If we were still together, I would tell her to fuck off. But right now, I choose to avoid them all. "Just been busy," I lie. My life has never been more boring.

"Well, how are you and Julian?" she asks.

I walk over to the elevator and push the down button. "It's Ryder, Mother. He goes by Ryder," I tell her for the hundredth time. "He's good," I say not wanting to go into detail on my broken love life.

"Good," she says happily. "When am I going to get to meet him? Your cousin Angela posts so much about him from the internet that I feel like I already know him."

I roll my eyes. "I'm not sure, Mom." The elevator dings, letting me know the doors are about to open. "I gotta go. I'm about to get in the elevator, and I'll lose you."

"Okay, honey, I hope you have a great Monday. I love you."

The doors slide open, and I take a step toward it but come to a stop when I see a set of green eyes narrowed at me.

My heart pounds in my chest, and it's hard to breathe. My palms instantly start sweating.

"Ashlyn?" my mother calls out in my ear. "I said I love you."

"I love you too," I whisper, swallowing the lump in my throat. And then drop the phone from my ear before hanging up.

My heart still pounds in my chest as I look at him. He's wearing a dark blue button up tucked into a black pair of slacks. His hair is styled to perfection in that messy way, and his face is freshly shaven. He looks perfect, and that makes it hurt even worse.

I quickly look around the elevator to see if he's alone, and I let out a long breath when I don't see a half-dressed woman in there with him. I'd cry if there was.

His eyes look me up and down, and his lips pull back with disgust. As if he has finally realized he was way out of my league. It hurts more than his words ever could.

I swallow nervously and take a step toward the elevator. "Ryder …" My voice cracks on his name, and I curse myself for being like this. I was doing better. I thought I was gonna be able to get over him, but seeing him right here and now proves I never will. He'll always be the one who got away.

Instead of saying anything back, he steps over to the right and presses the button on the elevator, and then he squares his shoulders as he places his hands in the pockets of his slacks, giving me a "go to hell" look right before the doors slide shut on me.

I stand there half dazed as realization dawns on what he just did. He hates me so much that he can't spend one minute with me in an elevator? Did he seriously just close it on me? The moment of panic I just had is replaced with rage.

I shove the door open to the apartment so hard that it bangs on the wall. I hear someone hiss *shit,* but I ignore them.

"That bastard," I hiss.

"What's wrong?" Becca asks.

I look at her as Jaycent excuses himself from the room. "He just shut the elevator door on me," I growl.

"Who?"

"Ryder," I explain, gripping my cell. "I was on the phone with my mother. The doors slid open, and I went to step in it but paused when I saw Ryder already standing inside the elevator. He just gave me this 'go to hell' look, and then as I went to step on the elevator, he reached over and pressed the button for it to shut." My arms go wide. "On me. He's being a child!" I'm shouting as my temperature rises.

"You've got to be joking." She sighs.

I shake my head and then run a hand through my hair. "Nope."

She walks over to me and places her hands on my shoulders. "You have got to make him hear you."

"What's the point?" I ask, pulling away.

"The point is that this is not who you are." Her voice rises. I narrow my eyes at her. "Jesus, Ashlyn. You are not this woman who lets a man treat her this way. Make him listen. Make him see that he is being an ass. That he has been wrong for long enough. Quit being this woman who lets a man make her feel small and doubt herself. You did nothing wrong, and he needs to see that."

I let out a long breath and look over to see Jaycent has reappeared. "You're right," I growl.

"Yes, I am," she says with a nod.

I've let this go on long enough. I smooth my skirt down and then push hair from my face. "I am not that kind of woman. And I'm tired of letting him make me feel that way."

He just thinks he hates me. Wait until I'm done with him.

CHAPTER SIX

RYDER

I stand at one end of the long conference table with the Manhattan view to my left. Men fill the seats, and my father sits at the other end.

I lean over it, my hands flat on the black surface. My hair is washed and fixed, I actually shaved this morning, and I didn't pick my clothes up off the floor. I look well put together for once, but I feel like shit inside. *I love you, too.* I knew the moment the elevator came to a stop on her floor that it would be her standing there, but nothing could have prepared me for what I saw. Or what I felt.

She looked so gorgeous, and the thought of him having her made me want to punch a fucking wall. Or myself. I knew the moment I saw her dressed in his shirt and the way she called him *baby*, I had lost her. But *I love you*? Nothing and I mean fucking nothing could have prepared me for that punch to the gut. I'm still having trouble breathing. I can't get it out of my head. *I love you too* ...

"Ryder?" my father calls out, clearing his throat.

I look up at him and stand up straight when he arches a brow in question. *What the fuck are you doing, Ry?* You're supposed to be working. You had the weekend to drink yourself into a stupor, but now, it's time to man up.

"Gentlemen," I say, straightening my black suit jacket as if it wasn't already in place. "Let's get started, shall we?" I sound so unaffected. As if I haven't had a major loss. As if I came to work prepared when all I wanna do is hide under my desk and drown in a bottle of Jack.

They all nod as they look up at me. I open my mouth to speak when I hear Kelly speaking loudly outside the conference door. "Miss ... he's in a meeting ... you can't."

"One sec, gentlemen," I say, already making my way over to the door. It swings open and about hits me in the face.

"Mr. O'Kane, I'm so sorry. I've called security ..." Kelly begins, storming in behind the last person I expected to see.

My heart races, and my eyes widen when I see the beautiful blonde standing before me as if my mind summoned her. "Ashlyn?" I ask in a high pitch voice.

She narrows her blue eyes up at me, and she pulls her shoulders back. My eyes run up and down her in a way that I should be ashamed of, but I'm not. "We need to talk, Ryder," she demands.

My father clears his throat, and I realize I'm standing in a room full of men who see me as a professional running a billion-dollar company. I pull my shoulders back as well and clear my throat. "I'm busy," I say, trying to sound like a boss, but my eyes drop to her chest, and I lick my lips at the way her tight black blouse hugs her tits.

Why would she think I want to talk to her? Did she not get that hint when I shut the elevator door on her this morning? It was a little low of me, but I couldn't chance being in there with her alone. I'm trying to keep from falling to my knees to beg her to pick me. I don't have much confidence in myself right now either.

She places her hands on her hips. "This won't take long."

"Ash—"

"I'm tired of you acting like a child!" she snaps, interrupting me.

I snort. "Me acting like a child?"

"Yes!" she shouts, and I ignore the men shuffling uncomfortably in their seats behind me. "Not only have you been ignoring me but you've also been ignoring your sister."

I run a hand through my hair as my jaw clenches. I can't deny that. But all she wants to discuss is Ashlyn. Hell, that's what everyone wants to discuss. I've even been ignoring Jaycent.

"I've come to tell you that Bradley and I—"

"Are what? In love? Getting married?" I snap, interrupting her.

"Well, I wish you the best …"

She jams a fist in my chest that I wasn't prepared for, and it actually knocks me back a step. "Quit interrupting me," she shouts.

I regain my footing and step up into her, my chest bumping hers, and I can feel her heart pounding against mine. My eyes narrow as I look down at her.

Kelly's eyes go back and forth frantically, no doubt wishing security would hurry their asses up.

"I didn't *fuck* Bradley," she growls.

My father clears his throat. "I think we need to—"

I snort and interrupt him. "I know what I saw."

"You know nothing." She stabs her finger in my chest this time, but I don't budge. "All you know is what you think you saw. And you're wrong, Ryder." Her voice softens for a moment, and she lowers her hand to her side. "Bradley is long gone. He walked out right after you did. The only difference is that I didn't chase him out the door."

I stand before her breathing heavy with narrowed eyes. But they soften at that statement. Could I really have been wrong? "No!" This is a trick. "I heard you telling him you loved him this morning."

She throws her head back laughing, and it's like a knife in my chest. That sound, I've missed it this past week. She straightens and looks me in the eyes, that laughter now gone. "That was my mother," she replies flatly. "I was on the phone with my mother." She huffs. "I would have told you that had you given me the chance to speak. And not run like a little boy!"

Just then, the door opens quickly and two men dressed in blue security uniforms enter panting as if they took the stairs. "Mr. O'Kane, is there a problem?" the bald man asks, his hand on his wide hips.

I just shake my head as I stare at her, trying to make sense of what she just told me. "But you—"

"I tried to tell you when I followed you out," she interrupts me this time. "But you couldn't give me two seconds of your precious time to explain myself."

I open my mouth, but the security guard speaks. "Mr. O'Kane?"

All I can do is shake my head. Could I have been wrong all this time? Jaycent has told me so many times just to call her. Talk to her. Could it have been that simple?

"I'm leaving," she says and then looks down as she starts digging in her purse. Moments later, she pulls something out. "Here. In your haste, you forgot to take what belongs to you." She drops the bracelet in my hand and then spins around, and I follow her without even thinking twice.

"Wait ..." I run to the elevator where she stands. "Ashlyn ..." I don't know what to say 'cause no words can express what I'm feeling right now.

She steps into the elevator and turns to face me. And I hate she has no tears in her eyes. No sign of sadness. Just satisfaction that she finally got to tell me what really happened. That I had been wrong all along. "It's over, Ryder. It's been over. But at least now you know I never betrayed you," she says flatly. "That is what hurts the most." She tilts her head to the side as if in thought. "That you could possibly think I thought so little of you." She licks her lips. "At least now we don't have to wait to see how it ends." And with those words, the elevator closes.

ASHLYN

I walk into work with a big smile on my face, and my head held high.

"Whoa, someone looks great," Thomas says, looking me up and down. "What did you do?" he asks skeptically.

My smile widens. "Something completely irrational and borderline psychotic," I tell him. And then my smile falls as I realize what I did. In front of his dad and complete strangers.

He takes a step closer to me. "Giiirrrrllll, what did you do?" he asks with worry now in his voice.

I look up at him. "I made a complete ass of myself in the middle of Ryder's business meeting."

"What?" he asks wide-eyed. "Why?"

"'Cause I was tired of feeling bad over something I didn't do," I growl. "He has been treating everyone like shit!"

He crosses his arms over his chest, and I sigh. I was wrong. I did it mainly for myself. I wanted him to know I hadn't betrayed him, but it was also because I put all my cards on the table that night I called him, and he never said anything back to me. That hurt more than him walking out on me when he found Bradley at my apartment. I wanted to hurt him too. And the look on his face after I told him the truth just made it worse. He had felt bad.

"I just need to work," I tell Thomas. "Get my mind off him."

An hour later, I'm still sitting at my desk when a man walks through the front door. A glass vase in his hand with beautiful red roses and a clipboard in the other.

"Miss Whitaker?"

"That's me," I say as I stand, wondering who could have sent me flowers. My first thought is my mother. The second is Nick. We do have a date tonight, after all.

"Oh, so pretty," Thomas says, coming up beside me. He takes the flowers as I sign my name on the clipboard.

"Thank you. You have a great day," the man says as he turns to leave.

"Who are they from?" I ask, turning to face Thomas. He already set the flowers down on the desk and is reading the card.

He looks up at me, and he gives me a big smile. "The king."

"What are you talking about?" I yank the card from his hand and read it.

I'm so sorry for everything. Please accept these roses and forgive me for my childlike behavior.
Yours, Ryder

I growl as I slam the card down on the desk and pick up the roses. I throw them in the trash can that sits beside it.

"What are you doing?" Thomas gasps.

"I don't want them!" I snap.

He runs over to them and pulls the vase out, but the flowers fall to the bottom of the trash. "This is a Waterford crystal vase," he says in disbelief as he hugs the vase to him tightly.

I wave him off. "Then keep it."

I'm more pissed that he sent me flowers than anything else. We have both decided it was over. Can't we just leave it at that? Can't we both just take our broken hearts and move on?

My phone rings, and I pick it up without looking at it. I bet it's Ryder. "What?" I snap.

"Oh, uh …" a male's voice stumbles. "I … is this a bad time?"

"Who is this?" I demand.

"Oh, so sorry. It's Nick."

I sigh and run a hand through my hair. "I'm sorry, Nick. It's just one of those days," I say, falling down into my chair. I look up to see Thomas still cradling the vase like it's his firstborn.

"Typical Monday, huh?"

Not really but I say, "Yeah."

He clears his throat. "I just wanted to make sure we were still on for tonight?"

I roll my eyes. "Yes." The man sounds so nervous. Not sure why since it's just dinner. I'm not gonna blow him under the table or take him back to my apartment. I think I need to close my legs for a little while. Obviously, I don't know what I'm doing.

"Okay. And you said you liked Chinese food, right?"

"Yes."

"Okay. Great." He laughs nervously. "I just want it to be perfect."

I let my head fall forward and close my eyes. "Nick, I don't know what you're thinking, but it's just dinner—"

"Oh, I know." He interrupts me with another uneasy laugh. "Please don't think I have any expectations."

"I hope not because I don't," I say truthfully.

I'm gonna kill Becca and Thomas for making me say yes to this date!

"What time should I pick you up?" he asks quickly. "Reservations are for seven."

"I'll meet you there," I tell him.

"Are you sure? I don't mind …."

"I'm sure," I say before he can keep talking. "I'll see you then," I assure him and then hang up.

I look up at Thomas, and he smiles down at me from the other side of the desk. "I'm gonna kill you."

His smile widens. "Make sure to bury me with this vase." Then he turns around and all but bounces out of the room with the vase in his hands.

"What the fuck are you doing, Ash?" I can't help but ask myself. But even I don't know what I'm thinking.

CHAPTER SEVEN

RYDER

I look down at my phone as Milton drives me home from another long day of work.

Me: *Please call me.*

I had sent that to Ashlyn twenty minutes ago and no response. I've been calling and texting her all day and nothing. She has officially written me off.

I decide to call Jaycent. He's the only one I haven't apologized to.

"What's up, man?" he asks, sounding tired.

"You sound like your day is going about as good as mine," I say with a sigh.

"Is yours going like shit?" he asks flatly.

Shit would be a good day. I haven't had one of those in over a week. "Is it Monday?"

That gets him to chuckle. "Yes."

I sigh again and lean back in my seat. "I saw Ashlyn today," I decide to tell him.

"How did that go?" he asks.

"I'm calling you, aren't I?" I growl.

He laughs, but I don't find this situation funny. "And I'm guessing it's because you got something to get off your chest, so let's hear it."

I don't waste another second. "She came crashing into my meeting this morning, told me off, and then stormed right out with this 'fuck you' look on her face," I growl.

"And?" he urges.

"And after she left, I felt bad. I've treated her and Becca like shit for the last week, so I wanted to make it up to them. So I sent them both flowers today.

Becca sent me a thank-you text, but Ashlyn sent me nothing."

"Did you really think flowers were gonna save the day? Week?"

"No." I sigh. A long silence stretches over the phone before he speaks again.

"Ryder, I tried to tell you that night we went out that you needed to call her. Talk to her. If you want to save whatever it was that you guys had, you are gonna have to go the extra mile."

Yes, I know this! But somehow rubbing I told you so in my face doesn't help. I let out a long breath. "I know. But ... fuck, I've ignored her for the last seven days, and I'm not sure how to get back to where we were. Or if she even wants to."

I hear him sigh on the other end as if he's contemplating telling me something. "Ryder, that night we went out, and I took you back to your office ..."

The night I almost slept with another woman? "What about it?" I ask.

"She had called you. You looked at it and threw the phone to the ground and I know I shouldn't have, but I answered it. She just started spilling everything. I tried to stop her from talking, but by the time she was done, she hung up."

I sit up in the back seat. So that's why I didn't remember having a conversation with her. He had been the one to talk to her. "What did she say?" I ask slowly.

"She said what you thought you saw and what happened were two very different things." He pauses. "... and that she loved you."

"She what—" I demand.

"I told you," he interrupts me. "After she had hung up, you looked right at me, and I told you, but you didn't say a word."

My heart is racing and my head is spinning. "She loves me?" I ask softly.

"That's what she said."

I let out a growl that he didn't tell me this the next morning when I saw him in my office. Or the day after that. Or the one after that. I open my mouth to ask him what the fuck but stop myself. It's not his fault I was a dick. It's not his fault I let it go on this long. "That was over a week ago. Of course, flowers aren't gonna fucking fix that!" I snap. "What am I supposed to do now?" I ask as if he has an answer.

"Fight. If you love her, fight for her. If she loves you as you love her, then she'll appreciate that more than distance."

"Yeah," I say, nodding my head to myself. She came to see me today. That has to mean something. "I ... Thanks, man. Thanks for being my best friend."

Minutes later, the Escalade comes to a stop, and I jump out of it then take the stairs to the building two at a time. I run through the lobby and press the button to the elevator a hundred times before one finally opens. I've already got my key out before it even stops on their floor.

I walk in their front door and come to a stop when I see Jaycent in the kitchen wearing just his boxers. "What the ...?"

"What are you doing here?" I ask confused. His eyes widen, and he drops his hands to the front of his boxers. "And where the fuck are your clothes?" I demand.

"Ryder." He raises his hands, but then lowers them again quickly. "It's not what you think."

What I think? What I think is he's in the wrong apartment. Why would he be here in his boxers? But as I look him over, a thought hits me. He never told me that Ashlyn had said she loved me. He never once told me that I had fucked up and pushed me to tell her I was sorry. My eyes narrow on him, and I take a step toward him. "Are you seeing her?" I growl. "So this is what you've been doing? Fucking her behind my back?" I demand. I didn't need to worry about Bradley at all because my best friend was too busy with her.

"Ryder ... I ..."

"So this whole time, I've been worried about the wrong guy," I snap.

He frowns at my words as if he's confused. Then his eyes widen, and he starts shaking his head. "I'm not seeing Ashlyn ..."

"Ryder." I hear my sister yelp as she comes running down the hallway, interrupting him. "What are you doing here?" Her green eyes narrow on me, and she places her hands on her hips. She's in an all-black lace teddy and a pair of black heels to top it off.

"Becca, what the fuck?" I growl, not wanting to see that. "Go put on some clothes!" I hold up my hand to block the view of her half-dressed.

Wait ... *I'm not seeing Ashlyn* ... My eyes widen as I look back at him and then to my sister. "Why are you not dressed?" I shout at her.

"Why do you keep entering *my* apartment like you own it?" she demands, her voice rising with every word. "Get out!"

"What the fuck is going on, B?" I demand. My eyes go back to Jaycent again, and I point over at her. "You've been fucking my sister," I shout, and he flinches.

"Ryder, I—"

"What and who I do is none of your business," Becca interrupts him.

I look at her wide-eyed while I point at him. "How long has this been going on?" I demand.

She crosses her arms over her chest. "Again, none of your business."

"Becca," I growl.

"What?" She arches a brow. "Don't like being kept in the dark?"

I take a step toward her. "What does that fucking mean?" I snap.

She smiles at me, and I think she's enjoying this way too much. I, however, wanna punch my best friend in the face. "Why are you here, Ryder?"

I'm here for Ashlyn ... I run a hand through my hair as I look over her again in a fucking teddy and my best friend is only in boxers. I don't have time for this. I place my eyes on the floor, so I can concentrate. "I came to talk to Ashlyn," I say through clenched teeth.

"She's on a date."

My eyes snap back up to hers. "With Bradley?" I demand. "Because she told me that was over." Had she been lying? Payback for what I've done the last week?

She snorts. "It is. Some new guy she met at the club Saturday night."

I fist my hand down by my side. "Where did they go?"

She takes a step toward me and holds out her right hand. "I want your key," she declares. I grind my teeth. "Is she worth the key?" she asks, and I growl.

I take the key out of my pocket and toss it onto the kitchen counter. It slides off and lands down by Jaycent's feet. "Where is she?" I demand.

"At the Chinese Kitchen," she says happily.

I spin around and go to open the door but stop and look over my shoulder at them. I look at the guy I've called my best friend all my life, and I feel as if he has stabbed me. How could he be seeing my sister behind my back? Had I been so wrapped up in Ashlyn that I never saw it? Or was tonight gonna be their first time? That makes my teeth clench. "I'm going to call you in thirty minutes, and I expect you to answer," I say and then look back over at Becca. "And you're going to go along with whatever I say." I'm gonna need a backup plan. I've watched Ashlyn work when it comes to revenge, and I'm gonna use her own moves on her. But I need Jaycent to pull it off. He arches a brow at me, and I add, "You owe me that much." Then I walk out, slamming the door behind me.

ASHLYN

I sit at the table across from Nick as he sips on his glass of wine. I take a gulp of mine, trying to loosen my tense muscles. This thing with Ryder is taking more of my time than I want to give it. It's over. Not sure why I can't stop thinking about him.

"Ashlyn?"

"Hmm?" I ask, placing my wine glass on the table. "I'm sorry."

"You okay?" he asks as his blue eyes search mine.

I nod. "Yes."

"You just seem far away tonight," he observes.

"It's my parents," I lie. This man doesn't know me so I could tell him anything, and he would have no reason not to believe me.

"Are they okay?" he asks with worry in his voice.

"Yes. I just haven't seen them in forever."

"Where do they live?" he asks.

"Seattle."

His brows lift. "That's a long way away. Are you from there?"

I nod and pick up my glass of wine again. "What about the rest of your family? Do you have brothers and sisters in Seattle or here?"

"I'm an only child," I tell him.

He frowns. "What brought you here then?"

"Work," I say although that's a lie. I came here mainly because of Becca. I wanted to get away and work at Talia's. Guess that saying about be careful what you wish for is true.

I just set my wine glass down when something hits the table and has my wine glass tipping over, white wine going all over my dress.

I jump up from my seat. "What the …?"

"Sis, come quick," a man shouts.

I look over to see it's Ryder. Why is he here? What is he doing? "Ryder?" I growl.

"Come quick, sis. Mom needs us," he says in a rush.

"Sis?" Nick asks. "I thought you were an only child."

"I am," I assure him.

Ryder reaches up and grabs my left hand, yanking me across the table toward him. I let out a huff at his force. "How can you say that, sis?" He looks over his shoulder to Nick. "She's embarrassed by me," he says, pouting.

"Ryder," I snap, yanking my hand from his hold. "What the hell are you doing here?" Even though my voice sounds annoyed of his presence, my body recognizes his touch and begins to heat up. God, I miss him.

"I've been calling you."

Yes, he has, but I haven't wanted to talk to him. Did he not get that when I sent him to voicemail every time?

"My phone died," I snap, lying. "Leave. Now."

"I can't. Not without you. It's Nibbles," he says breathing heavy as if he like he just came. And that thought makes my legs weak.

"Who is Nibbles?" Nick asks with confusion on his face.

"Nibbles is our mother's pet rabbit," Ryder answers, sniffing.

"He's lying," I say flatly. "Ryder, leave." I say but not sure it's believable.

"Sis, how can you say that?" he asks and places his fist in his mouth and pretends to bite down on it. He sniffs again. "How can you speak of Nibbles that way?" he asks, and then I see tears in his eyes.

Enough of this bullshit! I slam my hands down on the table and lean over it.

"Are you drunk?" He leans into me, and a slow smile spreads across his face. He's fucking playing with me. And I realize this is my payback from barging into his office this morning. "This is not funny," I hiss, my eyes narrowing on his.

His smile fades, and he sticks his bottom lip out as it quivers. "I'm not laughing, sis. This is serious. Mom is just heartbroken. We have to get home now."

"Isn't your mother in Seattle?" Nick asks confused.

I watch Ryder's jaw clench, and I smile. Yep, I've told him quite a bit about myself already. And now I'm glad I did.

Not wanting him to get the best of me, I throw him one last *go to hell* look and take a deep breath before falling down into my chair. I smile over at Nick. "What's the rush? Nibbles is already dead." I shrug carelessly and flip my hair over my shoulder. My dress may be covered in wine, but I'm gonna smile like I don't give two shits that Ryder is here making a fool of himself. "Where were we, Nick?"

I look up at Ryder, and he glares down at me. I ignore him as he yanks his phone out of his pocket. I'm not going to let him win this battle. He types away at his keys, and I watch Nick look up at him confused. Poor guy. He has no idea he's in the middle of a war.

I know Ryder is just trying to pay me back from what I pulled earlier. And I'm not even gonna say I don't deserve it because I do. I was way out of hand to barge into his work like that, but this is different. We both have said what we needed to say. Now, there's nothing left.

I clear my throat, and Nick looks at me. I lift my eyebrow in question for him to answer my question.

"I, uh … a drink," he finally answers me nervously and then swallows. "Maybe get you a new drink?" he asks, sounding unsure of what to do.

"I think that's a great idea," I say since I'm wearing the other one I had. Nick slowly raises his hand as he looks around the packed restaurant timidly as if he's one of those students who isn't sure they know the answer but wanna participate, and I hold in a sigh. The man is not gonna stand a chance up against Ryder. He's gonna eat him alive.

All of a sudden, Ryder's phone starts ringing. I lean back in my chair. Oh, this'll be good. "Hello, Mother," he says softly.

My head snaps up to look at him. His mother? He doesn't talk to her. Well, he hadn't when we broke up a week ago. Could that much change in a week?

I place my elbows on the table, very unladylike, and rest my chin in my hands. Will this end? "Hang on, Momma. I'm gonna place you on speakerphone."

My eyes widen at that. Why would I want to hear what the woman has to say? She hates me! The feeling is mutual after what I now know she did to Becca. That woman can go to hell.

He hits a button on his phone and pulls it away from his ear. "I'm here with Ashlyn," he says and then holds it down to my face. I see Jaycent written across his screen, and I narrow my eyes up at him.

Oh, that son of a ... "It's Mother," he says loudly probably letting Jaycent know he's on speakerphone. "Momma, Ashlyn is here."

I look up at him with pure hatred as he stares down at me with amused eyes, but he manages to contain his smile. "Ashlyn?" I hear Jaycent squeal, and it causes me to jump back in surprise. "Oh God, Ashlyn, Nibbles is dead," he cries, and I cringe at how badly he sounds like a woman. Nick can't possibly believe this is real. A quick look over at him tells me I was wrong. The idiot believes it.

"Tell her what happened," Ryder orders.

"Uh ..." Jaycent pauses. "Your father ran over him ... her. Ran over her. She was just hopping along ..." The voice breaks, and I roll my eyes as Nick's widen. "Tire marks ... over her back ..." Ryder chokes back a sob, and I roll my eyes again.

"Kill me now," I mumble embarrassed.

"Oh God," the voice over the phone wails at my words, and I blow some loose blond hairs from my face. I can't believe I actually took my time to get ready for this.

Nick's wide eyes finally meet mine. "Ashlyn, you should go. Your mother needs you. We can have dinner another night ..."

"Oh, what a sweet boy," the whiny voice adds. "I need my babies, Ashlyn. Ryder, please. Come home. We must have a … burial."

I ignore them both and look around the restaurant. How stupid can these two be? I just told Nick that my parents live in Seattle and can't he tell that's a man disguising his voice? God, this guy is an idiot. And Ryder is just an ass!

I can feel Ryder's eyes on me, and when I look back at Nick, he nods encouragingly.

I bite the inside of my cheek, push my chair back, and glare up at Ryder. The fucker actually winks at me! God, I want to scream! But I remember I have the best revenge right in front of me. I get up and walk around the table. I grab Nick's hand and pull him to stand.

"I'm so sorry, Nick," I say, sounding sincere. Not like this date was going to lead to anything but still, Ryder doesn't know that. I lean in to give him a kiss on the lips, but I'm yanked away instantly.

"Gotta go sis," he says tightly, and I give Nick a smile as I allow Ryder to drag me through the restaurant.

As soon as we reach outside, I shove him away. "What the fuck was that?" I shout.

"I'll call you tomorrow," he says into his phone and then hangs up.

"You are unbelievable, you know that?" I snap. "I can't believe …" I fist my hands down by my side.

"I needed to talk to you, and you've been ignoring my calls all day."

"Because I don't wanna talk to you," I scream, wide-eyed. I feel they may pop from my anger. "How hard is that for you to understand?"

"Babe …"

"Oh, don't you dare"—I point at him—"start that shit! You cannot just walk in and call me babe."

"I'm sorry," he says in a rush as if I'm going to interrupt again, but I don't 'cause I literally have nothing to say.

I can't help but look him over. He's wearing the same suit he was wearing this morning, but now his top two buttons are undone and his sleeves are rolled up, sans tie. He looks so good that it makes my heart beat faster and also makes me want to stomp my foot like a child throwing a tantrum and kiss him at the same time. This is so not fair.

I take a deep breath and pull my shoulders back. You can do this, Ashlyn. "I told you everything I wanted to tell you this morning in your office. I have nothing else to say to you." Then turn around, giving him my back, and walk off down the sidewalk.

"Ashlyn, wait!" he calls out. I don't stop.

I hear him call out my name a few more times, but I make my way through the busy Manhattan crowds not even sure where I'm going. I think home is the opposite direction, but I'm not about to turn around. I need to get away from him.

I have to slow down as the crowd gets thicker, and I feel a hand wrap around my upper arm and I'm yanked off the sidewalk between two buildings.

"Ryder!" I snap.

He pushes me up against the red brick building and pins my body with his. Before I can move, he places both of his hands on my face, and then his lips are on mine. "Ryder ..." I mumble as I try to shove him away with my hands on his chest.

He releases my face, and I think for a second he's gonna back away.

Instead, he grabs my hands and pins them above my head against the brick wall. Desire pulls between my legs. "Kiss me," he says breathlessly as those dark green eyes look down into mine. "Kiss me, baby. Please," he begs, and I growl in frustration. He can't do this! I won't let him! "I'm ..."

"Shut up, Ryder," I growl against his lips. He presses his lips to mine again, and I struggle with the decision to kiss him back or shove my knee into his groin.

"Ashlyn?"

Hearing my name makes me panic. I lift my knee and Ryder lets go of me, stumbling away and bending at the waist. He coughs from the unexpected turn of events.

"Ashlyn?"

We both look at where my name was called, and I see Nick standing over on the sidewalk, staring at us wide-eyed.

"Nick." I say embarrassed of what he just saw.

He stands there with a to-go bag in his hand, and his eyes dash back and forth between us. I let out a sigh. "I'm so sorry, Nick. I didn't mean for tonight to go like this," I tell him.

He drops the bag, and it hits the ground as he takes a step back. "You kissed your brother," he says horrified.

Ryder snorts, and I glare at him before I look back at Nick. "I can see it looked that way, but that's not what happened."

Nick looks at Ryder for confirmation, but he just licks his lips and then gives him a wink.

"Really?" I snap, turning to face Ryder. He just smiles at me, and I turn away from him. "Nick." He starts shaking his head real quickly and then wipes his lips with the back of his hand.

"You kissed your brother," he says with disgust.

"We do more than just kiss," Ryder says with a cocky smile on his face.

He gasps at his words. "Nick, he's joking ..." I say, taking a step toward him, and he takes a step back with his hands raised.

"I know what I saw," he argues.

"Nick, don't ..."

"Goodbye, Nick," Ryder says, interrupting me and raising his right hand to wave. Without another word, he turns and runs off into the crowd.

I spin around to face him. "What the hell is wrong with you?" I demand. He just laughs as he walks over to the bag of food Nick dropped. "I'm serious, Ryder."

He picks it up. "Hungry?" he asks with a smile.

I narrow my eyes at him and place my hands on my hips. "I'm no longer hungry," I respond flatly.

His eyes drop to my legs, and he licks his lips. "I'm all of a sudden starving."

"Well, you're going to starve to death," I spit out and then walk out of the alleyway and onto the sidewalk. I look him up and down with disgust as I pass him, and he smirks at me.

"I'm not gonna play fair," he warns me.

I come to a stop and slowly turn to face him. My eyes catch sight of the bracelet in his hand and then go back to his eyes. "I'm not going to play at all," I say and give him my back once again.

"Did you know that my sister is dating my best friend?" he demands over the crowd.

I come to another stop and sigh. I turn back around once again and face him. "Yes," I say, simply refusing to lie to him.

He takes a step back and runs a hand through his spiked hair. "How could you …?" He stops himself then takes a deep breath and lets it out. "How could you not tell me?"

I take a step toward him and narrow my eyes. "How could I not tell you?" I repeat. "You haven't spoken to me for a week. When would I have had the chance to tell you?" I demand.

"So you're saying you've only known for a week?" he asks, eyeing me skeptically.

I look away from him and bite my lower lip. "Thought so," he says with a snort. "Everyone is keeping secrets from me," he adds.

My head snaps back to look at him. "Maybe if you hadn't shut everyone out—"

"You wanna know why I shut everyone out?" he demands. "It's 'cause all they ever wanted to do was discuss you. And I couldn't stand it anymore," he shouts.

"Then why are you here?" I shout back. "If you can't stand the thought of me, why the hell did you ruin my date …?"

"Because I love you!" he shouts, fisting his hands down by his side.

I hate the way my body instantly hums at those words. And my chest tightens at the lie. I want it to be true so badly, but he's trying to manipulate me. He doesn't love me; if he did, he would have told me that when I called him the other night. But I hate the way my heart beats faster, wishing it was true.

I take a step back, shaking my head. "I don't need to hear this." This time when I walk off, he doesn't try to stop me.

CHAPTER EIGHT

RYDER

I beat on the door again. I've been standing outside the girls' apartment for over ten minutes and no answer. I pull out my cell and dial my sister's number. It rings several times and then eventually goes to voicemail. So I call Jaycent's. I know that fucker is in there. He answers on the third ring.

"Hello?" His voice is rough from sleep.

"Get your ass up and answer the damn door," I growl.

"What … Where are you …?"

"I'm at the fucking door!" I snap and demand, "Now answer it!"

"Who is that?" I hear Becca's sleepy voice, and I pound on the front door again.

"It's Ryder," he tells her.

She sighs. "Hang up on him …"

"Jaycent, don't you dare …"

The door swings open just as I speak. "What in the fuck are you doing?"

I'm surprised to see Ashlyn standing in front of me. Her eyes sleepy but narrowed at me as she tightens a robe around herself.

I storm in past her and hang up my phone. "We're having a family meeting," I say as I stomp down the hallway. Without knocking, I open Becca's door and find her in bed with Jaycent.

"What the fuck, Ry?" she shouts, trying to shield her body behind

Jaycent as he turns to face me.

"Get up, get dressed, and get your asses to the living room." Then I slam the door shut.

"Have you lost your mind?" Ashlyn demands, and I hate how good she looks. Even just rolled out of bed, she still takes my breath away. "It's four in the morning," she adds, in case I didn't already know what time it is.

"No. For the first time in a while, my mind is pretty clear," I tell her, and she rolls her eyes.

"I'm going back to bed," she states.

"Nope. You're part of this meeting as well," I say, grabbing her hand and dragging her over to the couch. She sits down with a huff but doesn't argue.

Minutes later, Jaycent and Becca come walking out both fully dressed, thank

God. "Why are you here at four in the morning?" Becca demands.

"We're having a family meeting," I say, narrowing my eyes at Jaycent.

Jaycent looks from me to Ashlyn. She sits there, arms crossed over her chest with a look of pure hatred on her gorgeous face. When his eyes meet mine, he smirks. "Guess my phone call didn't work." Jaycent adds with a chuckle.

Before I can respond, Ashlyn speaks. "We're not gonna talk about that."

He shakes his head with a satisfied smile on his face. "I'll start the coffee."

"No," Becca says, grabbing his arm. "We're not having a meeting, Ryder. Have you lost your mind?"

"Why do people keep asking me that?"

"Because you have," Ashlyn answers.

I turn to face her, the open floor plan allowing me a bird's-eye view. "No. I'm not. But I am tired of not sleeping."

"What does that mean?" Becca asks.

"I've been up for over a week over what happened between me and Ashlyn, and yesterday, I found out that all I had to do was talk to her. And then I also find out that my best friend is fucking my sister, and we need to talk it through."

"Stop saying it like that," Jaycent says from the kitchen.

"How should I word it?" I snap. "Because that's how I see it."

"Ryder." Ashlyn says my name in warning.

I look at my sister and demand, "Why didn't you tell me?"

"Because of this reaction," she says as if it's obvious.

"Well, of course, I'm gonna react this way. He's my best friend and seven years older than you are."

"I'm seven years younger than you are, and you didn't have a problem *fucking* me," Ashlyn says with an arch of her brows.

"That's ..." *Fuck!* "Different ..."

"Why?" she demands, standing. "Because I was just a fuck?"

My shoulders slump. "I didn't mean that, and you know it."

She places her hands on her hips. "Actually, I didn't know that, so why don't you explain it?"

"I was mad at you," I say as if that justifies my actions.

"And that makes it okay?" she snaps.

"Stop!" Becca calls out. "Both of you just stop." She points a finger at me. "I'm not gonna let you tell me who I can and can't love."

"Love?" I ask with a snort. "You can't possibly ..."

"I hooked up with Jaycent four years ago, Ryder," she declares.

My mouth falls open, and I look over at the man I call my best friend. "Four years ago?" I ask breathlessly, and he hangs his head as if he didn't want me to know that.

"Yes," she answers me, and I look back at her. She narrows her green eyes at me, and then she smiles. "And we've decided to move in together."

I start shaking my head. "You can't be serious—"

"I am!" she snaps, interrupting me. "And you have no chance at changing my mind, Ryder." I open my mouth, but she continues. "Now, my ass is going back to bed. Good night." Then she turns and gives me her back.

I turn to face Ashlyn and Jaycent. He faces me as the coffeemaker turns on. He leans his back against the countertop and places his arms over his chest as if daring me to say something. To challenge him.

And I'm not gonna pass this up. I've got an entire week of rage built up in me. I walk over into the kitchen and come to a stop in front of him. I take a deep breath and try not to just go off on him. Four years? He slept with her four years ago. She would have been …what? Seventeen? Eighteen?

"How could you not tell me this?" I say, trying to keep my voice down now that Becca went back to bed.

"Ryder, I wanted to—"

"No! You didn't!" I interrupt him. "Or you would have!" I snap.

He takes a step toward me as he narrows his brown eyes at me. "I tried!" he growls. "But then you were too busy feeling sorry for yourself over Ashlyn."

"This has nothing to do with Ashlyn," I argue.

"It has everything to do with her." He points over at where she sits on the couch. "You haven't cared about anyone else but yourself for a week, and now all of a sudden you want to know what Becca and I are up to?"

"That's because I didn't know about the two of you. It's obviously been going on for a while," I snap. "Believe me, I would have been all over it."

"Why because you wouldn't have allowed it?" he growls. "Like we need your fucking permission."

"Of course, I wouldn't have!" I snap. "I've seen how you treat your whores." His eyes widen before narrowing into little slits. "You think you can make her happy? That you're better than Conner?" I ask, shaking my head. "You're not. You're gonna break her heart and then what? You're just gonna walk away from her like you did Jasmine."

The next thing I know, his fist connects with my jaw, and the power behind it knocks me on my ass. Sprawled out on the kitchen floor, I look up at him.

His jaw clenches as he stares down at me with pure hatred, and I realize I may have made a mistake.

"Jaycent …" I sigh.

"I'm not having this conversation with you, Ryder," he says through gritted teeth. "I don't have to justify why or how I love her. Because it really just comes down to I don't give a damn what you fucking think." And then he walks out, leaving me sitting on the cold floor.

I sit up and touch my jaw and hiss in a breath from the sting of his punch. I look up as Ashlyn walks in, stepping over my legs and walking to the fridge. She pulls out an ice pack and then hands it to me.

Taking it from her, I press it to my face. "Thanks," I mumble. My face is not the only thing hurt. My pride is pretty bruised.

She leans against the countertop and sighs heavily as she drops her head to look down at me. "You're mad at the wrong person," she says, and I frown.

"He kept a secret from me. A big one," I argue.

"You should be mad at yourself," she says, and I start shaking my head. "Yes," she argues. "There's so much you don't know, Ryder." I frown at her words. "Your sister is in love with a man who treats her right and loves her back. And you and I both know he is a much better person than Conner." She looks away, taking a deep breath, and I hate that he was right. That I pushed everyone away because of her. That I didn't have to go this past week without her. I could have been with her all along. Now my chances are smaller than they were when I thought I had lost her to Bradley. "That man loves her. That man wanted to tell you a hundred times, but he didn't because she was too afraid if you found out that you would ruin the best thing that ever happened to her."

"Ashlyn ..." I start as I stand, removing the ice pack from my face.

"Have you ever stopped and listened to anyone other than your father?" she asks softly. I frown. "What does that mean?" What does my father have to do with my sister being in love with my best friend?

She runs a hand through her hair. "It means if it doesn't have potential to make you money, you ignore it."

She's not the first woman who has said something along those lines.

"That's what's wrong with all of you." Leslie looks from me to Jaycent and then back to me. "All you care about is what you can buy. Nothing to you holds value."

I remember Leslie saying those words to me as she stood inside my apartment. But at the time, I didn't understand. Now that Ashlyn has come along, I can see the meaning behind the words.

"That's not fair," I say but don't argue because she's right.

She looks away from me and lets out a laugh that holds no humor. "Life isn't fair. And neither is love," she adds. "Everyone in her world seems to be against her love for Jaycent."

"Nobody knows about it except for you and me," I say confused by her words.

Her blue eyes meet mine, and I hate the way they look so cold. Not like the ones that looked at me a week ago when she was chasing me out of this apartment. Those eyes held desperation, and now I understand why. She was afraid of losing me. But somehow, over the course of a week, she's moved on. "Yes, they do. Your mother knows. Your father knows …"

"What? How in the hell am I the last to know about this?"

"You were too busy ignoring her because of me, and you missed out on so much." She runs a hand through her messy blond hair. "You have a choice, Ryder. Either accept it or not. That's up to you. But when she pushes you away, it will be nobody else's fault but yours, and you won't only lose a sister but you'll lose a brother as well. Because he'll take her side. That's how it should be when you love someone." She turns to walk away.

But I reach out and grab her, pulling her to a stop. "Why are you for their relationship?" I ask, wanting to understand. There must be something here that I'm missing.

She looks down at my hand wrapped around her arm and then her eyes meet mine. "The real question is why are you against it?"

ASHLYN

I turn and give him my back and walk to my room.

"And you?" I hear him ask.

"Me what?" I ask as I turn around, holding in a sigh. "I already told you how I feel about them."

"I know. I'm talking about us." He places the ice pack on the counter. "How do you feel about us?"

Us? He thinks there's an us? He walks out of the kitchen, and my heart beats faster as he nears me. Now that we are all alone, I haven't been able to stop thinking about those three words he said outside the restaurant—*I love you!*

My lips part, and I suck in a long breath, trying to calm myself, but it doesn't work. He's had this effect on me since I first saw him, and the time apart hasn't helped.

He comes to a stop, and those dark green eyes look me up and down slowly. My robe isn't flattering in the least, but the way he licks his lips makes me think he is remembering what I look like underneath it.

"Ryder ..." I whisper as my legs start to shake. *Don't get sucked back in, Ashlyn. He left you when things got tough. He'll do it again. He didn't even give you a chance to explain yourself.* But then again, he did say *I love you.* Is that all it's gonna take to get me back? Three little words?

All these things go through my mind, but then he raises his right hand and brushes some loose blond strands behind my ear, and a shiver runs through me. "I love you, Ashlyn." My knees buckle.

"That's not fair," I manage to whisper.

He gives me that panty-dropping smile. "I told you I wasn't going to play fair."

I let out a long, ragged breath, and his face grows serious. "Please tell me there's still an us, baby," he whispers, taking a step closer to me. His chest now pressing into mine, and I'm breathing heavily. "Tell me that you've missed me as much as I've missed you."

"I've missed you," I say without thought as I look into his dark green eyes. I'm almost in a trance. Unable to pull away. Unable to push him away. I lift my hands and fist his black t-shirt. I expect a cocky smile, but instead, he cups my face with his soft hands, and I lean into him even more. My legs turning to Jell-O, and my head going foggy. This is what I have wanted for a week. This is what I've been dreaming about, and here it is, coming true.

"God, I wanna kiss you," he says softly, and his eyes drop to my lips as he licks his.

My hands let go of his shirt, and they wrap around his neck. I pull him into me and tilt my head. He lowers his lips until they graze mine, teasing me, and I beg, "Please kiss me."

His hands on my face pull me toward him as his lips capture mine in a rough kiss. His tongue meets mine, and I moan into his mouth.

All of a sudden, he pulls away, and I growl in protest as his hands let go of my face. They go to my sash around my waist, and yanks my robe open.

"Jesus!" He hisses when he sees I'm naked underneath it.

I don't know why, but all of a sudden, I feel nervous. Insecure. I grab for the sash and go to tie it when he pushes my back into the hallway wall and presses my hands above my head.

"Ryder ..." I pant as I shake my head side to side. My pussy tightens, and my lips part. God, he can get me so wound up in a matter of seconds.

"Don't hide from me, baby," he says, grinding his hips into mine, and I can feel how hard he is. "I wanna see you." His hands cross my wrists, and he holds them both above my hand in one of his. "I wanna feel you," he moans, running his nose down the side of my face until his lips touch my neck. My head falls back against the wall. "I wanna fuck you."

My eyes spring open, and I rip my hands from his grip. "Ashlyn, what ...?"

"Stop, Ryder," I demand, pushing him away, and he takes a step back.

"What's wrong?" he asks.

I swallow the lump that forms in my throat because I realize just how pathetic I am for him. He has ignored me all week, and all of a sudden, I'm willing to spread my legs for him. Hell, I was on a date with another man less than ten hours ago, and now here he is, and I'm all ready to take him back.

I look down to grab my sash and quickly tie it. Looking back up at him, I straighten my back and lift my chin. "I told you there is no us." The words are hard to say because I don't want them to be true. Now that I know I have such strong feelings for him, I can't push them to the side. But this is my only option. What is done is done. "You promised me that you weren't going to hurt me." His face falls. "And you also said we were the exception. Turns out it was just a lie, and we are nothing but an average couple who failed one another."

I push off the wall and give him my back as I walk to my room. It takes everything I have not to turn around and run into his arms, begging him to take me to bed.

CHAPTER NINE

RYDER

It's been two days since I made a fool of myself at the girls' apartment. And I've concluded everyone was right. It's all my fault. I pushed them away, and I wasn't there when my best friend or little sister needed me. I think I should have been the first one she told about her and Jaycent. But I understand why she didn't. I would have still made an ass of myself.

And then I couldn't leave it at that. I had to go and make an even bigger fool of myself to Ashlyn. I tried to get her into bed. It's not like that was all that I wanted, but it was the only thing on my mind at the time. And just as I thought I was about to succeed, she woke up and pushed me away.

So I've let them cool off—all three of them. I've continued to jump back and forth between Becca and Jaycent being in love to the woman I love not wanting me. I can't stop one and can't force the other. It's a bitch. But all I can do is accept it. And although I'm not a hundred percent sure I can, I have to try. I have to hear Becca out and find out what it is I'm missing.

So for two days, I've been blowing her phone up wanting to see her. She has done nothing but ignore me up until an hour ago. She finally responded with a very short and clipped answer.

Becca: *Yes.*

Was all it said when I asked her to please come by my work and give me ten minutes. Of course, I need more time than that, but if I told her I needed an hour, she would have refused.

I've been pacing back and forth in my office ever since she responded, trying to think of what to say. Of what to ask. Ashlyn said there was so much I didn't know about, and I knew better than to ask her what I'm missing. Only Becca can fill me in, and I need to know.

I come to a stop when my door opens. Becca walks in and shuts it behind her. She crosses her arms over her chest and lifts her chin. Not a good sign. She's already on the defense.

"Have a seat," I say, gesturing to one of my chairs.

"I'll stand," she responds flatly.

I sigh and rub the back of my neck nervously. "I … I'm sorry." Might as well get this part out of the way.

She snorts and looks away from me.

"I truly am sorry," I tell her. "I …"

"What exactly are you sorry for, Ry?" she asks. "For making a fool of yourself? For barging into my apartment at four in the morning? Or for calling me one of his *whores*?"

My jaw tightens. "I didn't mean it like that."

She pushes her right hip out. "Then what did you mean?"

I throw my hand out to the side in surrender. "I don't know. I was pissed, okay? Do you think I want you with Jaycent?"

"What is wrong with Jaycent?" she demands.

"He's my best friend," I state the obvious.

"He is." She nods, agreeing with me. "But tell me what the problem is. Tell me why he's okay to be your best friend but not okay to be mine."

"Ashlyn is your best friend," I say, rolling my eyes.

"She is. But so is Jaycent," she says, taking a step toward me. "Ashlyn was not only my best friend but my *only* friend for so long," she whispers, lowering her voice. "She was all I had when I was with Conner." She looks away and sighs. I can see her eyes start to well with tears. "Jaycent took up for me when no one else did."

"Took up for you how?" I ask. "What did he do that I couldn't?" I'm her big brother, after all. I should be the one who takes up for her.

She looks back at me, opening her mouth, and then shuts it, looking away again. "What is it?" I ask. "Ashlyn said there was so much I didn't know about. What do I not know about, Becca?"

"She's right," she says, and the first tear falls down her cheek.

I hate to see her cry. Normally, tears don't bother me, but when they're my sister's, it tears at my heart. I walk over to her, and she allows me to wrap my arms around her. She hugs me back tightly as a sob breaks through.

"It's gonna be okay," I say, rubbing her back. "Here, let's sit down." I walk her over to my couch and sit down beside her.

She turns to face me, her green eyes glossy and her cheeks wet. She lifts her hands to wipe them away. "I need to know that you support us, Ryder," she whispers, and I sigh. "I tried to be all tough the other night, but I want you to know it means a lot to me that you're okay with this."

"Sis ..."

"I love him," she says through fresh tears. "I love him, and he loves me. That's enough for me. And it should be enough for you."

I think about what Ashlyn told me—how I would not only lose a sister but I would also lose a brother—and she's right. I have always considered Jaycent my best friend and my brother. And it's not that I don't agree with them being together, it's the fact that he hid it from me. But that is a conversation I need to have with him. Not Becca.

I take her hands in mine and smile, hoping she doesn't see that it's not a hundred percent real. "I could never not support you, sis. I love you. And if you're happy, then I'm happy for you."

She throws her arms around me and gives me a big hug, continuing to cry on my shoulder. After a few minutes, she pulls away and wipes her face.

"Now tell me what I don't know," I urge.

An hour later, I have canceled two meetings and declined countless phone calls due to listening to my sister pour her heart out to me. And I'm more pissed off than I was at four a.m. the other morning.

I realize I have missed a lot. I thought my life was falling apart by losing Ashlyn when my sister was the one truly hurting. She filled me in on things about her relationship with Conner. Things that I would have never guessed. I mean, I hated the guy, but I had no idea just how horrible he was to her. She filled me in on how Conner told Jaycent that my mother had paid him to practically fuck her. Then the fact that Vicki knew about it. And how when she confronted our mom, she didn't even try to deny it.

I just sat there, shaking my head at times and fisting my hands. Pure hot rage went through me at what my mother had put her through. For no fucking reason other than being a selfish bitch!

I pace back and forth, running my hands through my hair as she tells me about how she called my father crying 'cause she had run into Conner at a Starbucks and how he then called Jaycent.

I come to a stop and turn to face her. "He what? When was this?"

She goes to open her mouth but shuts it the moment that my office door opens. "Ryder, what in the hell …?" My father cuts himself off as he spots my sister. "Becca, what are you doing here?" he asks, trying to hide his surprise.

"I needed to talk to Ryder," she says, sniffing and then wiping her wet cheeks. "I'll go …"

"No," I tell her. "You're fine. You can stay as long as you want."

She shakes her head. "I need to go. I'm meeting Jaycent for lunch." She walks over to me and gives me a big hug, whispering, "Thank you, Ryder. For everything." And then she pulls away, giving me a small smile, and it's the first smile I've seen on her face in a while. "I love you," she says, walking to the door.

"I love you too," I tell her, watching her hug our father and promising to call him later.

She comes to a stop at the door and turns back to face me. "I'm here to help you, Ryder. Let me know what I can do."

I know she means with Ashlyn, so I just nod, and then she leaves, closing the door behind her.

"So you finally found out about Jaycent," my father says.

"No thanks to you," I snap.

He shrugs. "I knew she would tell you when she was ready."

"Well, she didn't," I say. "I caught them."

He smiles at that. "So I'm going to assume that Jaycent was the one who gave you the shiner," he muses as his eyes look over my left cheek.

I look away from him, hiding that side of my face. "What do you want, Dad?"

"I was wondering why you canceled two very important meetings and weren't taking my phone calls."

I gesture to the door that my sister just walked out of. "Well, now you know."

"And Ashlyn?" he asks curiously.

"What about her?"

"Have you patched that up as well? She seemed pretty pissed when she took over the meeting the other day."

I sigh. "Nope."

"Too bad."

I laugh at all the craziness that has become my life. "You sound like you actually care."

He nods. "I do."

I snort. "This coming from the man who lied to me." He had the perfect opportunity to tell me what was going on when we were on his plane on the way back from Philadelphia, but instead, he chose not to.

He goes on. "Just so there's no confusion and you don't come to me later on pissed off at me for keeping secrets from you, Ashlyn has found out that O'Kane's is buying Talia's, and she put in her two weeks' notice."

"What?" I demand. "When the hell did this happen?"

"I spoke with her last week about it," he says with a careless shrug. "I talked her into giving me a month. Told her this process would take time and not to throw in the towel so soon."

"That doesn't make any sense, Dad. The auction is weeks away. The moment we buy it, you're tearing it down. So where does that leave her?" I growl.

"It leaves her here with you." He slaps me on the shoulder. "So you'd better come up with a way to keep her here before she packs up and heads back home. Word on the street is that that's the plan." Then he turns away from me.

"Word on the street?" I ask skeptically. "You mean Becca."

He doesn't respond as he continues to walk toward the door.

A thought hits me. "Dad?" He stops and turns back to face me. "Did the decision to divorce Mom have anything to do with what she has been doing to Becca?"

He doesn't smile nor does he look surprised by my question. "I can handle a lot, son. Most think this company is all that I care about. And I do care about it very much. But no one, and I mean no one, will tell you or your sister how to live your life. You guys are one of the main reasons I put so much into this company." He crosses his arms over his chest and lets out a sigh. "When it was time for me to go to college, I asked my father if he would be disappointed if I didn't plan to one day run the company, and he said no. That nothing I could do career-wise would disappoint him. That I controlled my own future and where it took me. And I feel the same way about you and Becca. If you didn't want to be here, then I'd understand. Although I would be lying if I said I didn't enjoy getting to see you every day." He uncrosses his arms and runs a hand down his already straight tie. A sign that he is getting uncomfortable with this conversation. We've never been the type of guys to open up to one another. "But it took your mother paying a man to date my daughter and her current boyfriend telling me he beat him up to realize I am not like my father. That I have only supported you guys financially, and that is not how I want our relationship to be." Then before I have a chance to respond, he walks out.

I turn to face the floor-to-ceiling windows that overlook Manhattan and sigh. "Fuck," I hiss. It seems like one thing after another. I have to get back into the know. I need to call Jaycent and set up a time to talk to him. I need to call my mother and tell her to go to hell. And I need to talk to Ashlyn and find out just what it is that's going through her head 'cause my dad is right. If she leaves the gallery and goes back home, I'll lose my chance with her.

As my eyes scan over the buildings of downtown Manhattan, something catches my eyes, and I smile.

Grabbing my phone off my desk, I dial my sister's number. She answers immediately. "Hello?"

"Still wanna help me?" I ask, sitting down behind my desk.

"Of course," she replies.

"Good. 'Cause I have a plan."

ASHLYN

Four days go by with no word from Ryder, and I can't decide if I'm relieved or mad. I mean, the guy ruined my date and then had me half naked and all hot and bothered. Then nothing! But it is all my fault, I walked away that time.

It's been the only thing on my mind all week. I'm just thankful that it's Friday, and I don't have any plans tonight but to lie in bed and watch a movie with Harry.

I walk into our apartment and find Becca standing in the kitchen pouring a glass of wine. "Hey, girl. How was work?"

"Exhausting," I answer, dropping my purse on the kitchen table. "We have a showing next week, and we have to get ready for it."

She hands me the glass of wine, and I thank her before taking a big gulp. She turns to fix herself a new one. "Have plans tonight?"

I shake my head.

"Good," she says, and then a big smile spreads across her face.

"Why is that good?" She has something in mind. And by the look in her eyes, I'm not gonna like it.

"Because I have tickets ..." I'm already shaking my head before she can finish. "To *Romeo and Juliet*. The play."

"What?" I ask wide-eyed. I saw a billboard the other day on my way home from work and wanted to go so badly. "How did you get those?"

"A friend," she says with a careless shrug. "Wanna go?"

"Absolutely!" I say excitedly. "Is it tonight?"

She nods. I start jumping up and down. It's the first thing I think I've actually been excited about in two weeks. "This is awesome!" I all but shout. Finally, something I can look forward to. "Thank you. Thank you. Thank you," I say, wrapping my arms around her tiny frame. Careful not to spill wine down her back.

"Don't thank me just yet," she says with a laugh.

I pull her away, and the smile drops off my face as I eye her skeptically. "Why not?"

She starts biting her lip nervously. "Becca?" I say her name with a sigh. "What is it?"

"Well ..." She pauses. "I'm not supposed to tell you."

"Not supposed to tell me what?" I ask before taking another drink of the cool wine.

"I'm supposed to tell you that I'm taking you to the play. You know, a girls' night." I just stare at her 'cause I have a feeling I know where this is headed, and I already don't like it. She sighs when I narrow my eyes at her. "Ryder called me three days ago and told me to give you these tickets—"

"I'm not going!" I say, interrupting her before giving her my back and making my way to my room.

She barges in behind me before the door can shut all the way. Harry meows at me as I flip on the light while he lies on my pillow. "Just hear me out."

"Nope," I say, shaking my head.

"Please, Ashlyn. Just give me a second—"

"What the hell is that?" I ask, interrupting her again when I see a black garment bag hanging on the outside of my closet door. *It's not mine.*

"That's the dress you're wearing tonight to the play," she answers.

I turn to face her and go to open my mouth to refuse when she beats me to it. "You're going, Ashlyn!" I arch a dark brow. "He got these tickets for you three days ago." I roll my eyes. "I know what happened in the restaurant, and I know how badly you wanted to forgive him when he came over to our apartment." I let out a huff at her argument. I should have never told her that I almost slept with him. "It's clear you still want him."

"I do not—"

"Yes, you do!" She's the one interrupting now. "I see you moping around here. Hell, I spoke to Thomas today, and he even said that you've been moping around at work."

"That's 'cause I'm losing my job soon." Not a total lie.

She places her hand on her hip. "Thomas also told me that has been a rumor for years." Well, hasn't Thomas been a little chatty Kathy. He and I need to have a talk. "Maybe it won't happen like my father thinks it will." She takes a step toward me as her hand falls from her hip. "Please go." I shake my head. "You don't even have to talk to him." She shrugs. "It's a play. Just sit there and enjoy a once-in-a-lifetime opportunity."

"And then what?" I ask.

"Then you're the better person," she adds. "He's sorry. Just like you were sorry when he caught you half-dressed with Bradley."

I narrow my eyes at her. "That isn't even the same situation."

"It is. You just don't want to admit that," she says softly, and we both know she's right. "Get dressed up. Go to a play and enjoy a night with the man you love." I snort. "What do you have to lose?" she asks.

I look away from her and sigh, looking at Harry. He rolls onto his back and stretches. "If I go, then he wins," I say as my shoulders fall.

"Wins what?" she asks.

I look back at her. "We both know what will happen if I go tonight." I don't need to tell her that I love the man. That going with him to the play will put me back in the same place I was just a week ago. And that it will take more willpower than I have not to sleep with him.

She gives me a soft smile. "You could be doing much worse than spending time with the man you love, Ash. He loves you too, and he's sorry. Let him prove it."

• • •

Two hours later, I hear the doorbell ring, and I go to answer it, silence filling the apartment. Becca left after she talked me into going with Ryder tonight. She told me she and Jaycent were staying at his house for the evening, and then she winked at me. Not sure if that was for her or for me.

I take a deep breath and square my shoulders as I turn the doorknob. And my knees buckle at the sight I find once I open it. Every reason I wanted to say no earlier is now screaming yes. I spent a week crying over him, and now all I want to do is smile. At times, it was hard to breathe, and now I feel like I can fly. He does this to me, and at this very moment, I wonder why I was ever scared to fall for him.

Ryder stands there in the hall, wearing a black and white tuxedo that fits him like a glove. He's slicked back his normally spiked dark hair and sports a five o'clock shadow, just how I like it. A bouquet of red roses in his right hand and a box of chocolates in his left.

"Hello." My voice is breathless, and a smile spreads across his face at the sound of it. I don't even have the power to be mad at his cockiness.

"Hello," he says, looking me up and down. I'm wearing his usual overly large t-shirt. I had just gotten out of the shower when the doorbell rang, and I grabbed the nearest piece of clothing to slip on. My hands go to the hem of it, and I tug it down a little, hoping to shield myself from him, and he chuckles. "You don't seem surprised to see me."

"Becca told me your plan," I say and clear my throat. Why do I sound so affected by him? How does he have so much power over me?

"I figured she'd pick your side." His eyes land back on mine. "That's why I decided to show up early."

"Why ring the doorbell? Trying to be a gentleman now?" I ask, and I can't help the smile on my face.

He grunts. "Becca took my key away," he says, and I frown. *When did she do that?*

"May I come in?" he asks.

"Of course," I say quickly and take a step to the side. "Make yourself comfortable. I have to finish getting ready," I say, closing the door behind him. Before heading to my room, I go to the fridge and grab the wine out of it and then two glasses.

"Would you like a glass of wine?" I ask him.

"Yes. Please."

I fill two glasses and then hand him his as I take a sip of mine. His eyes rake over my bare legs as he tips his glass back. "I'm gonna get ready," I say before turning and heading to my room. Needing to take a deep breath. One that isn't filled with the scent of him. That same one that makes my pussy wet.

I walk to my bedroom and grab my phone off my bed. I send Becca a thank you for letting me borrow a dress once again. I tried to tell her that I could wear something of my own, but she explained to me how people dress up for opening night. And I needed to dress more formal than club wear. I thought I was gonna be overdressed for the play, but now I'm thankful for her.

I toss my phone onto the bed and walk into my bathroom. I pick up the makeup brush that still has black eyeshadow on it and start to blend it into my crease. I'm starting the second eye when I hear Ryder walk into my bedroom. "You couldn't have waited somewhere else?" I can't help but ask. I need to be able to clear my thoughts. To try to give myself a pep talk so that way I at least make it to the play before I jump him.

I hear him sigh heavily. "Ashlyn … I'm sorry."

Placing my hands on the countertop, I hang my head. Why are those words enough? How is it that three words can make me want to hug him? Kiss him? It shouldn't be this easy to forgive him.

"I know I messed up," he continues. "I just need one more chance."

"Ryder, I …"

I hear him start screaming at the top of his lungs.

I push off the countertop and run into my bedroom to see him standing on my bed in his tux, his gorgeous face as white as a ghost. His glass of wine still in his hand, but it's empty. "What the hell are you doing?" I yell as my heart races. He had screamed like a little girl.

He places his hand on his chest and looks at me wide-eyed. "I just saw a rat." My eyes widen. "And I'm pretty sure it was wearing a fucking sweater," he adds, breathing heavy.

What? "A rat? Where did it go?" I ask, looking around and not seeing anything on the floor. I'm pretty sure he's mistaken. The occupants in this building pay millions of dollars for these apartments. I doubt they would pay that much if rats were running around.

He points at my closet. "It touched my leg," he says in a high pitch voice. He bends down and starts dusting off his black pants as if it left germs on him.

I slowly push my closet door open all the way and flip on the light. I look around and don't see anything but my shoes on the floor. I go to the very back where my jeans hang so low they almost touch the floor. I push them back and laugh when I see what had almost scared him to death. "Come here, Harry," I say, picking up my cat.

"You named it?" he demands from my room.

I laugh as I pet his back over his shirt. His green eyes are wide, and his ears are back. Ryder scared the crap out of him as well. I walk back out, and Ryder takes a quick step back when he sees me holding it. "Put that down, babe," he demands. "Those things have diseases."

I laugh. "Ryder, this is Harry. He's my cat."

"Your cat?" he asks, looking at it while tilting his head. "Doesn't look like a fucking cat to me."

"He's a sphynx," I say. "A hairless cat."

He lets out a long breath. Seeing this macho man dressed in a tuxedo standing on my bed like a scared child makes me laugh. "And you named him Harry?"

I nod with a smile. "And he *is* wearing a sweater." I look down and read it: *This pussy is loved*. I guess I can see where he thinks he was a rat. He's still a kitten and very small.

He nods his head. "Well." He straightens his black bow tie trying to act unaffected now. "He looked like a rat when he ran into the closet. I've been in your apartment multiple times. Why am I just now seeing him?"

"Bradley brought him here. I had to leave him behind because he had an appointment with the vet to get fixed." Just saying Bradley's name has changed the mood in the room. The air is thicker, and my heart feels heavy for the friend I lost and the guy who came between us.

Without another word, I turn and walk back into my bathroom, taking Harry with me.

• • •

An hour later, I'm standing back in my extremely large closet looking at myself in the full-length mirror. My blond hair is teased at the crown. I've pulled it to the right where it lay over my shoulder and pinned the big curls in place. I've put more makeup on than I normally wear on any given workday but as much as you wear for evening. My eyes are more of a neutral color with a touch of black in the crease. I went with winged eyeliner and natural blush. Topped off with black mascara and a dark red lipstick. It's not a look I've done often, but I find that I like it.

I turn to the right and unzip the garment bag hanging on the rack. I pull the dress out that Becca let me borrow and slowly start to put it on, sliding one leg in at a time. I bring it up over my hips and stomach and gently slide one arm in, being careful not to rip it. There's no way I would be able to put this on over my head and not mess up my hair or makeup. I bend down and place one heel on at a time.

I turn and look at myself in the mirror one last time and take a deep breath. I have to come out of this room sooner or later. I've kept him waiting long enough. I take one more drink from my wine glass, finishing off my third glass.

I walk out of the closet and through my bedroom to find Ryder standing in the living room in front of the floor-to-ceiling windows overlooking the city. It's lit up from the city lights. I look over at him as he stands there with his hands in his front pockets of his black pants. He has removed his black jacket and laid it on the back of the couch.

I slide my sweaty hands down my dress and try to muster up the courage to say something. I feel so out of my element. I have ever since I walked into this extraordinary apartment weeks ago. I didn't think I fit in here—that I was in over my head—and this just confirms it. Standing here in a dress that isn't mine trying not to love a man who is way out of my league. I feel like Cinderella. But the only difference is I'm not gonna get the guy. Our love story is more like Romeo and Juliet—when he walks away, I'll wish I was dead!

I roll my eyes at how dramatic I sound. Come on, Ashlyn. You can do this. It's just one night out with the guy you love. How hard can it be? I clear my throat before I have another second to think about it and say, "I'm ready."

He turns slowly to face me, and I hold my breath as his eyes look me up and down slowly as if he's trying to memorize me. His eyes finally meet mine, and I give him a soft smile. He doesn't return it. I go to bite my lip—nervous habit—but refrain so I don't mess up my lipstick. Is he mad that I mentioned Bradley earlier? Has he changed his mind about tonight? Maybe he regrets ever giving me the tickets. Or maybe he regrets ever meeting me.

He walks toward me, his hands still in his pockets, and my heart races at the intense look he's giving me. "Everything okay?" My voice shakes showing my nervousness. My stomach is flipping, and my heart is racing.

He pulls his right hand out of his pocket and lifts it to run his knuckle over my cheek, and I hold my breath. "It is now."

CHAPTER TEN

RYDER

I can't help but stare at her. Well, I guess one would call it gawking. She's wearing a long black dress that flares as it hits her knees, giving what my sister calls a mermaid look. It's a black one-shoulder dress that shows off her thin waist. I thought she was beautiful the day I met her on the beach, but tonight, she takes my breath away. And I'd gladly die just looking at her. The black fabric against her tan skin makes her blond hair glow, making her look like an angel.

I had to trick her. Lie to her. I knew there was no way she would go with me to this tonight no matter how much she would love to. I had a feeling that Becca would rat me out, but thankfully, the tickets were enough to get her to agree.

"Sorry it took me so long to get ready." She blushes as she looks down at her dress. I knew she would look amazing in this dress when I saw it. Another thing Becca helped me out with.

"No need to apologize," I say truthfully. After I had freaked out over what I now know is her cat, I spent the time in her kitchen having a couple of glasses of scotch while she locked herself in her bedroom getting ready. It was well worth the wait.

"I'm ready when you are."

I look her up and down one more time, thinking of how much I'd love to pick her up in my arms and carry her back to her room where I'd take my time undressing her. Take my time loving her. Every inch of her. But I shake my head to clear that thought. I know that sex is the last thing I'll be getting from her tonight.

We make our way down the elevator and out to the car where Milton waits for us. "A limo tonight?" she asks in surprise.

I nod. "Only the best for you," I say, opening the back door for her.

She crawls in, and I enter after. She thanks Milton before he closes the door.

Once we are situated, she looks over at me. "I didn't need a limo, Ryder. We could have taken a cab."

I snort. She doesn't understand how these things work, and I get that, but you don't show up to a Broadway play on opening night in a cab. Not when you're Ryder O'Kane, anyway, and with a gorgeous woman who you love on your arm. You pull out all the stops. And a limo was one of them. "Would you like a glass of champagne?" I ask, already reaching for it.

She nods, not looking over at me. "Yes, please." I have a feeling it's more to calm her nerves than to taste.

I grab the bottle out of the bucket of ice and grab two flutes. I see Milton has already uncorked the bottle. I pour her a glass and then myself. We hold them up and toast. "To me being a douche," I say.

She laughs, but I can tell it's a nervous one. "You don't have to—"

"Yes, I do," I say, interrupting her and getting serious. "I overreacted when I had no right to," I say, and she gives me a soft smile.

She clicks her glass to mine and then takes a drink. After she swallows a good part of it, she looks over at me. "Hungry?" I ask, and she nods. "I was thinking sushi," I tell her.

"Can I make a request?"

I smile, letting her know I would take her anywhere. "Of course."

"Can we go to sushi some other night?" And that makes my smile widen even more. As if I'll get to see her again tomorrow.

"Whatever you like," I assure her.

"The other day, I ate lunch at this amazing Italian restaurant. I'd like to go there for dinner. I've been craving it all day."

I nod my head and get Milton's attention as she tells him where it's at. We pull up to the fancy restaurant and get out of the limo. "Well, crap," she says sadly. "I didn't think about it being packed." There's a line down the sidewalk and people are seated at a few round tables outside waiting to be seated indoors.

"That's okay," I say, grabbing her hand and pulling her toward the entrance. Her heels clapping on the concrete to keep up with me. I see the man standing outside the door dressed in a suit and tie with a clipboard and pen. He is looking down at it, marking out a name as we come up to him. "Hello. I would like a table for two," I say.

"I'm sorry. The wait is currently sitting at an hour," he says, not looking up at us. Ashlyn squeezes my hand and tries to pull me back, but I don't budge.

"Maybe you can check again," I insist.

He sighs heavily. "I don't need to check …" His words cut off as he looks up at me. "Mr. O'Kane," he says in surprise as he fixes the glasses on his face. He looks over at Ashlyn wide-eyed and then back at me. He nods quickly. "Table for two, you said?"

I nod. "Yes. Please."

He turns, giving us his back as he mumbles into his headset. When he turns back around to face us, he has a big smile on his face. "Go on in, Mr. O'Kane. They have a table waiting for you."

I remove my right hand from my pocket and shake his. His eyes widen when he feels the hundred dollar bill I just slipped him. "Thank you," I say before letting go of Ashlyn's left hand and placing my hand on her back. I guide her into the well-known restaurant.

"Ryder," she whispers harshly. "We just cut in front of twenty people."

I ignore her as another man takes us to the corner of the restaurant to a table set for two. I thank the man and then hold out her chair for her. She thanks me, but her eyes are narrowed. "I thought you would be happy," I say, sitting down across from her.

She shakes her head, mumbling, "Becca used to tell me about this."

"About their pasta?" I ask.

She snorts. "No. Well, yeah… She is the one who told me and Thomas about it." Then she shakes her head quickly. "But that's not what I meant. She told me how people treat her differently once they know who she is."

"I paid him for his help."

Her mouth falls open. "So you think that's better?" she demands.

"Because you threw some money at him?" She places her forearms on the dark red table cloth and leans in to me. "Do you always use money to get your way?"

"If it calls for it."

She lets out a laugh that tells me she thinks I'm an ass. And honestly, I can't argue with her. Because I have used money many times to get what I want. "How did you hear about this place?" I ask, looking around the rather large restaurant and wanting to change the subject. It has round tables, and all of them draped with dark red tablecloths along with two chairs. A few of them have four. The lighting is dim, giving off that romantic atmosphere. And it doesn't hurt that we are in the corner all alone. For a wait that was an hour, this place isn't all that busy. "You said Becca?"

"Yes. She told me and Tom about it, and we came here the other day for lunch," she states, still sounding pissy.

I stare at her with a tight jaw as she looks around as if embarrassed to be seen with me. "Tom? You sure do spend a lot of time with him." I know she works with the guy, but they seem to spend a lot of time alone outside of Talia's.

She shrugs. "He is my only other friend here besides Becca." "I'm not your friend?" I question.

"You are, but you have been absent for a week."

I swallow and nod. "Can I ask you a question?"

"Sure."

"That night I broke up your date with Rick …"

"Nick," she corrects me.

I wave a hand in the air. "Was that your first date?"

She nods. "It was."

"How did you meet him?" I ask, needing to know. It's like I want to torture myself.

"Becca and Tom set me up with him." She tilts her head to the side in thought. "Well, I guess they didn't really set us up. The three of us went to Seven Deadly Sins, and I met him there …"

"Wait?" I ask, holding up my hand. "You, Becca and … Thomas went to Seven Deadly Sins?" She nods, and I curse myself. Thomas was the nice guy Milton was trying to tell me about. Fuck, Ryder. So many times I could have found out the truth if I had just let people explain.

Dinner went smoothly after that. She seems to loosen up, and I was able to relax knowing that there never truly was a reason to worry about Bradley. We make our way back out to the limo that waits by the curb. "How was it, Ashlyn?" Milton asks her with a smile.

"Delicious. But I'll let you be the judge of that," she says, handing him the extra meal she had ordered.

"For me?" he asks wide-eyed. She nods with a smile. "Thank you, Ashlyn," he says with a smile of his own.

She stays quiet as we make our way to the theater. I don't push her to talk because I already see the inner struggle. I can hear it in the way she spoke to me at dinner. And I can see it in the way she looks at me. She's still unsure if coming tonight was the best idea, but I am on a mission to prove to her that it is.

We pull up to the theater and get out. Her eyes widen as she sees *Romeo and Juliet* light up the marquee that stands tall above the theater. I take her hand in mine, and I'm thankful when she doesn't pull away.

"Good evening, sir," a man dressed in an all-black three-piece suit says as he holds the door open for us to the Grand Theater. "Miss," he adds, bowing to Ashlyn.

"Thank you," we say in unison as we enter.

Coming to a stop, she drops my hand and slowly spins around as she looks up at the gold and cream walls. The ceiling has a picture of a champagne-colored crown. I watch her in awe as her eyes light up and her lips part, sucking in a deep breath.

"Ryder, this is …" She can't finish the sentence as her eyes drop to the floor, and she takes in the blood red carpet.

People dressed in their finest Kiton suits while their wives don just as expensive designer evening gowns are walking around and talking to one another. I spot a man I know, and he gives me a smile as he sees me. "Mr. O'Kane," he says, reaching out to shake my hand. "Surprised to see you here. Thought you steered clear of these places," he says with a chuckle.

I nod. "Well, I figured I've lived here all my life. This time is as good as any to try it out."

He laughs and looks over at Ashlyn as she silently stands beside us.

He reaches his hand out to her. "And who might this beautiful woman be?" he asks.

I place my hand on the small of her back. "Mr. Tucker, this is Ashlyn Whitaker."

"It's nice to meet you, Mr. Tucker," she says, shaking his hand.

"Ashlyn just moved to New York," I tell him.

"Oh, really?" he asks, giving her a big smile. "Well, I hope it's living up to your expectations."

She smiles. "Yes, sir."

"Mr. Tucker is the mayor of New York," I inform her.

Her eyes widen, and he laughs, looking back at me. "Call me next week. I'm still waiting for my chance to beat you at another round of golf."

ASHLYN

I stand at Ryder's side in amazement and pretty tipsy from the wine and champagne. But I'm trying to sober myself up because the man knows everyone here! I've met a senator, the mayor, the district attorney, and a judge. A woman who looked like she belonged in a movie instead of here at the Broadway play insisted I have lunch with her. I'm not sure what she does or who she was, but she seemed important. Two women and a man stood behind her as if waiting for her approval to move. One man we stopped and spoke to went on and on about his daughter who has the lead role of Juliet in this play. And I was happy to know that she had just got engaged to the very man who plays her Romeo.

I stand next to Ryder as he makes his way through the people talking here and there about anything and everything under the sun.

Ryder leans down and whispers in my ear. "You okay?"

I pull away and look up at him. Yes, I'm okay. I'm just speechless. One man he spoke to said that Ryder hated these things. He came here for me, and I didn't realize how much that meant to me until he had said it. I nod my head and give him a smile, so he doesn't think I've gone mute.

"Ryder," a man calls out, getting his attention.

"George." Ryder says excitedly. "It's been a long time." They shake hands.

"It has. Funny I see you here. I was going to call you next week."

"Oh?" Ryder asks, pulling me to his side. I don't think he knows he's even doing it. He isn't being overly handsy or anything, but he can't help but hold my hand or touch my back. As if he's making a claim to me for every man to see, and I hate how much I like it.

"Yeah. I have a piece of property you may be interested in."

Ryder smiles. "I'm always interested."

The man he called George fixes an already straight bow tie. "One word; Hamptons."

Ryder chuckles as he nods his head once. "Well, give me a call and we'll set up a meeting."

We make our way over to a bank of gold elevators. "Where are we going?" I ask Ryder quietly.

"To our seats," he says simply. He strikes up another conversation with a man and woman in the elevator. When it opens, he ushers me down a hallway and then through a door. I gasp when I see we are up in a box looking down on the stage. Just the two of us.

"Ryder," I say breathlessly as I make my way over to the gold rail.

He comes up behind me, runs his fingers lightly over my exposed shoulder, and leans down to whisper in my ear. "You like it, sweetheart?"

I spin around in his arms and look up at him. He places his hands on my face, and I smile. "Thank you," I whisper.

He smiles as he leans down, pressing his lips to mine. "No thank you is needed." He runs the pad of his thumb over my bottom lip, and my breath catches in my throat. "Seeing that smile is thanks enough." Then he leans down and gently kisses my lips. And I realize, once again, I couldn't fight this man if I tried.

CHAPTER ELEVEN

RYDER

I sit back in my seat and watch her. I haven't even looked at the stage once. I couldn't care less about the play. I'm here because of her. If not for her, I would never see another one. It's not that I don't like them; it's just that I don't have the time in my busy schedule to see one. But for her? It's worth it. She hasn't quit smiling once, and I don't even think she knows she's doing it. Her eyes are lit up, and she's sitting on the edge of her seat as if she doesn't know what's going to come next.

Even though I can hear the actors talking, I still don't stray from her. But I can tell it's nearing the end. I watch Ashlyn as she smiles brightly. I frown as I try to figure out this woman. How can someone find this romantic? Or even somewhat related to love? How can she see this as a romance and not a tragedy? They die. Both of them commit suicide due to lack of communication. What kind of woman can fall in love with such heartbreak? Isn't love supposed to be rainbows and sunshine? Not dark and deadly.

She stands quickly and starts clapping enthusiastically. I look around to see the actors and actresses bowing with smiles on their faces, and I stand, not wanting to look disrespectful when everyone else in the theater is.

She turns to me, her blue eyes lit up and a smile on her face. Her blond hair curled over her shoulder makes her look like a goddess. She is the most gorgeous woman in the building. And she's here with me!

"Thank you, Ryder." She throws her arms around me and hugs me. "Thank you so much," she whispers.

I pull her away and lean down, pressing my lips to hers. Just a soft and gentle kiss, not wanting people to see just what she does to me. When I pull my lips from hers, I lean my head on hers. "You're very welcome, sweetheart."

We make our way down the elevator and out the doors after only being stopped a few times here and there to talk to people I know. When we get into the back of the limo, she's laughing.

"What's so funny?" I ask as Milton pulls away from the curb.

"The fact that I told Becca I wouldn't come to this with you," she states, laughing even harder.

I arch a brow. "So she did have to talk you into it?"

She nods. I reach over and cup her face, her laughter dying instantly. "I'm glad you came."

"Me too," she whispers.

"I want another chance, Ashlyn," I say without giving her any time to think about what is happening.

She closes her eyes for a brief second. "Ryder, we both know where this will lead."

"A happily ever after?" I question with a charming smile.

She chuckles. "There's no such thing."

I frown. "How come you believe in Romeo and Juliet so much, but you can't believe someone could love you like that?"

She stares at me unblinkingly. "What does that mean?"

"It means that you believe two people can die for one another, but not live."

She starts shaking her head. "They would never be happy. Not with the way their families hated one another. Death was inevitable. In peace, they are one."

I snort. "That's bullshit!"

She gives me a half-smile. "Can you think of a better love story?"

"I can, as a matter of fact."

"And what's that?" she asks.

"Ours," I say simply, and I see the pain flash across her face. I take her hand in mine. "You once told me that you want that soul-crushing, all-consuming love. You said that you don't know who you are until you lose yourself." I lick my lips. "And Ashlyn, this past week, I lost myself. And it did exactly what you said it would; it drove me crazy." Her eyes search mine, but she remains quiet. "Can you honestly say that you didn't feel a difference? That you didn't feel a piece of you missing?"

She looks away from me. "You know I did."

Hope makes my heart speed up. I release her hands and dig my right hand into my pocket. The last surprise I have for her tonight. "Please?" I beg, holding it up in front of her. "Take me and this back. I promise I won't let you down again."

She looks at the bracelet she had returned to me earlier this week and gives me a small smile. "You know what they say…"

"What do they say?" I ask with a frown, confused where she is going with this.

She gives me a slow and sexy smile. "A king is nothing without his queen."

I laugh at her statement and nod. "You are correct. I'm nothing without you." Smiling, I add, "You are my queen."

"You know all the right things to say," she says, but it wasn't meant as a compliment.

"We both know that's not true, or I would have never lost you."

She hangs her head, and I lower my hand that holds the bracelet. My free hand goes to her chin, and I lift it to make her look me in the eyes.

My eyes drop to her dark red lips, and I love the way they look on her. She licks them, and my eyes land back on hers. "I can't live without you," I say. "Please don't make me," I beg.

Her eyes search mine, and I feel her lean closer to me. I hold my breath, afraid of what she may say. "You said you love me?" she asks.

"More than anything."

A slow smile spreads across her face. "Love is a very dangerous game."

Her words catch me off guard, but I return the smile. "I don't expect you to play fair."

"Nothing about love is fair," she says, bringing her hands up to my chest. Her eyes drop to her hands as she starts undoing the buttons on my tuxedo.

When they meet mine, I arch my brow. "Plan on teasing me, do you?" I question, not choosing to comment on the fact that she just said love. I know Jaycent told me she said it, thinking I heard it, but she hasn't said it any other time. And I'm not going to rush it. She'll tell me again when she's ready.

"Who said I was gonna tease you?" She chuckles as her hands slide up my chest and over my shoulders, pushing my jacket off on the seat.

"Well, baby. I'm all yours," I say, making her laugh.

"Then don't keep me waiting," she says, batting her eyelashes and puckering her red lips.

A growl forms deep in my throat as I feel my cock start to harden. I reach over with my free hand and press the button to put up the divider, blocking Milton's view of us.

I lean forward, pressing my face in her neck, and kiss her soft skin while my hand takes hers and places it on my achingly hard cock. "You do that to me."

She whimpers as her hand massages it over my black slacks. "Please," she begs as she arches her back, lifting her ass up off the leather seat.

I slide my hand into her dress and cup her bare breast. "Fuck." I sigh.

"Ryder," she moans as I massage it.

"I wanna taste you so badly, baby," I admit.

She places her hands on my chest and pushes me backward. I place my hands up in surrender, not wanting to rush her. If she's not ready, I won't push her. But fuck, my cock is so hard for her it's painful.

She surprises me when she drops to her knees before me. With my hands still in the air, I ask, "What are you doing?"

Her hands go to my waist, and she pushes up my cummerbund and unbuttons my pants all while staring up at me with a mischievous look in her eyes.

I grab her hands. "Stop."

"What? Change your mind already?" She cocks her brow at me in challenge.

"I wanna please you." I want my head between her legs. I wanna taste her while she comes on my tongue.

"You have. Now, I wanna please you." Her voice drops to a

whisper as her eyes fall to the outline of my hard cock inside my pants. "Please," she begs, and it's my undoing.

I let go of her hands and reach out, sliding mine into her hair. I pull her head back, and she sucks in a breath; my cock twitches as I watch her lips part while she breathes heavily. My other hand reaches out and cups her cheek while my thumb runs over her parted lips. "What do you want, baby? Tonight is all about you." *The rest of my life is gonna be about you.*

"I want to taste you," she moans, and I smile.

I pull away, and she looks up at me through heavy eyes. "Lie on the floor," I order.

She doesn't argue as she lies down in my limo in an expensive evening gown. My smile widens, glad I chose the Escalade limo over any other. The cut out of the mini bar to the right where the back door is gives me just the right amount of room to do what I have planned.

I undo my seat belt and slide off my seat to the floor at her feet. She pulls her knees up, and I grab the hem of her dress. I slowly raise it up and over her legs allowing my knuckles to graze her smooth legs. I moan when she lifts her hips for me to raise it higher. She has on a pair of black lace panties. Her legs fall open when I place my hand on her inner thigh and run it up along her flesh to the black lace.

"Ryder," she breathes as she runs her hands through her curled blond hair.

"Shh," I whisper. "I know, baby."

I very slowly place my hands on either side of her hips and lift one leg over hers to straddle her. This limo isn't ideal for sex, but it's doable. I just gotta keep in mind that Milton is driving, and this is New York. He can fling me face first into the floor at any moment.

I place her arms above her head. I come to a stop when my legs are on either side of her upper chest.

I let go of her arms, and she leaves them above her head, unable to move them with my body pinning her chest and shoulders.

I reach down and unzip my pants. She licks her lips as she watches me pull my hard cock out of my zipper. I wrap my hand around the base and start to stroke it. Fuck, it hurts; I'm so hard.

She whimpers, and her body shakes as a tremor runs through it. I position myself up on my knees and lean forward. "Open those pretty red lips," I order. She opens for me, and I guide the head of my cock between them.

I moan as her tongue licks around the tip of it before she wraps her lips around the head. She pulls back and licks up the shaft while her eyes stay on mine.

I growl as if I'm an animal about to attack its prey. I press forward, pushing more of my cock into her mouth. I grind my teeth when she lifts her arms awkwardly and places them on my upper chest.

I grab them and pin them down to the floor at her forearms. I readjust my knees, squeezing her chest between them, and press forward. It forces her to take more of me without being able to pull away.

Her body lies incapacitated on the floor of the limo. All she can do is take what I'm giving her. She tries to tilt her head side to side to free her mouth of my cock to get a breath, but she can't. "You feel so good," I tell her, closing my eyes. "Your mouth. Your tongue. Fuck, baby, I can't go easy," I admit.

She moans around my cock, and I start to move—faster and harder. Her body thrashes under mine, and every now and then when I push it to the back of her throat, she closes her eyes and makes a choking noise, and I find it hot as hell. Her at my mercy. Her serving me.

My legs are starting to go numb from my cramped spot, and I know her hands must be going numb.

I look down at her, and tears slowly fall down the sides of her face as her mouth is open to me. It's my undoing. I come in her mouth with a grunt as my balls tighten, and I bite my lip to keep from screaming out her name.

ASHLYN

I walk on shaky legs to the elevator in the Q's. The doors close, and I look at myself in the mirrored walls. When this evening started, I must say I looked pretty damn good, but now that it's over, I look like a woman he picked up on the side of the road for a couple of hundred bucks. It's sad how soft I am for him. But the bad part is that I'm not even embarrassed about it.

My long blond hair has lost its curl, and the part where I had teased it looks like it was in a windstorm. The bobby pins long gone. My black eyeliner is running. But instead of running down my cheeks, it ran down the side of my eyes to my ears from lying flat on my back in the limo. Ryder placed his jacket over my shoulders before we got out of the limo, thank God, or you'd be able to see red marks on my upper arms from his hands.

The elevator dings, and the glass doors slide open. We stay silent as he places his hand on my lower back and guides me to the door. Good thing, too, because I'm not sure I could talk if I wanted to. My throat is sore, and my cheeks still burn. I like it. I liked the way he was in the limo. Unable to control himself. How he controlled me. I'm wetter now than I was earlier. Pleasing him makes me feel powerful because he loses all control.

I'm not sure why he chose my apartment to stay in tonight, but that's where we are. I dig into my purse and hand him my key since I know Becca took his from him.

He walks past me into the living room. He sits down on the white leather chair and starts to undo his bow tie.

"What are you doing?" I ask then clear my throat.

He smiles at me and tosses his tie to the floor. "You're my queen," he states proudly. "And every queen needs a throne."

I blink. My mind still fuzzy from alcohol, and my body still humming with need. "I don't …"

He leans forward in the chair placing his elbows on his knees. "Come here, my queen. Your throne awaits." He licks his lips, and I smile at him as realization dawns.

I drop my clutch on the floor and make my way over to him. His dark green eyes look me up and down with heat in them. When I come to a stop before him, he places his hands on my hips and runs them up and down. He leans his head forward, and the chair he sits in along with the height of my heels puts my sex right in front of him.

He inhales sharply. "I can smell how wet you are," he whispers proudly.

I place my hands in his hair and wrap my fingers around the brown strands. I yank his head back, and he hisses in a breath as he looks up at me. "What are you gonna do about that?" I ask.

He smiles, making his eyes light up with mischief. He leans back in the chair pulling me with him. He reaches up and pulls my hands free of his hair. Then he scoots down, positioning his head by my lower belly as I straddle him. He pushes me up the chair, and I spread my legs for him, placing them on the armrests.

He shoves my dress up and around my stomach, and then I feel his hand on my hip. He grips the thin black lace of my panties and yanks on them. I yelp in surprise as the fabric burns my skin from the force of his hand tearing it apart. My head falls back to look up at the ceiling, and I pant as I feel his breath on my sex.

"I'm been craving you all week," he states, placing both of his hands on my hips.

I cry out when I feel his lips on my pussy. He's not gentle. His tongue makes long strokes, and my body tightens as his tongue enters me. My dress falls over his head, and I place my hand on the back of the high back chair, gripping it tightly.

"Ryder." I gasp as I feel his teeth nip here and there. "Oh God …" I suck in a deep breath as my hips rock back and forth as I ride his face.

He growls against my sex, and his fingers dig into my hips. I lose track of time. I close my eyes and lose my sight and hearing. All I can do is feel. I feel every stroke of his tongue. I feel the power in his fingers holding me in place. And most of all, I feel his desire to please me.

I come on his tongue, screaming out his name and panting as I open my eyes. Colors look faded and objects come in and out of focus as I come down from the highest orgasm I've ever had.

When he releases me, I fall against the chair. He sits back up, wraps his arms around my waist, and stands from the chair, carrying me down the hallway.

He walks into my bedroom, slamming the door shut with his foot, and lays me on the bed. I lie there, still breathing heavy, and my sex swollen as he rips his shirt open, buttons hitting the hardwood floor. He kicks off his shoes and strips out of his pants.

Then he's on top of me. His hands in my hair. His hard cock pressing against my throbbing sex. I go to speak, but his lips are on mine moments later. He kisses me desperately, and I kiss him back, tasting myself on his lips.

"Taste that?" he asks, running a hand down my cheek. "That's the taste that drives me wild," he states.

I go to speak, but he removes the back of his hand from my face and wraps it around my throat. I arch my back and suck in a ragged breath before he takes it away. He lowers his face to mine and whispers, "I'm just getting started, beautiful."

CHAPTER TWELVE

RYDER

She's lying next to me in bed naked as I run my hand up and down her bare arm. Silence fills the room as we lie in darkness. Not sure what time it is, but I'm not tired. I'm afraid if I close my eyes that I'll wake up and she'll be gone. Like this night was just a dream.

"Are you awake?" I ask.

A long silence follows as I continue to rub her arm softly. I think she has fallen asleep when she finally whispers, "Yes."

I shift so I'm facing her. Even though I can't see her, I still want her body against mine. My hand covers the small of her back, and I pull her to me. Her right leg slides over my hip as she gets closer.

"There's so much we need to discuss," she says softly.

"It can wait," I tell her, just wanting to enjoy this moment with her.

"It can't," she insists.

I let out a long breath. "Okay. You go first."

"Bradley proposed to me."

My hand comes to a stop, and my heart beats wildly in my chest. "What did you say?" I must have heard her wrong.

"What do you think I said?" she asks.

I pull away from her and sit up. Reaching over, I flip on the light on her nightstand and turn to face her. She blinks a few times and slowly rises to a sitting position. "I'm serious, Ashlyn," I growl.

"So am I."

I run a hand through my hair and throw the covers off me. My body heat rising all of a sudden. "Fuck, Ashlyn," I snap, getting out of bed and pacing; I need the movement. The thought of them together makes my skin crawl.

She gets out of bed as well, and I look over at her. She's naked, of course. Red marks cover her upper arms. A hickey on her chest from where I couldn't stop kissing her and another one on her hip and inner thigh. My mouth waters at the thought of leaving more.

Focus! "Why would you tell me that?"

"Because this time if you choose to walk away, it's gonna be because you know the truth," she growls.

"I'm sorry!" I shout. "How many times am I gonna have to apologize?" I growl.

"I don't know," she snaps. "Until I feel you're truly sorry."

I snort. "You think this is just some big elaborate show? You may not forgive me, but that doesn't mean I don't truly forgive you."

Her eyes widen, and her mouth falls open. "Forgive me?" she says slowly, and it makes me think I might have said the wrong thing. "I understand that not telling you Bradley was coming was a big mistake on my part. But you walked out. You wouldn't even give me two seconds to explain." I open my mouth, but she continues. "And then I called you. I even told you that I loved you and nothing!" She's shouting again. "And then a week later, you find out I'm on a date, and all of a sudden, you care again."

"That's not true!" I snap, mad at myself all over again.

"Then what is, Ryder?" she demands, crossing her arms over her chest. "Please tell me what I'm missing here."

"I didn't know you called me."

"Bullshit!" she snaps.

"I swear on everything," I say, holding my hands up. "I didn't know you called me until Monday night when you had your date."

She snorts. "Unbelievable. You think I'm going to believe you …?"

"Jaycent answered my phone when you called me. I was too drunk due to the fact that I thought I had lost you to Bradley. He was the one you told I love you to. But he never told me." She stands, staring at me with confusion in her eyes. "You came to my office throwing your fit and made me see the truth. I had called Jaycent later that evening to bitch about you and how you ignored my flowers and my calls. That's when he told me that you had called and said I love you."

"No ..." She trails off.

"Yes," I say, taking a step toward her. "I was a dick! An ass! I get that. But I would have never ignored you if I had known how you truly felt." She swallows and looks away from me. As if she finally understands how fucked up all this has been. And how easily it could have all been avoided. "How could you ever doubt how I feel about you?" I ask, and her eyes meet mine again. "I have tried from day one to be more than just a fuck to you. But you were the one who pushed me away at every turn. Every time. It was always these rules, and you kept me at arm's length." Her eyes have filled with tears, and she licks her lips. "I love you, Ashlyn," I say, swallowing and taking another step toward her. "No matter what happens between us or how mad at me you get, know that loving you is the easiest part of my day." I come to a stop in front of her, and a tear slides down her face. I cup her face and brush it away. "Even when I thought you didn't want me, I still loved you."

Another tear falls and her lips part as she sucks in a deep breath. "I love you, Ryder," she whispers. "I'm so sorry ... for everything ..."

I take her into my arms and kiss her. Pulling away, I run my hand through her blond hair.

"I told him no," she says softly.

I pull back and look at her, and a tear runs down her face. "I was so mad at myself from what happened between us, but I was mad at him too." I wipe a tear away. "He was supposed to be my friend. He wasn't supposed to want more."

Giving her a soft smile, I tell her. "As much as I hate to admit it, I don't blame him." I cup her face with both of my hands. "Ashlyn, I fell in love with you that weekend in Panama. I knew then that you were the one for me."

"Why me?" She sniffs. "I can't give you anything that you don't already have." Licking her lips, she continues, "Even Bradley knew you were too good for me."

My teeth grind together that that bastard would even think that. He just felt that way 'cause he wanted her too. "Is this why you pushed me away?" She nods. "Ashlyn, listen to me. You are everything!" She closes her eyes for a second, and when she opens them, another tear runs down her face. "You think I care about what I have? It would mean nothing without you." I realized that when I didn't have her. My apartment. My job. None of it mattered while a piece of me was missing. "You are everything to me," I say again, in case she needs reminding. Taking a deep breath, I watch another tear fall, and I hate that she's hurting. That she could think this after everything I've tried to prove otherwise. "You asked why you? Because, baby, in a world full of ordinary, you're magic."

ASHLYN

Saturday morning comes, and I can't quit smiling like a fool. I stand in our kitchen making the man I love breakfast. He sits at the kitchen table going over emails on his phone, and I can't help think of how we got here. Somewhere along the past four weeks, I fell head over heels in love with a man who was way out of my reach but somehow fell for me in return.

I pile up the pancakes and place them on a plate along with bacon and some scrambled eggs. I walk over to the table and place the plate in front of him.

He sets his phone down and looks up at me with a smile. "This looks delicious." Then he grabs my arm and yanks me down so I fall across his lap. I laugh, and then his lips hit mine.

One hand snakes around my back while the other slides between my legs. I let out a moan as he deepens the kiss and gently bites my lip. He rubs my pussy over my pajama pants, and I hate that I even have them on.

"Whoa, looks like someone made up."

I jump off Ryder's lap when I hear Becca's voice. I clear my throat as I fix his overly large t-shirt when I see her and Jaycent standing by the front door. "Good morning," I say cheerfully. Not all that embarrassed they caught us.

She laughs. "Good, indeed."

Ryder clears his throat and stands from his chair. "Can I speak to you for a moment?" he says, looking at Jaycent. Who isn't smiling like everyone else.

He crosses his arms over his chest but gives no answer.

Becca and I look back and forth between them. I think Ryder wanted them to go outside and talk, but it looks like that is not an option. So Ryder begins.

"Becca filled me in on everything you did for her. And although I don't agree with how you guys kept things from me, I do understand why." He looks at Becca, and her eyes plead with him to accept what he can't change. And I have to agree with her. What's done is done. They can't go back and fix it. "And I want to thank you." I look at Jaycent, and he uncrosses his arms from his chest. "Thank you for being there for her when I couldn't. Thank you for ... everything."

Jaycent walks toward Ryder, and I stiffen. Is he going to punch him? 'Cause I have a feeling this time Ryder will fight back. But instead, Jaycent reaches out his right hand. Ryder shakes it as they pull each other in for a one-handed hug, and they slap each other's backs.

"I'm sorry too, man," Jaycent says as they pull away.

"So is everyone okay now?" Becca asks with a big smile. "Everything is back to normal?"

I laugh, and Ryder nods his head. "As normal as things can be, I guess."

Becca claps her hands and then hugs Jaycent. When his lips touch hers, Ryder turns away to look at me, and I give him a soft smile. I know seeing them together will take time, but I do think he is okay with it. "Who else wants breakfast?" I ask.

CHAPTER THIRTEEN

RYDER

Monday morning, I walk into work whistling a tune. "Hello, Kelly," I say to my assistant who sits behind her desk.

She eyes me skeptically. "Hello, Mr. O'Kane."

"What do we have going on today?" I ask her, picking up my mail out of her basket.

"Well, right now your father is looking for you."

I drop the mail and walk toward his office, still whistling. I enter without even knocking. He sits behind his desk holding the phone to his ear and wearing a pissed-off look on his face. He gestures for me to sit, so I plop down.

"You can try," he says into the phone. "But it won't help you."

I take my phone out of my jacket pocket and send Ashlyn a quick text.

ME: *How about takeout tonight and a movie in bed?*

My father all of a sudden starts laughing, and I look up at him with one eyebrow raised. He really isn't the kind of guy who randomly starts laughing. He doesn't even find jokes funny. He's always been pretty uptight. No matter the situation.

He slowly stands from his chair with his office phone still glued to his ear. "You think you're smarter than I am?" he asks, laughing at his own question. "I guess we'll find out." He chuckles. Then he slams his phone down.

He straightens his suit jacket as he fully stands, no longer laughing. He walks out from behind his desk and over to his office door and slams it shut.

"Are you okay?" I ask, truly worried for his sanity. I see my dad every day, and for some reason, his behavior is extremely off.

He plops down and runs a hand through his hair. His eyes look heavy and his lips thinned. He's either really tired or pissed. Possibly both. "Your mother is fighting me on this divorce."

I snort. "Well, I could have guessed that was gonna happen. What is it that she wants?"

"The company."

I blink twice. "Come again."

He places his forearms on his desk. "She wants fifty percent of the company. She says she is *owed* that."

I start shaking my head. "She can't … Can she …?" My mother owning half of this company will be the biggest mistake ever! She doesn't know a single thing about it except that it makes money. And not to mention she would be up my ass every fucking day! "What are you gonna do …?"

He holds up his right hand. "I have a solution."

"I'd love to hear it." I snort, sitting back in my chair.

"Give her what she wants."

"What?" I demand. "You're gonna give her half the company?"

He shakes his head. "Either I give her half or I walk away."

"Why would she want you to do that?"

"'Cause she wants me as miserable as she is, and she knows how much this job means to me."

"That's not a solution. You can't walk away …"

"No, but I can demote myself. Make it look like I've stepped away for now. And you're gonna take my position."

I sit there and stare at him more confused than I was a minute ago. "This is not a joke, Dad," I decide to say.

"I'm not joking." He stands up and turns to face the windows that overlook Central Park. He places his hands in his pockets. "I've made up my mind, Ryder. All you have to do is tell me if you can do it or not."

I run a hand through my hair, not really knowing what to do or say. "Dad, this company is your life."

He slowly turns around and walks around his desk. He leans back against it. "I can't argue with that. I have put a lot of time into this company, but it has also taken a lot from me." He sighs. "I missed so much of your and Becca's life. And I would say if I could go back in time and do things differently, I would, but that isn't an option." He looks away from me and swallows. "I know I give you a hard time as your boss and as your father, but you're ready, Ryder." He looks back at me. "You know what it takes. You've seen what it takes. The question is, are you willing to give it what it needs?"

• • •

The only lights in my apartment are what's streaming into the floor-to-ceiling windows from Manhattan as I sit on my couch. I'm still dressed in my suit, and I have a glass of whiskey in my hand as I think about what my father told me earlier. And my anger for my mother rises. For her to do this to him. She won't give him what he wants unless he walks away. She wants him to lose just as much as she would.

"Babe?" I hear Ashlyn call out as the front door opens. "I picked up the pizza."

"In here," I say, looking down at my almost empty glass not in the least bit hungry.

She comes into the living room and looks down at me with a wide smile. The moment her eyes meet mine, it falls. "What's wrong?"

I sigh, and she plops down next to me. "What's wrong, Ryder?" she asks more concerned.

"Today, my father told me he wants me to take over his position at the company," I say softly.

She gasps and grips my hand tightly. "That's great news, baby."

I wish I felt her excitement. She doesn't know that it has to do with my mother, and I feel that part isn't important right now. I let go of her hand and stand, making my way over to the window. I look out over the town that I have grown up in, the only place I call home, and I feel a pain in my chest.

"Why do you not sound happy about this?" she asks, her excitement now gone.

I turn around and face her. "I'm not sure I can do it."

She frowns. "Why would you say that?"

I toss back what's left of my drink. "I've seen what my father gave up in order to make that company what it is today. And I don't want to disappoint him," I tell her truthfully.

She frowns. "Why would you ..." She looks away from me and trails off. "I see."

I go to take another drink, but remember that it's empty.

She slowly stands and walks over toward me. In the midst of my dilemma, I allow my eyes to rake over her black dress. It hugs her chest, showcasing her great tits, and stops at her knees. She wears a pair of bright red heels that matches her lipstick. Just like every time I see her, she takes my breath away.

Once she reaches me, she places her hands on my chest. "It's gonna be okay."

I wish I could be as optimistic as she is. "I'm not gonna choose ..."

"You don't have to," she tells me. Reaching up, she runs her hand through my hair, and I close my eyes as her fingernails scrape against my scalp, making my body break out in goose bumps. Her fingers grip my hair so tightly I hiss in a breath, and my eyes spring open. She stands before me, her blue eyes staring hard up into mine. "You're gonna do this! And I'm gonna be here for you. That's what *I love you* means, Ryder."

"Ashlyn—"

"Wait!" she says, interrupting me. "I'm all in. I'm standing here, telling you that I'm all in. No matter how hard it is, if we try, we can make it."

As I look into her eyes, I realize just how lucky I am to have a woman like her. One who supports me and my dreams, but what will they cost me? I refuse to be my father. I admire him for his work ethic and what he has accomplished. But look what he had to give up in order to do that. I want to be optimistic like Ashlyn. I want to believe I can have both. The only question is can I?

"I love you," I say as my hands find the black material right below her ass. I start to pull it up over her thighs.

She laughs and pulls away from me, the black material falling back down into place, and I frown. "Give me five minutes," she says and then takes off to my bedroom.

I take my phone out of my suit pocket and send my father a quick text.

Me: *I'm in.*

He sends me back a response before I can put it away.

Dad: *We'll sign the papers next Monday.*

I let out a long breath, trying to convince myself that my life isn't about to change, but it is. I'm just not sure it will be for the best.

ASHLYN

I lie in Ryder's bed with my eyes wide open as I stare up at his ceiling. He's passed out, slightly snoring. I run a hand down my face, releasing a sigh.

He's going to take over his dad's company. It's something I keep repeating in my mind. It's a hurdle I didn't see coming, but I was telling him the truth when I told him I'm behind him a hundred percent. Having him back in my life reminded me just how much I do love him. And that hole in my heart when he was gone has been patched. I'm not saying it will be easy because I already know it's going to be hard, but I'm ready. I'm going to stand beside him and support whatever decision he makes. Even if it means taking time from us.

The next few days went by rather fast. I didn't get to see Ryder very much, considering he had a lot going on at work now that he and his father were preparing for him to take over. And I have thought to myself that this will be the rest of my life, not getting to see him much. But I know he wants this. And I was being honest when I said I would support him on this new path.

Thursday morning, I wake up and leave him in bed to sleep and go make him breakfast. I'm halfway through cooking his eggs when there's a knock on the door. I walk over to it and look through the peephole to see Jaycent and Becca standing there. I open it up and smile. "Good morning, guys."

They walk on in without an invite, and I notice that Jaycent is pulling a suitcase behind him. "Going on a trip?"

They both frown and exchange a look that could only be confusion. "Yes," Jaycent answers slowly.

Becca places her hands on her hips and narrow her eyes a bit. "Ryder didn't tell you?"

"No." I spin around to see Ryder coming down the hallway interrupting her. He wears a pair of sweatpants, and that's it. I lick my lips as I imagine pulling them off him. "I have not," he says to her and then looks at me. A big smile spreads across his face as he comes to me. "Good morning, gorgeous." He wraps me in a hug and kisses my forehead softly.

"What is going on?" I ask skeptically, not returning the affection.

"We're going on a trip."

"You and Jaycent are going on a trip?" I haven't heard anything about this, but I'm not surprised. I know they do a lot of work together.

"No, silly. All four of us are," he says, holding out his hands.

I look back at Jaycent and Becca, and she is nodding her head excitedly with a big smile on her face. He still holds her Louis Vuitton suitcase.

"It's Thursday," I say, trying to understand what is going on. "I can't miss work ..."

"It's already taken care of," Ryder says.

"What?"

"I spoke to Thomas, and you are all good to go." He smiles down at me, his green eyes lit up with happiness. I hate to ruin it for him or seem ungrateful, but I'm just a little confused right now.

"Okay. I haven't packed," I tell him.

"No need; it won't take you long to pack." He looks down at his phone in his hand. "We have an hour before the plane leaves."

"An hour?" I ask wide-eyed. "This airport is huge. We should already be there if our plane leaves in an hour."

Jaycent laughs and so does Ryder. I feel like they know some inside joke I don't. "We'll be fine, babe. Go pack."

"Where are we going?" I ask. "I'm not sure what to bring."

"One sec." He opens up his phone and types on it then speaks. "It's eighty-nine degrees and a chance of rain today and tomorrow."

My brows pull together. "Are you not going to tell me where we're going?" I ask, and he shakes his head.

"It's a surprise."

I smile up at him because I think I know where we're going. He's taking us back to Florida.

• • •

Exactly forty-five minutes later, we pull up to a gate. Ryder pulls up an app on his phone and types in a code and the gate opens. I look around out the side of the Escalade window from the back seat. "This isn't the airport," I state.

Becca laughs. "This is where Ryder and my dad store their planes," she says simply.

"Store *their* planes?" I ask, looking around at the big steel doors lined up one after another. It reminds me of going to a storage facility. Where all the garage doors are one after another. But these doors are much, much larger.

The Escalade comes to a stop in front of an open hangar. Milton gets out and then we all climb out one by one. "Where are we …?" I trail off as I look up at a private plane that sits right outside the open bay door. If possible, it looks fancier that the hundred-foot yacht I boarded weeks ago.

It's mainly white with a blacked-out front window. It has eight circular windows down the side, and the door is open with a set of black stairs to enter. G550 is written across the tail section in big, bold black letters. "What is that?" I ask in awe.

"That's Ryder's private jet," Becca whispers, leaning into my side.

I look over at him as he and Jaycent unload the luggage from the back. "You have your own jet?" I ask wide-eyed.

He smiles a cocky smile. "Of course."

CHAPTER FOURTEEN

RYDER

I'm not gonna lie. This is a part of her that made me fall in love with her. That she isn't used to the type of lifestyle I live. The women who I grew up with had parents just as rich as mine. Just to take them on a date, you had to go above and beyond to impress them. Ashlyn isn't that way. Although I do love the look on her beautiful face when she looks at me like I'm her king giving her a key to my kingdom. I want to share everything I have with her.

"How else did you think we were going to get there?" I ask as I watch her stand there staring at me.

"A commercial airliner. Like us normal folk." She makes a joke, and I laugh.

"We will be ready in ten, Mr. O'Kane," Milton announces.

"You're going too?" Ashlyn asks him with excitement.

He gives her a warm smile. "Of course. Who do you think is gonna fly it?" Then he turns and walks off before climbing the stairs to board the aircraft.

She turns to face me wearing a sly smile on her face. "What?" I ask.

She arches a brow. "So you have your own jet, but you can't fly it?" I open my mouth, but she continues. "There *is* something you can't do." Then she spins around and starts to climb the stairs.

I chuckle and call out, "I have my pilot's license."

I make my way onto the plane and close the door behind myself, looking around the plane I bought three years ago. I had a very important meeting in California, and my father was away on his private jet in Colorado. I ended up missing my meeting in California due to the delay of my connecting flight, and it cost me millions of dollars. Solution—buy my own damn plane so that it won't happen again. And so far, it's worked.

"Want a glass of wine?" I hear my sister ask Ashlyn as they find a seat in the back.

"Yes, please," she says, nodding her head quickly.

I stand in the middle of the aisle and watch her big blue eyes take in the white carpet and white leather seats to the right. On the left is a couch that fits four people. She sits down and reaches out, placing her hands flat on the black table top and slowly running her fingers against it.

I rub my finger over my lips to cover my smile. She looks like a kid experiencing Disney World for the first time—awestruck! I walk toward her and sit down in the seat directly in front of her, facing her.

She removes her hands quickly as if I caught her doing something wrong. "Sorry," she says, licking her thumb and then rubbing a smudge off.

Holding back a laugh, I smile at her and how unsure she seems. "No worries."

She pulls her phone out of her back pocket and asks, "What kind of plane is this?"

"It's a Gulfstream G550," I answer.

She types a few things into her phone and then her eyes widen. "Holy shit!" She gasps.

I know what she's doing, and I chuckle.

Her eyes meet mine, and they're huge. "Oh my God, this thing is outrageously priced. I mean, it's awesome, but damn!"

"I stole it," I assure her. She looks up at me through her lashes.

"I doubt that …"

"I only paid twenty," I tell her.

She lets out a long breath. "Twenty thousand is a steal," she agrees with a nod.

"Million," I correct her, and her mouth falls open again.

selfless

• • •

The plane touches down, and after a few minutes, it comes to a stop. Milton comes out from behind the door and opens the stairs. "We're here, ladies and gentlemen," he says, gesturing us to exit.

Becca goes first followed by Jaycent and then Ashlyn. I come to the last step as she makes a circle looking around. "Wait …?" She trails off. "This doesn't look like Florida."

"Florida?" I ask, arching my brows. "What made you think we were going to Florida?"

"Well, where else would we be going …" Her voice trails off as a black limo pulls up onto the tarmac. It comes to a stop and the back door bursts open. A blur of dark hair and a woman squealing follows.

ASHLYN

"Mom?" I ask in shock.

She reaches me and wraps her arms around me, almost picking me up off the ground. "Oh, my God," she squeals in my ear.

I gently pat her back. "What are you doing here?" I ask slowly.

She pulls away from me and turns to face Becca, pulling her into her arms as well.

"God, I have missed you two so much," she exclaims, gripping her just as tightly as she did me.

Becca laughs. "We've missed you too."

I turn to face Ryder and see he is helping Milton remove our luggage. He gives me a quick look over his shoulder and then a wink. I take another look around at the snow-covered mountains and take in a big breath of the fresh Seattle air.

He brought me home?

I go to open my mouth to speak to him when an arm drapes over my shoulder. My mother yanks me to one side and Becca to the other. "I can't tell you how glad your dad and I are to have our girls home," she says and then sniffs.

I feel my eyes start to sting, and my throat tightens as I realize just how much I have missed them. "Me too, Mom." I hug her this time. "Me too."

She walks us over to the limo, and I see my father standing by the open trunk helping the guys load our luggage. He spots me, and a big smile spreads across his face. "There's my girl," he says, walking over to me. I let go of my mother to hug him.

Minutes later, we all crawl into the back of the limo with the exception of Milton. He gets in the passenger seat.

I take Ryder's hand as I settle in next to him, and I can't help the big smile on my face. "How did you all pull this off?" I ask in amazement.

My mother smiles over at Ryder. "Ryder called us yesterday and asked if we were available this weekend. He wanted to surprise you by bringing you home."

I tighten my hand on his. "Aren't you sneaky?"

He chuckles and nods.

"I'm glad we didn't blow it this morning," Jaycent says. "We weren't in on the surprise."

My mom smiles over at Becca. "And who is this, Becca?"

"This is Jaycent." She pats his leg. "My boyfriend."

"Well, it's nice to meet you, Jaycent," my mother says.

"You too, ma'am." He nods once, and she giggles like a teenager. I can't help but laugh.

"I assume this is the man you were telling me about."

I feel Ryder shift in his seat beside me at the fact another person knew about them together when he had no clue.

I take my free hand and place it on his chest as I lean into his side. "Thank you," I whisper softly so only he can hear as my mother talks to Becca about their relationship.

He leans in as well and kisses me softly on the forehead. "You're welcome, beautiful."

Thirty minutes later, we are walking into my childhood home, and I kick off my shoes, taking in a deep breath. The smell of vanilla hits my nose, and twenty-five years of memories comfort me. It's like I never left.

"Okay, ladies. I'm making your favorite tonight!" my mother exclaims. "All of you go and wash up. Dinner will be ready in an hour."

"Sir?" Ryder and I turn to see Milton standing by the front door. "I will be on my way ..."

"Where are you going?" my mother asks him.

"I have a hotel—"

"Nonsense," she interrupts him, waving her hand in the air. "You'll stay here with us."

He shakes his head. "I couldn't—"

"I don't take no for an answer, Milton," my mother interrupts him again, and he sighs as if he already knows this. "We have four bedrooms, and each room has its own bath. You will stay here with us, and you will also quit calling me ma'am."

He gives her a soft smile and nods his head once.

"Come on," I say, grabbing Ryder's hand and practically yanking him up the stairs to the second floor. I enter the first door on the right and then close it behind us.

I make my way to the adjoining bathroom, removing my clothes, and he silently follows my lead. I open the glass shower door and turn on the water. He closes the door behind him as he steps in.

I whirl around on him and place my hands on his hard chest. The warm water spraying my back. "Why did you do this?" I can't help but ask.

He smiles softly and reaches up, placing some of my hair behind my ear. Pieces of it already wet from the sprayer.

"You deserved this," he says.

I shake my head. "How did you ... Why would you ...?"

He wraps his arms around my waist and pulls me to him. His eyes search my face, and I can already feel his cock harden against my lower stomach. "I want you to be happy."

"I am," I tell him. "I was."

He shakes his head and lets out a long sigh. "When I was in the elevator and I watched you say I love you." He licks his lips. "I heard the longing in your voice. I could see the sadness in your eyes. And at the moment, I had thought it was Bradley. But later on when you told me that was your mother, I realized just how much your life has changed for you over the past month. And honestly, I didn't know what I could do to make it better."

"You didn't have to do anything," I tell him softly as my hands slide up his chest and wrap around his neck.

He guides me to the left until my back hits the cold shower wall and the water comes down on our sides. He removes his hands from my back and places them against the wall on either side of my face as his head leans closer to mine. "I don't think you understand how much I love you, Ashlyn." I swallow at his words, and he cups my right cheek. His hand holding my hair back. "I would give you the moon if you wanted it," he whispers.

"I don't need the moon," I say breathlessly as his thumb softly caresses my face.

"Then what do you need?" he asks, his eyes dropping to my lips and then rising back to my eyes. "All you have to do is name it. And it's yours." His voice is deeper, rougher.

I stay silent as my eyes search his, trying to process everything that has happened to me in the last month. I stood in this very shower a month ago the night before we flew out to New York, and I would have never guessed I'd be back here with Ryder. My heart pounds harder in my chest.

As if he can hear it, he lets go of my face, and his fingertips very lightly trail down over my chin and along my neck. My lips part, and I start to breathe heavily, and it's partly due to all the steam filling the shower. His hand stops on my chest, and he smiles. "You know what this reminds me of?"

"No," I answer softly.

"Being in this shower with you reminds me of my birthday. That afternoon on my balcony in Panama City. You. Me. And nothing but the rain." My knees start to buckle at that memory. He lowers his head to my neck, and I close my eyes and lean my head back, hitting my head on the wall. His nose trails up my neck, and my head falls to the side. "God, you took my breath away, baby," he admits as his hand makes its way back up my chest and to my neck. I grip his muscular biceps straining against my fingers. "I knew right then and there you were gonna destroy me."

"I'm sorry," I rasp, knowing exactly what he means. I felt the same way so many times.

"Don't be sorry, baby." His hand on my neck snakes around to the back and grips my hair. I suck in a breath, and my pussy throbs as his hard cock presses into me. "I'm sorry," he states and pulls his head away from my ear. His dark green eyes glare down into mine, and I cling to him. "I'm sorry that I'll never be able to walk from you again."

I try to shake my head to tell him that's no reason to be sorry, but his hand in my hair prevents me from moving.

"Tell me I'm yours," he orders.

"I'm yours," I say breathlessly. "I love you."

"Fuck." He hisses at my words. "I thought I'd never hear you say that."

"I love you," I repeat. "I love you …"

He cuts my words off when his lips smash into mine. I open my mouth wide on a moan, and his tongue enters my mouth as he tilts my head more to the side. His free hand grabs my thigh and yanks my foot off the shower floor. I grind against him the best I can as his mouth devours mine in pure need.

The warm water beats down on us; my soaked hair clings to my back, shoulders, and chest. And I can't help but shiver even though my body is on fire.

I let go of his shoulders, and my hand slides between our bodies and grabs the base of his cock.

He pulls his lips from mine quickly. "We can't."

"We are," I argue still breathless.

"Your parents."

"We're both adults."

He goes to argue, but I let go of his dick and shove him to the side. His back hits the wall not expecting my next move. Now he's under the sprayer, eyes open, and water running down a hundred percent of his body like a waterfall. And all I want to do is dive in.

I step in front of him and run my nails down his chest. He hisses in a breath. "You can't stand there and tell me you don't want me."

He arches a dark brow. "I would never …"

"Then take me!" I demand.

I'm not sure if it's the challenge in my voice or the naughty smile on my face, but in the next instant, his lips are back on mine and he's got my back pinned against the wall.

"God, I missed this so much." Becca moans through a mouthful of food.

We all laugh. "Are you girls cooking for one another, or are you eating takeout?" my mother asks us. I look at Becca as she takes a bite of bread, and my mother sighs. "I figured."

"Hey, now," I say, taking a drink of my glass of wine. "I cook."

"Yeah." Ryder dabs his lips with the napkin. "She cooked me breakfast twice this week."

"Breakfast, huh?" My father speaks. "You guys living together already?"

The room falls silent, and I swallow the large bite I had just put in my mouth without even chewing it. "Nnnoo," I choke out before taking another drink of my wine to wash down the bite of lasagna that was stuck.

"Not for my lack of trying," Ryder exclaims.

"Ryder!" I say his name in shock. We haven't discussed living with one another.

I stand in the kitchen making him coffee, and he walks out of his bedroom. "You keep spoiling me like this, and I'll have you moved in."

That was the only time he has ever mentioned it. Hell, just last week, we weren't even speaking. When has he had time to think about us living together? Let alone, us discuss it?

"What?" he asks with a shrug. "Are you saying you haven't thought about it?" he asks, arching his dark brow.

I open my mouth, but nothing comes out.

"I didn't know it was that serious," my father says, looking back and forth between us. He doesn't sound mad or disappointed. Just curious.

"It is," Ryder answers since my mouth still can't speak.

"Well, I think that would be nice," my mother says, nodding her head in approval. My parents aren't old fashioned. They know I'm not a virgin, and they probably think we already spend every night together.

"But …" I manage to get out.

"But what?" Ryder asks. I look at Becca, and she smiles widely at me. Jaycent puts his head down and pretends to study the food on his plate. "Becca and Jaycent are moving in together," he states and then looks over at them. That gets Jaycent's head up. "Are you moving in with Jaycent, or is he moving in with you?" he asks.

"She's moving in with me," Jaycent declares, and it's almost as if there's a challenge there. For Ryder to argue that to see if he truly is okay with them being together.

He doesn't. Instead, he looks back at me. "See," he simply says before taking a bite.

I got the message. Becca is moving out. Timothy will sell the apartment, and I don't have a place to live. That sinking feeling comes back that I just need to move back home. Soon, I'll have no job and no housing. How long will Ryder stay after that?

Thankfully, my mom ends that awkward conversation by turning her attention to the man sitting at the other end of the table. "What about you, Milton?"

"I don't cook, ma'am." he jokes, and everyone laughs, breaking the awkward silence.

"How do you know my girls?" she asks, and I watch Becca smile proudly that she refers to her as one of her *girls*.

"I have known Becca and Ryder for twelve years now. I've worked for the O'Kane's since I was thirty," he states.

I take another bite of my food, looking over at him. I know nothing about Milton except that he drives Ryder around and can fly a plane.

"Really?" my mother asks with interest.

He nods. "Timothy, Ryder's father, hired me out of a favor." He takes a quick sip of his water. "And what was supposed to be temporary became permanent."

CHAPTER FIFTEEN

RYDER

Becca and Ashlyn are in the kitchen doing dishes as I sit in the living room with Jaycent and Milton. All three of us drinking a beer with her dad.

He's telling us about his new golf clubs when I spot a picture on the mantle. I set my beer on the coffee table and stand. I walk over to it in order to get a closer look.

It's a baby. A baby boy. He's wrapped up in a blue blanket, lying in a white crib. He's sleeping and looks to be only days old. I pick it up, examining it more.

"That's Henry."

I look up to see Margaret standing next to me. "He's beautiful," I tell her. "Yes. He was."

I place the picture back at her words and swallow nervously for looking at it. "I'm sorry …"

"No need to be sorry," she assures me and picks it up herself. "I took this the day we brought him home."

I frown. "Ashlyn has never mentioned a brother."

"She didn't know him," she says, placing the picture back. "We got pregnant with Henry very young. I was in my last year of law school and already working at the firm full time. He was busy working all hours of the day and night." She turns to face me. "We weren't ready for the surprise, but we were happy." She sighs. "But we didn't understand what a child meant. We still worked our lives away. We hired a nanny, so he wouldn't have to go to daycare. One day, we got a phone call that she had found him dead in his crib."

"I'm so sorry," I say, feeling awful for bringing up such a bad time.

Her eyes meet mine, and she smiles softly. "So were we." She then sighs. "We decided that what we needed and what we wanted were two very different things. We both cut back at work. Sold our house and downsized. We decided that our careers could wait." She chuckles "Why work your life away when you can live it? Anyway, three years later, we found out we were pregnant with Ashlyn. And she was our second chance. To do things right. To see what truly matters." She places a hand on my shoulder. "She didn't replace him, but she gave us a second chance to do things right. And not everyone gets that."

As I listen to Margaret, I can hear the girls laughing and talking in the kitchen.

"Take care of her, please. Her father and I worry about her so much."

With that, she walks away. I run a hand through my hair and release a sigh. I feel like she was speaking about me. The second chance she gave me after I walked away from her, and the fact I'm about to give up more of my life to take over O'Kane's. Because she and I both know you can't have both. One will always suffer.

• • •

I pull the purple sheets back on Ashlyn's queen-size bed and crawl in while she takes off her makeup in the adjoining bathroom. I can't seem to get what her mother told me out of my head. Second chances. What if I fuck up again? Will she give me a third? A fourth? How many times am I gonna fuck up before I realize that she is more important than my career?

"What's on your mind?" she asks, interrupting my thoughts.

I look up to see her standing at the end of the bed with a smile on her face.

I pat the space beside me. She crawls up the bed and lies down facing me. "Talk to me. I can tell by the look on your face something is wrong. Is it work?"

"No," I tell her.

"Is it me?" she asks, playfully shoving my shoulder.

"Yes," I say honestly, and the smile drops off her face.

She sits up and crosses her legs in front of her. "What is it? Do you regret coming here?"

"What?" I sit up quickly. "No! Nothing to do with coming here. I'm glad we came here."

She reaches out and runs her hand up and down my arm. "Me too. Thank you for this. It means so much to me."

I grab her hand and bring it to my lips, softly kissing it. "I was serious."

She tilts her head to the side. "About what?"

"You're moving in with me," I say, not wanting to put this conversation off any longer.

She pulls her hand from mine, and her head falls forward as she looks down at her legs. "I don't think that's a good idea …"

"We both said we were all in," I remind her.

She looks up at me. "We did."

"Then what's the problem?" I ask.

She sighs and gets out of her bed. She starts pacing as she runs a hand through her blond hair. "Because words and actions are completely different things, Ryder."

"So I tell you I love you, but you don't believe I do?" I ask, slowly trying to figure out what she means.

"I believe it," she growls, getting angry. "But if I give up my freedom …""Freedom?" I ask, getting out of bed myself. "You feel you'll be a prisoner if you move in with me?" I cross my arms over my chest.

She stops pacing, and she narrows her eyes at me. "You didn't let me finish."

"By all means."

She looks at me for a few seconds and then turns away from me. "Never mind," she mutters to herself, heading to her bedroom door.

"Oh, no!" I state and grab her upper arm, spinning her around. "Whatever you're thinking, you're gonna tell me."

She sighs heavily as her eyes meet mine. "You walked out on me.

I then found out I will be losing my job." She brings up the one thing we haven't talked about since we got back together, and I'm not sure what to tell her. "And now Becca is moving in with Jaycent. If I move in with you, what will I have left?"

I take a step into her. "You're not losing your job," I say, and it's complete bullshit! We both know that, but it sounds good. We can work that out later. "And you're not losing me."

"You say that now." She rolls her eyes.

"And I'll keep saying it," I assure her.

"Ryder, I—"

"Please," I interrupt her. "Please move in with me." I'm begging her 'cause I know what will happen once we get back to New York. I'll be working twenty-four seven and never see her. That company is gonna take all my time, and having her live with me is the only thing I care about right now. I want to know that when I walk in my door, no matter what time it is, she will be in my bed. Not across town or back here in Seattle. I need her, and that is me being selfish, but that's the truth.

She slowly gives me a soft smile, and I almost fist pump the air. "What about Harry?" she asks.

"I love that little rat," I say, and she laughs.

I pull her into me. "So ... yes? You'll move in with me?" I ask, needing to hear her say the words as I run my hand through her hair.

"Yes." She laughs. "I'll move in with you."

I bend down and pick her up before tossing her onto the bed. She laughs as I land on top of her. "This is insane," she says.

"I know." I have to agree with her but for different reasons. She thinks we're moving too fast. I can't believe I was lucky enough to find the one in a million. A woman who makes me feel like the king of the world. Her world.

• • •

It's been a week since my father told me the news about his plans for the company. Seattle was exactly what I needed. Her parents took us out and showed us the town during the day, and then the girls took me and Jaycent out at night to show us their favorite bars and places to shop. It was nice to relax. Forget about the busy streets of New York. I have always loved Manhattan but being in Seattle made me wonder what my life would be like if Ashlyn and I had a home with some land. Cars in the driveway and kids in the backyard. How simple life would be without the hustle and bustle. And if you ask me, it would be great.

Now we're back, and things are what they always have been—work. I've always wanted this, but things change. And Ashlyn is my game changer. Losing her would be worse than anything. I know; I've felt what that was like once.

But as I sit at the conference table reading over the papers that my father's lawyer wrote up, I find myself smiling. And it's not the words on the paper, but the words written across the screen on my phone.

Ashlyn: *You can do it. Don't doubt it, believe it. I love you.*

"Ryder?" my dad calls out.

I blink and look up at him. "Yes, sir?"

He points his finger down at the paperwork. And I sign the last line.

"That's all, gentlemen," Duncan, my father's lawyer says. "Ryder?" I stand. "Congratulations." He reaches out and shakes my hand.

"Thank you, sir," I say with a swift nod.

My father and he say their goodbyes, and then he turns to face me. "Well, I'll leave you to it," he says, slapping me on the shoulder.

"What?" I ask, and my voice is high, showing the panic I feel. "You're just leaving like that?" I ask.

He nods, sliding his suit jacket on. "I have somewhere to be," he says.

I go to speak, but his phone rings. I catch that it says blocked number before he answers it. "Right on time," he says as if he already knew who it was. "Yes." He lowers his voice. "I'll be there in twenty." Then he hangs up.

I follow him out of the conference room. "Where are you going?" I pry.

"I'll be back in a few hours," he informs me. "Don't let the place fall apart before then." He laughs at his joke, and I shake my head. Something is wrong with him.

"Who was that on the phone?" I ask as he presses the button for the elevator.

"Wrong number."

The doors open, and he enters. I follow. "You do know that I could hear you, right? Who was that?" I ask again.

He ignores me as he presses the lobby button. "Dad?" I snap.

He turns to face me. "What?"

I stare at him in disbelief. "What the hell is going on with you?"

"Whatever do you mean?"

My mouth falls open. "You … you just signed away all your shares to your company and stepped down as CEO, and now you're running off to God knows where, and you're making crappy jokes." He just stares at me, and I turn to fully face him. "Are you having an affair?" I ask. That's the only thing that makes sense to me at this moment. Mom knows, and she wants his company as revenge. He's finally found the woman he wants to be with, and he will give anything to have her. I know; I'd do the same for Ashlyn.

He chuckles. "No."

"I don't believe you," I growl, narrowing my eyes at him. He just shrugs as the elevator comes to a stop. The doors open, and I walk out behind him. "Have a good day, son," he calls out as he places a pair of sunglasses on his head and then walks out the glass doors without a care in the world.

I watch as he gets into his waiting car and then run outside. "Do you need me to call Milton for you, sir?" the doorman asks.

"No," I say and hail a cab. He looks at me strangely as I crawl into the back. "Follow that black Town Car," I order.

If I followed him in the Escalade, he would know it's me. This way, he can't see me.

An hour later, we pull into a neighborhood outside Manhattan. Traffic was a bitch, and it took us an hour to get where it should have taken us less than twenty. But I sit up straight when I see the car pull into a driveway. "Stop here!" I order, and the cab pulls up to the curb.

I watch my father get out of the back of his car as the front door opens to the yellow house. What I see has my heart pounding in my chest. A woman who I know very well steps out dressed in a long fitting dress that matches the house. Her black hair down and a smile on her face.

"What the …?"

A little girl runs out of the house and down the stairs. I see her little lips move but can't hear what she's saying as she runs to my father. He bends down and picks her up, spinning her around.

A pain forms in my chest at what I'm seeing. My father is having an affair, and it has resulted in a child.

I throw some cash at the driver and get out, slamming the door. I walk up to the house, and the woman spots me. The smile drops off her face, and her eyes widen. "Ryder …"

My father spins around, the little girl still in his arms. "What are you doing here?" he demands, realizing I followed him.

I let out a laugh, but it holds no humor. "You wanna tell me what you're doing here with Jaycent's sister?"

ASHLYN

I get out of the Escalade and thank Milton for the ride. Now that Ryder and I are back together, I don't have to take cabs anymore. One more thing to be thankful about since my life isn't in the hands of the crazy cab drivers here anymore.

"Good morning," I say with a smile on my face when I spot Thomas behind the desk. But he doesn't return it. Instead, he stands and meets me halfway.

"We have a meeting upstairs," he says.

I frown at his tone. "Did you wake up in a bad mood this morning?" I ask, but he doesn't answer. "Are you okay?" I ask, placing my hand on his shoulder. He shrugs it off. "Thomas. What's wrong?" I demand.

"Come on, Ashlyn." He gives me his back and starts to walk up the stairs.

I follow him and enter Mrs. Mills' office. She sits behind her desk with a set of paperwork in front of her. She stands as Thomas sits down in a chair. I sit beside him.

"What's going on?" I can't help but ask.

She sighs as she comes around the desk and stands in front of us.

"I have called this meeting because something has come to my attention."

My brows rise. I look at Thomas and then back at her. "Are we in trouble or something?" I can't help but ask with a chuckle. They both look so serious.

"We're closing," she announces.

"What?" I ask, sitting up straighter. No. Mr. O'Kane told me it would take time.

"I'm sorry," she says with a heavy sigh. "The owner did not want me to tell you due to procedure and lawsuits, but I want you two to have enough time to find somewhere to go."

Thomas snorts, and I stand. "How long do we have?" I ask as my mind spins.

"One week," she says.

"One week?" I ask wide-eyed. "So …what? In one week, you're just gonna close the doors?"

She nods. "I'm sorry." Mrs. Mills looks at me. "But you can't be this surprised. You put in your two weeks' notice three weeks ago. So you must have seen this coming …"

"Yes. I had been warned, but then I had also been told by Mr. O'Kane himself it could take time. And to give it a month." She looks away from me and clears her throat. I guess him telling me a month three weeks ago would fit this timeline. I've been too wrapped up in Ryder and me back together that I have lost track of time. "Have you spoken to him since you ratted me out?" I demand. I know she was the one who told him I put in my notice. Because I hadn't told anyone else.

"I have not," she answers my question. "But I can't discuss the situation at hand other than informing you of the closing."

I open my mouth and then close it. I slowly sit back down and try to figure out how in a matter of weeks I have lost my job. How could Ryder not warn me? A heads-up? I know he's busy with work, but still, this is my job. My future and for him not to warn me …

"So what do you plan on doing for us?" Thomas asks softly.

"Doing for you?" she repeats as if she didn't understand the question.

"Yes," he says with bite. "You know? We have rights when

termination is fulfilled. I can't speak for Ashlyn, but I have been here five years. I have health insurance through Talia's. Will we receive a severance package? Unemployment compensation?"

"I'm sorry; that's not possible."

"My signed contract stated that's what would happen if I was fired," he snaps.

"The circumstances have changed," she tells him, ending the meeting.

I call Ryder, but he doesn't answer. I sit down at the desk and try not to cry as the gallery phone rings.

CHAPTER SIXTEEN

RYDER

I hear my phone ring in my pocket, but I ignore it. My father very slowly lowers the little girl to where her feet touch the ground. I finally get a good look at her. She has brown hair and big green eyes. She looks so much like Becca did at that age it takes my breath away.

"We need to talk," my father says.

I just nod 'cause I don't know what to say at the moment. We all make our way inside the house, and I find the first seat I can and sit. It's the fireplace. Hanging my head, I run my hand down my face as bile starts to rise. Oh God, I slept with Rosie once. A very long time ago but it still happened, and now she's been sleeping with my father. I'm gonna get sick …

"Here," Rosie says, handing me a glass of water.

"Got any whiskey?" I ask roughly, and she nods before turning away.

"Son, it's not what you think," my father says, and I can't help but laugh. That's the same thing Ashlyn once said to me; although, at the time, I didn't believe her. For the life of me, I can't see this situation being anything other than what I see.

Rosie returns, handing me a glass of the whiskey, and I toss it back. "So this is why you gave over the company?" I ask, sucking in a deep breath from the drink. "So Mom wouldn't get it when she finds out you're leaving her for another woman."

"Ryder ..."

Rosie begins, but my father raises his hand to silence her just as the little girl runs into the living room. She has a blanket in her hand. It's so long she drags it behind her. I sit up straight as she comes to a stop in front of me.

"Hi," she says to me in the cutest little voice I've ever heard.

I swallow. "Hello." My voice still rough.

"You're my brother," she states, and all breath leaves my lungs. "Mommy gave me this." She holds the blanket up, and numbly, I take it from her. It's a picture of me, Becca, Jaycent, and Rosie. It's at Rosie's high school graduation. And my chest tightens at the way this little girl gives me a huge smile. And at this very second, I wish to be as innocent as her.

I nod at her 'cause what else is there to do?

"Maggie?" Rosie says, and the little girl turns around to face her. "Will you go play in your room for a little bit?" she asks. "Mommy needs to have an adult conversation."

She nods her head quickly, making her brown hair bounce. Then she takes off in a mad dash through the living room, the picture blanket dragging behind her.

I hang my head, running a hand through my hair, and then I throw back what's left in my glass. "How old is she?" I ask, clearing my throat.

"Five," Rosie answers.

"Ryder, I need you to listen," my father speaks.

"How could you?" I demand, standing. "How could you keep her from us?" I look at Rosie. "And you? Does Jaycent know?" She looks away from me, shaking her head.

My father stands and takes a deep breath. "Calm down. I didn't cheat on your mother."

I snort. "You think I give two shits if you cheated on her?" I demand. "I care that you kept this little girl from us." I'm not an idiot; I know my parents aren't faithful. Two people that unhappy won't have that much respect for one another.

"I had to," Rosie says as she starts to cry.

"Bullshit!" I snap.

"Enough!" my father roars.

I take a deep breath as Rosie stands and runs out of the room, crying harder. My father falls back down into his seat and sighs heavily. "She's not mine," he states.

I snort. "More lies."

"I'm not lying." He grinds out. "But she is your sister."

I roll my eyes. "How is that possible then?"

He lifts his head, and his eyes meet mine and I see something in them that I've never seen before. Regret. It's so heavy that I find myself sitting back down as well. "Maggie's mother had an affair with Rosie's dad. Your little sister is the result of that."

ASHLYN

I lie in Ryder's bathtub, music blaring and my bubbles so thick I can't even see my body. An empty bottle of wine sits on the floor beside me. It was the first thing I did when I walked into Ryder's apartment. And even though I drank the entire thing in a matter of thirty minutes, I'm not feeling much from it.

I'm in the middle of washing my legs when I see the bathroom door open. Ryder walks in with his head down. His hair is standing every which way, and his eyes look red.

"Babe? What's wrong?" I ask, immediately standing. He never did call me back today. So many times I picked up my phone to try again but didn't want to bother him.

He turns, giving me his back while gripping the black countertop, and drops his head. I watch the muscles in his back strain against the fabric of his white button up.

"Ryder?" I yell over the music as bubbles and water slide down my body.

I step out of the tub to go to him when he reaches over, grabs the UEBoom that plays the music from my phone, and throws it across the bathroom. It hits the wall with a loud thud and then the music stops.

I stand outside the tub, dripping wet, body shaking due to the cold air, and eyes wide—not sure what to do. Or what to say. So I just watch him. Now that his head isn't down, I can see him better in the mirror. And I was right; his eyes are bloodshot, and I take in a long breath and smell alcohol on him. Has he been at a bar? He's missing his black tie he left with this morning and his black suit jacket. His shirt has the top two buttons undone, and it's untucked.

Finally, he turns to face me, and I take a step back when he comes toward me. I see hurt flash across his face, and I practically run to him. I'm not afraid of him in the least. I wrap my arms around him, and he doesn't waste a second as he does the same, pulling my wet body to him and soaking his clothes. "It's okay," I say, knowing that whatever it is, it's bad.

Ten minutes later, I'm dried off, and he's undressed. We crawl into bed, and I cuddle up to him. "Talk to me, baby."

He lies on his back, staring up at his ceiling, me on my left side with my arm flat on his bare chest. "Did you have a bad day at work?" I know he was nervous today about signing the paperwork. He tries to be tough, but I think that would scare anyone. The fear of failure is stronger than love if you ask me. When you allow yourself to love someone, they have the power to break you. When you set yourself up high, only you can bring yourself down.

He takes a deep breath and finally speaks. "I have a sister."

I frown. "This is about Becca?" Is he still mad about her and Jaycent?

He softly shakes his head. "I have a five-year-old sister. Her name is Maggie."

I very slowly sit up and look down at him. His head falls to the right, and his eyes meet mine. "You're not making any sense, babe."

"I followed my father today after he stormed out of the office, and I found him at Rosie's house."

My frown deepens. "Rosie? As in Jaycent's sister, Rosie?" I ask, remembering her from when Becca and I went to her salon and spa.

He nods. "She is raising my little sister."

My eyes start to widen. "Rosie and your father have been having an affair?"

He closes his eyes, and I feel his heart start to beat faster under my hand that still rests on his chest. "My mother had an affair with Jaycent and Rosie's dad six years ago, and she had his child."

I can feel the heartbreak in his words. The way his muscles still strain as if he's in physical pain. And if that didn't give me enough clues, the fact that he said it all with his eyes still closed does. "Oh, God," I whisper.

His eyes open, and he looks up at me. "My mother gave her to Rosie when she realized her dad didn't want any more than sex. Now that my father wants a divorce, Rosie is afraid that my mother will come after Maggie just to be a bitch. And I would bet my life on it that she will. She would want that sympathy as a single mother."

"Wow!"

He nods. "And the kicker? I'm the only one who knows," he adds. "Well, you too."

I sigh for his father and Rosie. How hard must it be to keep that kind of secret from loved ones. "Did you meet her?" I ask softly.

For the first time since he walked into the apartment, he smiles as he looks at me. "She's beautiful," he says as he sits up. I can see the excitement in his bloodshot eyes. "She's so smart. She took me to her bedroom and showed me her stuffed animals. And told me how much she loves school. She's in kindergarten, by the way." His eyes light up, and his voice went from hurt to excitement as he tells me everything he knows about his little sister.

"That's awesome, babe," I tell him when he's done.

His face gets serious, and he sighs. "I was sitting in the cab when I saw her run out of the house to my father. He picked her up and twirled her around before kissing her on the cheek. I thought she belonged to him. And a part of me was mad. That I never saw him that way with Becca. And then I thought that was why he was so willing to walk away from the company. To give this little girl the dad he never was." He shakes his head. "But I was wrong."

"It's okay to feel that way," I tell him. "That's a lot to take in."

He wraps his arms around me and pulls me down onto the bed. "I want you to meet her."

I smile. "I would love to. But is that a good idea?" I ask. "If no one is allowed to know about her? How will your dad and Rosie feel about you telling me?"

"We're all going over to Rosie's house this weekend for dinner. Dad is telling everyone then."

As I lie beside him, listening to the sadness in his voice while he tells me about his secret sister, I realize losing my job is small in comparison.

CHAPTER SEVENTEEN

RYDER

My first week at running the company didn't go as planned. I've been distracted and off my game. By the third day, I had a rhythm down and was in the middle of a phone call when my father walks in. He's still here just as much as he used to be; it just doesn't look like it on paper.

"What did we decide to do with Hahn's property on Fifth Avenue?" he asks.

I end my call and sit up in my chair. "A hotel."

"Cancel it," he orders.

I arch my brow. "Why?"

I know I was pissed at my dad when I found out about Maggie. But all that went away when he sat in Rosie's living room telling me how his wife had an affair with his best friend, got pregnant, and then refused to keep the child. I had never felt so much respect for this man. Rosie has her salon, and I know she is set for life, but my father helps her out financially with Maggie. He said his best friend would have wanted that.

"I have other plans for that space," he answers.

"Okay. What is it?"

"I'll let you know when I get more details," he says, starting to walk out of my office. "Oh hey, Ryder?"

"Yeah?" I ask, looking back up at him.

"Is your mother still calling you?"

I frown at his question but shake my head. "I think she got the hint." I've learned a lot about my mother over the past couple of weeks, and I've concluded I don't want anything to do with her.

"Don't be so sure. Maybe she just plans to confront you in person."

I snort. "I won't be seeing her anytime soon."

"Yes, you will. Your cousin's wedding is next weekend." Then he walks out.

"Shit!"

Later that night, we lie in bed eating Cinnamon Toast Crunch out of the box. I got home later than she did and met her at her apartment. We decided to just stay here for the night since she hasn't officially moved in with me yet. Too much has been going on. We were too exhausted to cook or even order carryout. So we cuddled up in her bed, watched some TV, and she grabbed the cereal box out of the kitchen.

She's lying on top of my arm resting her body against my side when her cat jumps up on the bed meowing. He makes his way up my leg and over my stomach. He sits down on my chest, and she reaches up with her left hand to pet him. "I've always been a fan of the shaved pussy, but I must say this is the ugliest shaved pussy I have ever seen," I state, making her laugh.

"Oh, yeah? Have a lot to compare it to?" she asks, still laughing.

"I'm just saying." The ugly thing looks right at me with those big glowing green eyes and overly large ears. I woke up this morning when it was still dark outside, and he scared the shit out of me when I found him sitting on the bathroom counter when I turned on the light. I swear he does shit like that on purpose. The rat remembers our first meeting, and he's paying me back. "He looks like an old man's set of balls," I say with a frown.

I look over his little shirt she has him dressed in. It's the same color of his gray skin that makes him look like he has tattoos. The one on his chest says *I love my momma*. And one on his back that says *this pussy won't bite*. "You dress him every day?" I ask.

"Yes. I order him shirts and sweaters online."

"Why?"

"Because I don't want him to be cold," she says like I should have known that.

"It's summertime in New York."

"But he still gets cold," she argues as if the alien speaks to her.

I turn onto my side, and the cat takes off meowing at me. I look at her and smile. "What?" she asks as she eyes me skeptically.

"What are you doing next weekend?"

"Nothing that I know of. Why?"

"Good! We have a wedding to attend."

She laughs. "Oh, we do? And you're just telling me now?"

"I forgot," I say, "until my father reminded me today."

"Where is it?" she asks.

"The Hamptons." She smiles. Then I drop the bomb. "My mom will be there..." Her smile falls. "And Vicki."

"I'm not going," she states, shaking her head.

"Yes, you are!" She goes to argue when I add, "You're going, and that's that."

"When did you become so bossy?"

I lean and kiss her lips. "Since I got a girlfriend who wants to argue about everything."

I place my hand on her chest and pull it away when I feel crumbs on her skin. "What is on you?" She looks down at it and touches it. "I think it's the cinnamon from the Cinnamon Toast Crunch," she says with a laugh.

I lean in and run my tongue along her chest bone. "Hmmm. Cinnamon tits," I say, running my tongue along her nipple. "Best idea ever." I push her down onto the bed, and she giggles as I lick her clean.

ASHLYN

The rest of the week flew by. I was busy at work going on like I wasn't about to lose it. But Thomas and I couldn't hide the fact we knew the end was coming fast. We both made call after call, trying to get interviews anywhere, but we couldn't find anyone who was hiring. I had a few moments of panic but talked myself out of it by reminding myself that I had Ryder, the man I love, and that I was in New York. How bad can it be? I wouldn't stop looking for a job, but I also wasn't going to let

*sel*f*less*

it ruin me. And the thought of running back to Seattle was long gone. Ryder and Becca both needed me here.

Instead of worrying about my job, I've been trying to be the best girlfriend I can be. Which is very hard. Because in order to play the girlfriend part, the boyfriend needs to be around. He has been pretty MIA all week with work. Tuesday, he had to fly to California for the day and ended up having to stay the night. I went down to my apartment to spend the night with Becca like old times, but she was at Jaycent's. It's so weird how much things can change in a matter of a couple of months. And how much more they are gonna change next week when I'm jobless.

But finally, it's the weekend, and this morning, we woke up, had sex, ate breakfast, and then did it again in the shower. I could tell Ryder was tense just from the night before. He tossed and turned all night long, and I knew it had to do with finding out about Maggie.

"Where is she?" Becca asks as tears run down her face while we all sit in Rosie's living room.

"The nanny took her to the park. I didn't want it to be too much for her. She will be back here soon for you to meet her," Rosie tells her, her face also wet.

Becca nods as she sits on the couch next to her father. I sit over on the loveseat alone. Ryder and Jaycent both stand over by the fireplace. Ryder's face is clear of emotion while Jaycent's is beet red in anger. "You're letting a nanny raise her?" Jaycent snaps.

"I didn't want one." Her eyes slide to Timothy's for the briefest moment, and I feel like the nanny was non-negotiable. "But she does come in handy for things like this," she adds softly.

"How could you keep this from your family for five years?" he demands, looking at his sister.

"I didn't have a choice," she tells him. "There are legal documents. Documents that Gwenda and I signed. If I said anything, I could lose her."

"Who the fuck cares!" he shouts. "She didn't even want her!"

She narrows her eyes at him, and her lips thin. "I care!" she snaps. "At any second, she could have changed her mind," she argues. "You see it all the time in the news. Mother gets child back after x so many years …"

"You should have told me no matter what!" he shouts.

"Don't you dare yell at me," she shouts back at him. "You haven't been here."

"And whose fault is that?" he snaps back.

I watch as this family becomes divided by lies and secrets. And all I can think of is how did no one know Gwenda had a baby? I know Jaycent, Ryder, and Rosie were already adults and out of the house. But how did Becca not know? Or Timothy? Did he know the entire pregnancy that it wasn't his kid? Maybe he thought it was his?

She sighs heavily, and her shoulders start to shake as tears run down her face. "Why would I tell you?" she asks. "Were you going to help me?" He opens his mouth, and she raises her hand to stop him. "I never see you."

"I talk to you all the time," he argues.

"But we never see one another. I'm busy with work …"

"Apparently, you're busy with a lot of things." He growls, looking over at her boyfriend. That I just found out minutes ago no one knew about. But supposedly, they've been together for two years. I don't know much about Rosie except that she is a very private person. And given her circumstances, I can see why.

"Arguing isn't going to solve anything," her boyfriend defends her. "Now you all know."

"And that makes it better?" Jaycent snaps.

"Babe, please …" Becca begs as she stands from the couch. "Just stop," she cries.

He looks over at her and then at his sister. He then tosses his hands up in the air and storms out of the living room. Moments later, we hear the front door slam.

"I'll go talk to him," Ryder says softly.

"No!" his father says as he too stands from the couch. "I'll do it."

Rosie turns to Ryder and Becca. "You have to understand. My hands were tied," she says as fresh tears run down her face. "And I couldn't lose her …" She sniffs. "I just couldn't …" She bows her head and places her face in her hands.

"It's okay," Becca cries, running to her. "It's gonna be okay," she assures her, and I look over at Ryder as he watches them together. A look of worry all over his face. When his eyes meet mine, I can tell he doesn't share Becca's confidence.

• • •

I hang the last piece of clothing up in Ryder's, now our, closet and turn to see him standing at the door, staring at me. He wears a white t-shirt with a pair of blue jeans and running shoes. He looks just as good casual as he does in a suit. "You okay?" I ask.

The meeting at Rosie's didn't go as planned. Jaycent ended up leaving. I don't know what Timothy said to him, but it either pissed him off or scared him. And although I wanted to meet Maggie, Rosie felt that things needed to calm down before we got that chance. We all agreed.

He nods and leans his shoulder up against the doorframe. "So much is happening."

I give him a soft smile. "I know it seems like a lot, but they're all good things." He is taking over the company. He has a sister, and I've moved in with him.

"Are they?" he asks softly before his eyes look around his closet at all my clothes on the right side—my side.

The smile drops off my face. "If it's too much right now, I understand," I tell him as my chest tightens at my words.

He looks back at me and frowns. I gesture to my clothes. "Me moving in. I understand if you want to put it off now—"

"No!" he interrupts me and pushes off the doorframe. He walks over to me. "You are exactly what I need right now. We are where I've wanted us to be."

My smile returns. "Tell me what you want me to do?" I urge. "What can I do to make it better?"

He releases a sigh as he lifts his hand and runs it through my hair. "Love me forever." It breaks my heart that he feels so alone in this world. He has friends and family who love him, but right now, they are all so disconnected from one another.

I place my hands on his chest, and I feel his heart pounding. "Not loving you isn't an option," I tease him, trying to lighten the mood.

And it works. He gives me a smile as his eyes search mine. "Going to Panama was the best decision I ever made."

"Mine too," I agree.

CHAPTER EIGHTEEN

RYDER

I go to kiss her but hear a knock on our door. "I'll get it," I tell her, walking out of the closet to go answer it.

When I open the door, I'm not surprised to see Jaycent standing there. His eyes are puffy and red. He avoids meeting mine.

I take a step to the left and welcome him in.

"Who is it, babe …?"

We both look up to see Ashlyn coming into view, and she immediately grabs her phone off the countertop when she sees Jaycent standing there, turning away from her. "I'm gonna go see Becca," she states and then walks out the door that I'm still holding open.

I shut it and turn to face him. I don't say anything. I don't know what Jaycent is going through at the moment, but he's come here to talk to me. I'll let him take his time.

We were all upset to find out about Maggie. But the love I felt for her outweighed the madness I felt toward my father and Rosie from keeping her a secret.

He gets my attention as he starts to pace. "I didn't mean to interrupt anything," he says, and his voice is rough.

"You didn't," I assure him.

He runs a hand through his hair. "I just needed to talk to someone," he says with a head nod. "Becca doesn't understand …"

"I will," I tell him.

He nods his head again as if he's trying to convince himself of that. He stops pacing and turns to look me in the eye, and I see the hurt all over his face. "I knew Gwenda slept with my dad."

I frown. "So you've known about Maggie?"

He shakes his head. "No. But I knew they had an affair. I knew that your mother was in love with him."

"She loved him?" I ask confused. "I thought that it was just a one-time sort of thing?"

"I don't know how many times it was," he says with disgust. "But I caught them one day. At my parents' house." He shakes his head. "My mother had passed… He was lonely … weak …" He swallows. "She loved him, but he didn't love her." He growls as he starts to pace again. "Then he died." He sniffs. "I had no clue …" I go to ask what he's talking about, but he continues as he paces. "And then she went and paid Conner to keep her away from me," he growls, getting angry. "'Cause she knew I loved Becca. I could have prevented all of it had I just opened my fucking mouth," he snaps.

I take a step toward him. "Jaycent? I'm trying to understand, man. But you're not making much sense."

He stops and turns to face me. Tears in his eyes. "It's all my fault. Had I stood up for me and Becca back then, none of this shit would have ever happened!" he snaps.

I frown. "I don't understand …."

"Your mother loved my dad!" he shouts. "And when he didn't love her back, she got angry. She knew me and Becca had something, but she refused to let her daughter be with the son of the man she loved. So she paid Conner to move away with Becca." He's breathing heavy and nostrils flared. "Your father told Becca that he had taken care of Conner when I was the one who had him thrown in jail."

"You what?"

"I didn't want her mad at me more than she already was. I made some phone calls and found some old drug charges against him. Guess that was another reason he was so willing to get away from here and go to Seattle. Everything leading up to this point is my fault." He sighs.

"No, it's not," I say, shaking my head.

He narrows his eyes at me. "I never told anyone what I knew. If I had told your father ..."

"He knew."

"He knew about the affair, but Maggie ..."

"He knew about her too," I say softly. "He knew about our sister, and that was how Rosie found out about her." I take another step toward him. "Maggie is safe," I say, and my words cause him to fist his hands down by his side.

"Your mother wants her," he says through gritted teeth.

"What? How do you know that?" I ask.

"Your father told me when we had our talk outside at Rosie's earlier tonight. She's been threatening him about her."

I start shaking my head. "But why all of a sudden?"

He snorts. "Your father has filed for divorce. To her friends and the town, she looks like an idiot who couldn't keep her husband. But if she has a child." He shrugs. "She has sympathy."

That's exactly what I had told Ashlyn. "What is he gonna do?" I ask.

"He's going to give her what she wants, so she'll leave Rosie and Maggie alone."

I run a hand through my hair, letting out a breath. "How much does she want?" She had wanted him to step away from the company, so he did, but he can always go back to it. After the divorce is final, we can sign some more papers and everything be undone. What is the price she wants in order to walk away from Maggie?

He looks at me and says, "She doesn't want money." I frown. "He's called off the divorce."

ASHLYN

I sit on the couch in Becca's apartment as she sits beside me crying. "He's so mad." She sniffs.

I reach over and grab some tissue for her. "At your mother?" I ask.

She shakes her head. "At everyone."

I place my hand on her back and start to rub it. "He's not mad at you, Becca."

She nods. "He is. On the way home, he was talking all this

nonsense. About my dad and then Conner. And then he was yelling about me going to Seattle …" She sobs.

I pull her to my side and gently rock her from side to side. "He didn't mean it," I assure her. "There's just so much going on right now …"

The door to the apartment opens, and I look over my shoulder to see Jaycent walk in with a pissed-off Ryder behind him.

Now what?

Jaycent comes over to us and bends down in front of her. She sniffs and then wipes her nose with the tissue. Without a word, he takes her into his arms, and she sobs into his chest. "I'm so sorry, baby," he tells her softly.

• • •

We make our way up to our apartment without saying a word to one another. I walk in and go straight to our bedroom. I'm getting undressed and climbing into bed when he enters, holding a glass with dark liquid in it.

I hold in a sigh. "What's wrong?" It's a stupid question to ask because there is so much that isn't right at the moment.

He ignores me as he walks to the bathroom and shuts the door behind him.

I stare at it for a few seconds, debating whether to go in there or to just lie down and go to sleep. The stubborn part of me decides to get out of bed.

Storming into the bathroom, I find his white t-shirt on the floor while he bends at the waist to push down his jeans. He looks over at me as he straightens and kicks them to a corner. "Thought you were going to bed," he growls.

I come over to him and lean my hip up against the countertop. "And I thought you were in a good mood?"

He snorts. "I'm so fucking done with this day." Picking up his glass, he takes a big swig.

"Then come to bed with me," I say, reaching out and touching his arm softly. I can feel his tense muscles ripple under my touch. "This past week has been hectic, to say the least. Let's just go to bed and start over tomorrow."

He slams his glass down on the countertop. "Tomorrow won't be any better." Then he turns to walk over to the shower.

"Well, aren't you the little pessimist," I observe.

He enters the shower, once again shutting me out. The only thing I'm wearing is a pair of boy shorts, so I rip them off and go in after him. He's standing under the sprayer, his head tilted back and his arms lifted as he runs his hands through his hair.

And my sex clenches at the way the water runs down over his hard chest and defined abs. I want to fall to my knees and lick his defined V. I know sex should be the last thing on my mind, but I'm so unbelievably attracted to him. It makes me insane. His cock hangs between his thighs and makes my heart speed up. Even soft, it's intimidating.

I make my way over to him as he continues to run his hands through his hair, eyes closed. And I crave to know what he's thinking. What's going on behind that gorgeous face of his? Why will tomorrow be just as bad as today? I can't help but think I'm part of the problem. He told me earlier I'm not, but that doesn't help ease my fear. Am I in the way? Am I just another obstacle creating stress in his life? I know his workload has gotten bigger, but I also know that now he is gonna try to balance the two so our relationship doesn't suffer. And that alone could cause problems between us.

I reach out and place my hands on his hips. His eyes snap open, and he lowers his head to look down at me, his hands gripping my hips in a state of panic.

"Sorry," I say, realizing he didn't know I was in here. He is really out of it.

He pulls me to him, and I feel his cock start to harden against my lower belly. His hands leave my hips and find their way into my hair. I gasp as he tightens them, and his lips crash on mine. I can taste the lingering whiskey in his kiss, and it has my head spinning when he knocks my back into a cool shower wall.

I pull away panting. "It's okay," I tell him and his brows pull together in confusion. I just want him to take his frustration out on me. I want him to fuck me! We both need it.

He places his forehead on mine and closes his eyes, sighing heavily. "I'm trying …"

"Shh," I say, running my hands up and down his forearms. "It's just you and me right now, baby. Let go."

Without another word, his lips are on mine again.

CHAPTER NINETEEN

RYDER

"Good morning, Mr. O'Kane!" Kelly says cheerfully as I walk off the elevator.

I walk right past her and into my father's office, slamming the door behind me. "Tell me you were lying to Jaycent," I demand.

He sits behind his desk, his phone to his ear. The person on the other end must have said something because the next thing he says makes me narrow my eyes at him. "It's your son."

"She's on the phone?" I demand and all but run toward his desk. He hangs up the moment I go to reach for it. "So he was right?" I demand.

He sighs and says the one thing that makes my skin crawl. "You have to pick your battles, son."

I take a step back as if he hit me. "Pick your battles?" I ask in disbelief.

He nods. "Yes. And this is not one worth fighting."

I can't believe I'm hearing this! "How can you say that?"

"This is what is best for Maggie. If your mother …" He can't even finish the sentence. "She will be so lost. Confused. And I won't do that to her." He shakes his head quickly. "She needs to stay where she belongs, and that is with Rosie."

"So just let the bitch win?" I snap.

He slams his hands down on the table as he stands. "That is your mother!" he all but shouts.

I snort. "Yeah, some mother she is."

"Ryder …"

"First, she cheated on you. Had a baby with your best friend, which she didn't even want. And then paid a man to fuck your other daughter …"

"Ryder …"

"Now, she's blackmailing you to keep her reputation." I snort. "She's fucking pathetic. And so are you," I snap.

"Get the fuck out of my office!" he roars, pointing at the door.

"Gladly!" I shout, throwing my hands up in the air, and then spin around and walk out, slamming the door behind me.

"Mr. O'Kane?" Kelly asks timidly as she stands from behind her desk. "There's a call on line four …"

"Hang up on it!" I snap and get on the elevator. Taking the day off.

I walk outside the glass doors and see Milton still standing by the back door of my Escalade, having only dropped me off minutes ago. "Where to, Mr. O'Kane?" he asks.

"Talia's," I say, and he nods, closing the door.

I sit in the back of the SUV and remove my suit jacket and tear off my tie. I undo my cufflinks and roll up my sleeves along with undoing the top two buttons. I feel like I can't breathe. My heart pounds in my chest, and my palms are sweaty. I can't seem to catch my breath. I'm so wound up. So pissed. I'm spiraling out of control.

I pull my phone out of my pocket and look up my mother's number. My finger hovers over it for a few seconds as I think about what I would say to her. That I would finally tell her what I think of her, but instead, I close out the screen and throw it to the floor. She would just hang up on me before I could get the words out, and that would just piss me off more.

"We're here," Milton announces, and I climb out of the back seat.

"Hello, Mr. O'Kane," a man says as I enter Talia's. I've seen him before but don't remember his name.

I nod. "Hello …?"

"Thomas."

Ah, yes, Ashlyn has told me about him before. "Where's Ashlyn?" I ask.

His face falls, and I catch it before he can mask it. "Uh …" He looks around as if at a loss. Then his eyes meet mine, and he sighs. "She isn't coming in today."

"Not coming in?" I take a step toward him, and he takes a step back. "I just dropped her off here thirty minutes ago," I snap.

He nods. "Yes, but then she left."

I take another step toward him, not in the mood to be fucked with. "Where did she go?"

His shoulders slump. "She went to a meeting."

"Where at?" I growl. Is it a top secret meeting for NASA? Why in the hell is it like pulling teeth to find out where my girlfriend is?

"She went to the Belvedere Hotel," he finally says

"Thomas," I growl, "I'm in no mood to play games. So you said she left for a meeting and then you tell me she's at Belvedere." He nods quickly. "Explain."

"She has a meeting at the restaurant in the hotel."

"Why was that so hard?" I ask and slap him on the shoulder.

"Belvedere Hotel," I tell Milton as I get into the back of the Escalade again.

I try calling her twice but get voicemail both times. Just as we pull up to the hotel, I see her coming out, wearing a smile on her face. She comes to a stop and turns to her right and shakes the hand of a man dressed in a black suit with a bright yellow button up. He pulls her in for a hug.

My anger rises more than I thought possible. I'm out of the door before the Escalade comes to a complete stop.

I square my shoulders as I approach them. "Ashlyn."

She pushes the guy away from her at the sound of my voice and spins around to face me. "Ryder?" she squeaks. "What are you doing here?"

Walking up to her, I take her in my arms and give her a long kiss on her lips. It's totally a douche move, but at this point, I couldn't care less. I want to show whoever this man is to my right that she's mine. Pulling away, she stumbles a bit and I finally turn my attention to the man staring at me with narrowed brown eyes.

"Ryder O'Kane," I say, reaching out my hand to him.

"I'm very aware of who you are," he says in an annoyed voice. And I notice he places his hands in his pockets instead of shaking mine.

"Well, I don't know who the hell you are."

"Ryder," Ashlyn snaps. "I'm so sorry, Mr. Coats," she says, turning to him.

"It's quite all right, Ashlyn." He says her name with a smile on his face, and I fist my hands down by my side. Turning to face her, as if I'm not standing here, he gives her a bright smile. "I hope to hear from you soon, Ashlyn." Then he looks at me. "We would love to have you in Seattle." He walks off.

I whirl around on her. "What the fuck does he mean by Seattle?"

ASHLYN

Shit! How did he find me? "Ryder ..." His name comes out a little rough, so I clear my throat. "I can explain."

"Yeah, I've heard you say that one before," he snaps.

I let out a long breath. "How did you find me?"

"Really? I catch you at a hotel with another man, and you ask how I found you?" he asks with wide eyes.

My mouth falls open. "Don't go there, Ryder. You know damn well I wouldn't do that," I snap.

He takes a step back and runs a hand through his hair as he lets out a long breath. "I know," he says softly. "I just ..." He trails off. "What's going on, babe?" he asks confused.

I lick my lips as I look around, and Milton catches my eye by Ryder's Escalade. "Come on. We both need to get back to work," I say, taking his hand.

"Thomas said you were talking the day off."

So that's how he found out. "Well, I'm not. I'll explain on the way." I don't miss the fact that his hand is shaking in mine. I know something else is going on other than finding me here.

Once in the Escalade, I turn to face him. "We had a meeting at work on Monday, and your father was wrong."

He snorts. "About so many things."

I ignore that because I don't know what he's talking about. "Talia's has been sold."

He starts shaking his head. "No—"

"Yes," I interrupt him. "When I questioned the details, she said she could not disclose them. Why didn't you tell me that you bought them?"

"No!" he says, shifting in his seat. "I am the one dealing with the Anderson file, and it hasn't even gone to auction yet. The date is still out a month …"

"No, babe." I shake my head. "I'm not a hundred percent sure when the date is set for, but it's done with."

"Who bought it?" he growls.

"They wouldn't tell us," I say, lowering my head.

"How long do you have?" he demands.

"The doors close after today."

His hand softly grabs my chin, and he lifts my head to where I have to look up at him. "Why didn't you tell me?" he asks, his brows pulling together.

"I wanted to. But you came home and had just found out about Maggie …" He closes his eyes and sighs. "Ever since then, things have been nothing short of chaos." We both know that he hasn't been in the best of moods since he took over the company and found out about his little sister. Me losing my job was the last thing he needed to worry about.

"I'm so sorry," he whispers, looking back at me. "But that doesn't explain why that guy mentioned Seattle."

I take my hand from his. "He runs the Mason Gallery here in town, and Thomas was able to get a job there. So he got me an interview. But they aren't hiring anyone else. But they do have a spot open in their sister gallery in Seattle—"

"Absolutely not!" he interrupts me.

"Let me finish," I snap.

His jaw is set in a hard line, and he turns to look straight ahead, staring at Milton's head as if he can really see where we are going. "I told him no."

He turns back to face me. I reach out and grab his hands in mine. "I told you I love you. I told you that I'm all in. Hell, I moved in with you, and you still doubt how I feel?" I ask in complete disbelief. "When did the roles reverse?" I ask, trying to smile and lighten the mood.

He sighs. "Babe."

"I'm trying not to make things more difficult for you, Ryder, but you're making things hard for me. I'm trying to handle this on my own, so it's one less thing you have to worry about. Please, trust me."

"No," he says.

"No?"

He gives me a soft smile. "No," he repeats as he cups my face. "I won't let you do it on your own because part of my job is to take care of you. And I hate that you didn't come to me."

I shrug. "I just thought you bought Talia's and forgot to tell me through all the chaos."

"But I didn't buy it. But you can bet your ass I'm gonna find out who did," he assures me. "I will find you another job."

I sigh. "I've been calling for days now, and no one is even hiring. Thomas told me today that it's bad. In his search for another job, he was informed that other galleries are closing as well. That due to the easy access of internet, no one is going to the galleries anymore. They prefer to buy them from their phones or at home from their computer. He just happened to get lucky."

"We're here, Mr. O'Kane," Milton announces.

"Give us a second," he calls out.

Milton doesn't respond, but I watch him get out and stand over on the sidewalk in front of Talia's. I turn my attention back to Ryder, and he leans close to me. "Don't worry about anything. Okay? I will take care of it. I promise." I open my mouth to argue, but he places his finger over my lips. "The only words I want to hear are yes, Ryder."

I laugh and pull away from his finger. "Yes, Ryder," I say with a smile. It's crazy how this man can make me happy when I should be freaking out.

"Okay, so I lied. I want to hear one other thing," he admits.

"What is that?"

"I love you."

I wrap my arms around his neck and place my forehead on his. "I love you."

His hands slide up my ribs, and he gently presses his lips to mine. "You're mine, baby." I nod then give him a kiss of my own. "And I take care of what is mine."

CHAPTER TWENTY

RYDER

I walk back into my office and find my assistant sitting behind her desk on her office phone. "Kelly," I say, slamming my hand on her desk.

She looks up at me wide-eyed and whispers, "Gotta go," into the phone before hanging it up. "Yes, Mr. O'Kane?"

"Get me the Anderson file," I order. "Somehow, the auction has taken place without my knowledge."

She looks up at me. "They called."

"What?" I snap.

"The other day, I tried to tell you that you had a call on line four, but you ran out of here …"

"Why in the hell didn't you tell me it was for the gallery?" I snap.

She opens her mouth and then closes it before opening it again. "I …"

"Ryder?"

"What?" I snap, turning around to see my father's assistant, Jackie, flinch from my harsh tone. "What?" I demand again when she just stands there staring at me like a deer in headlights.

She holds out her hand. "I got some more information on that business for you …"

"At least someone is doing their job around here," I growl, yanking it free of her hands, storming into my office, and slamming the door behind me.

ASHLYN

I walk into the apartment and sit down. The silence of the room is deafening. I got a text from Ryder earlier that he would be working late just as I expected.

Harry meows as he jumps on my lap, and I rub his back. My phone lights up, and I pick it up to see a picture from Becca. It's a bottle of wine and a plate of spaghetti.

Becca: *Hungry?*

I let out a laugh and reply.

Me: *Be there in two.*

"I'll be back." I kiss him on his wrinkly head and place him on the ground then make my way down to my old apartment.

"Hey," I say as she opens the door for me.

"Hey," she says softly, and I hate that she too is still upset.

"How are things? Better?" I ask with hope.

She hangs her head as she walks over to the couch. "Not really."

I blow some blond strands off my face as I plop down beside her. "It can only get better," I say with a smile.

She laughs at me. "Since when did you become so optimistic? I don't remember you being that way."

"Since I had no other choice," I say truthfully.

"What do you mean?" she asks slowly.

I pick up the bottle of wine and pour some into one of the glasses already sitting on the coffee table. I hand it to her and then fill the other. "Since I lost my job," I say, lifting my glass in salute to her.

Her eyes widen. "What? When?"

"Today was my last day," I tell her.

"Oh, my God, Ashlyn. I'm so sorry."

I shrug. "I'll find another one." Then I tip the glass back not really sure I believe that statement.

I don't know how much time passes, but Becca and I are currently on our third bottle of wine. After we finished off her second one, I had to go up to my and Ryder's apartment to get another one.

We lie on the floor of her living room—why, I don't know—laughing when we hear the front door open. I know it's not Ryder because he doesn't have a key.

"Found them." I hear Jaycent's voice.

Becca and I both sit up and look over the coffee table to see Ryder and Jaycent both standing in the entryway.

"Hey," I say, raising my glass in salute. And Ryder surprises me by smiling at me. Maybe he ended up having a good day after all.

He walks over to me. "Having fun?"

I take a gulp of what's left of my glass in answer. He chuckles. "Come on; let's go home." He yawns. "I'm tired."

I say my goodbyes, and Becca tells me that we are going to hang out tomorrow since I have no other plans. Like a job. Ryder helps me up to our apartment, and I'm laughing when we walk through the front door.

"I'm guessing you had a good day?" I ask as the room tilts a little bit.

He bends down and sweeps me off my feet, and I squeal at the sudden movement. "Nope. It was pretty shitty."

I frown as he carries me off to our bedroom. "Then why are you smiling?" I ask when he lays me on the bed.

He falls down beside me, and his hand comes up to cup my face. "Because you were smiling."

I lick my numb lips and give him what I think feels like another smile. He laughs before leaning down and placing a chaste kiss on them. Then he lifts my shirt and flattens his warm hand on my stomach. I lift my hips off the bed and his fingers dip inside the waistband of my shorts, teasing me.

I close my eyes and say, "I wouldn't do that."

"Why not?" he asks, and my eyes are too heavy to open, but his voice sounds rough.

"Because you're tired," I remind him.

He pulls his hand away, and I let out a moan in protest. "Are you tired?" he asks, and then I feel his hands undoing my button and zipper.

"No," I whisper.

I lift my hips as he pulls my shorts down my legs, and then I hear them hit the floor. I jump when I feel his lips on my hip. "Then neither am I," he whispers against my skin as they trail lower.

With my eyes still closed, my hands run through his thick, spiked hair as my pussy tightens, knowing where he's heading. "Please," I beg.

He pulls my panties to the side. "I love when you beg for it, darling."

I grip his hair and lift my hips, but his hands push them down, keeping them in place. "So greedy," he whispers.

"I need you," I say, opening my eyes for the first time, and the room sways. Closing them again, I hear him chuckle.

I feel him sit up, and my hands fall from his hair. I lie there refusing to open my eyes, not wanting to get sick. He slides my panties slowly down my legs, and it feels like the delicate fabric is burning my skin.

"Ryder ..." I pant, running my hands up my stomach and lifting my shirt in the process to expose my breasts. I have a bra on, and I feel him pull it down right before his lips touch my nipple. I gasp as he sucks on it, making it harden. Then his teeth nibble on it, and I moan loudly.

He pulls away, and my body feels cold. His hands grip my hips, and his fingers dig into my skin. "I'm gonna take my time with you tonight, baby, and love you."

• • •

I spent most of the week with Becca. And it felt like old times again back when we lived in Seattle. We had school and work back then, but we would spend every free moment we had with either my parents or just chilling at our apartment. But since we moved to New York six weeks ago, I've spent all my free time with Ryder—besides that week we were apart. And she spends all her time with Jaycent. It was nice to have my best friend around. Even if I was jobless.

Friday finally came, and it was time to head to the Hamptons for their cousin's wedding. Ryder had somehow managed to take the day off since it was also Fourth of July weekend.

We woke up early Friday morning as if it was any other day, got ready, and was out the door by eight, luggage in tow.

We make our way down to the lobby, and I start to walk toward the front door when he takes a left. "Where are you going?" I ask, coming to a stop.

"To the parking garage."

My eyes widen. "There's a parking garage here?"

He chuckles as he waits for me to catch up with him. "You didn't know that?"

"I don't have a car." Why would I need to know that?

We take another left and walk down a long hallway. At the end, there's another elevator. "Thought we were going to the parking garage?" I ask as it opens, and he steps into it.

"We are." He scans his key card. "There is not much room for parking in New York, so the buildings that do have them are underground." I nod as if I knew that.

We go down a few floors, and the doors slide open when we reach the parking garage. I step out into the brightly lit garage and follow him since I have no idea where he is parked.

Then I see the SUV, but he walks right past it. "Aren't we taking the Escalade?" I ask, running to catch up with him.

"No. Milton will need it this weekend."

I frown. "Where is he going?"

"To see his family."

"How will he get it? Do we need to take it to him?"

He looks at me over his shoulder with a smile on his face. "He lives here in the building."

Of course, he does! I roll my eyes at myself. That makes total sense now.

He turns to the left, and I see his apartment number written in white paint on the concrete wall in front of a white car. "What kind of car is that?" I ask, looking at the sleek thing. It sits low to the ground with blacked-out windows and big black rims. My first thought is that it matches his private jet.

"It's a Bugatti Veyron," he says as if I should know what that is. I've never heard of it before.

He opens the passenger side for me, and I bend down, sliding into the white leather seat. He closes the door, and I feel like I'm sitting in the cockpit of a plane. The dash is solid black with a few silver accents in the center. It smells of expensive leather and brand new. He climbs in beside me. He starts it up, and the car hums from the deep sound of the exhaust.

A screen pops out, and he pulls out of his spot. "How often do you drive this?" I ask as he maneuvers us out of the very tight parking garage. It makes me nervous he's gonna hit a concrete barrier.

"I've driven it like twenty times."

"Did you just get it?" I ask.

He shakes his head as we start to climb a small hill, and I see a red gate ahead of us. "No. I've had it a little over two years now."

"Why even buy it if you never drive it?" I wonder.

He stops in front of the gate and reaches out, pressing a few numbers on a keypad. The gate rises, and he proceeds into a back alley. "You'll see," he says, looking over at me with a smile on his face.

Traffic is a bitch. I guess I never really pay attention when I'm in the back seat of the Escalade while Milton drives us around. But it's bumper to bumper for as far as the eyes can see. It is Fourth of July weekend, after all.

But I like that he is driving. I haven't seen him behind the wheel of a car. He has a baseball cap on backwards, just like the first night I met him in Panama. His hair peeks out from the sides, and he wears a pair of Aviators. His right hand is on the stick shift while his left lies carelessly over the steering wheel. He looks so carefree. So not the Ryder I've seen the past couple of weeks. He's got a pair of holey jeans on with tennis shoes along with a light blue t-shirt. The way the color makes his skin glow has my mouth watering. And every time he shifts, his arm muscles flex, showing me how defined they are.

The windows are down, and the radio is up. He comes to a stop at a light and looks over at me. Reaching over, he turns the radio down and smirks. "What?"

"Just admiring how gorgeous you are," I say, making him laugh.

"You're the only gorgeous one in this car," he says, reaching over and grabbing my hand from my lap.

"I'm pretty sure those are the same sunglasses and hat you were wearing the first night I met you on the beach," I say.

He smiles, not taking his eyes off the road. "Remember what you said to me?" I frown. "I told you that I could be anything you wanted me to be …"

"I said I wanted you to be mine," I say, remembering with a smile.

He brings it to his lips and kisses my knuckles.

I go to open my mouth, but his phone rings through the speakers. He presses a button on the screen, and the sound of a woman fills the car.

"Mr. O'Kane?" she asks nervously.

"Yes," he answers, rolling up the windows as the light turns green. He shifts, and we start to move forward through the intersection.

You can hear her take a deep breath. She seems nervous. "I know you have taken the day off …"

"I have."

"Yes, sir, but I have finally got a hold of those papers you were requesting."

"Email them to me."

He places his blinker on, switches lanes, and the roar of the car as he speeds up vibrates my seat. I refrain from moaning at the feel of it. I'm so turned on right now it's not even funny.

I reach over and place my hand on his thigh and very slowly move to the center of his legs. I feel his cock start to harden, and I smile to myself.

He clears his throat as he shifts in his seat. "Thanks, Jackie. Have a great weekend." Then he reaches over and presses end. The music once again fills the small car. "Ashlyn," he growls in warning.

I don't stop. "How long is it to the Hamptons?"

He clears his throat again as I squeeze him through his jeans. "On a normal day, two and a half hours."

I smile to myself as I remove my hand. He looks in his side mirror and changes lanes again, getting onto a highway. *Perfect!* Undoing my seat belt, I shift to my side and lean over. My hands pull his shirt up, revealing his defined abs, and I quickly undo his jeans.

"Babe …" he groans.

"What?" I ask innocently, pulling him through his boxers and wrapping my hands around the base of his beautiful cock. "We have plenty of time."

Realizing I'm not gonna give up, he sits farther down in his seat and throws his right hand over the back of my seat before I lean down and take him into my mouth.

CHAPTER TWENTY-ONE

RYDER

She sits next to me, a smile on her face as she sings along with the radio. She bounces up and down in her seat. I have the windows down and her blond hair blows around her face wildly as I drive through the Hamptons. And I smile at her. I've seen an entirely different Ashlyn than I knew. So much has happened in the past few weeks, yet she seems freer than before. It's almost if she has no cares in the world.

I slow the car as I come to a driveway. I pull into it, and she leans out of the car window. We pull up to a gate, and I punch in the code I was given. Once it opens, she gasps. "This is where the wedding is?" she asks in awe.

"No."

The look of shock on her face fades, and she frowns. "You said we were staying at the location of the wedding."

"I did say that. Plans have changed."

"Why?"

"Remember the guy at the *Romeo and Juliet* play? He said he had some property in the Hamptons for me to look at? He thought I would be interested in?" She nods. "This is it," I say simply. "I spoke to him last week, and he told me we could stay here so I could check it out."

"You plan on buying this?" she asks, looking back at the house as I come to a stop in front of the five-car garage.

If you like it. "Possibly."

I shut the car off and get out. I walk around and open her door, helping her out. I don't let go, but instead lead her over to the garage. I punch in the five-digit code he told me on the keypad outside the garage door, and the farthest one to the left opens.

"Wow," she says, stepping in and looking around the massive yet empty garage. "Who needs a garage this big?" she asks, her voice echoing through the emptiness.

"Someone who likes to drive a different car every day," I state, making her laugh. "Come on. Let's go look at the house."

I open the door off the garage, and we enter a mud room. We walk through a long hallway and come to an open kitchen. "Whoa," she says as she looks up at the high ceilings and smiles. "This place is gorgeous."

"It needs some work," I say, flipping on the kitchen light. The lighting needs to be updated along with the floors, wallpaper, and furnishings.

"I don't understand." She looks at me. "I thought you did business with companies? You buy homes as well?"

I shrug as I walk over to the big bay windows. I yank the dark blue curtains open to let the sun in through the huge windows. "I will buy anything as long as I can make a profit off it."

"So what ... you buy this house, fix it up, and then sell it?" she asks as she walks over to me and looks at the ocean through the window.

"That's the plan," I lie.

"May I?" she asks as she grabs the doorknob to the glass door.

"Of course."

She opens it up to walk outside, and I follow her. The house is built in a U shape. When you walk out onto the back patio, there's a swing, overly large couch, and a fireplace with a full-size outdoor kitchen to the right. An Olympic-size swimming pool sits in the middle with lounge chairs and tables with gray umbrellas. I look at Ashlyn, and she's already halfway to the ocean. I run after her.

She kicks off her flip-flops and runs until her feet are in the water. The waves gently roll in one after another. I come up behind her and watch her. She has her arms out wide, and her head thrown back as she looks up at the sky. She spins around and faces me, her blond hair whipping her in the face. "How could you sell this place?" she asks in wonder. "I mean, just look at it."

"The house is nice," I say.

She shakes her head. "Who cares about the house! It could be a shack for all I care." She turns, giving me her back again. "This ..." She kicks her feet around in the water. "This is what I would want. The sun, the ocean. This view," she says in awe as she looks at the blue water that seems to be endless. It makes me feel small, and for once, I don't mind that feeling.

I kick off my shoes and remove my socks before I step into the cool water, not caring that my jeans are getting wet. I come up behind her and wrap my arms around her waist. She sighs as she leans her back into my chest. "Some things money just can't buy, Ryder," she says in a whisper.

That's not the first time someone has told me that, but it's the first time I believe it. I lean down and kiss her neck. She moans as she lifts her right hand and wraps it around the back of my neck. "Ryder ..."

"Shhh," I tell her. I bite down on her skin, and she squeals as she yanks away from me. I reach out and grab her wrist. Pulling her to me, I bend down, throwing her over my shoulder.

"Ryder." She screams my name as she spanks my ass. I bend my knees as I pretend to drop her, and she squeals. "Ryder, you'd better not ..."

This time when I bend my knees, I let myself fall into the water. I close my eyes as the saltwater splashes my face, knocking off my hat and sunglasses. She lies next to me, breathing heavy and laughing. She shoves my chest, and I roll onto my back. The water maybe a couple of inches deep. She straddles me, placing her hands on my chest, and growls. "I can't believe you did that."

I laugh as I reach up and push her wet blond hair back. My laughter calms as I look up at her beautiful face; the sun makes her blue eyes shine just like they did when I met her in Panama. And my heart beats faster as a soft smile spreads across her gorgeous face. "You're so beautiful," I say, feeling breathless. She knocks the wind out of me. That smile, those eyes, and her voice—they make me weak in the knees and make me feel invincible all at once. She's the perfect storm, and she's all mine.

She narrows her eyes at me. "You're still in trouble," she tells me.

"Promise me something," I say as I search her face.

"What?" she asks skeptically.

"Promise me that you'll never leave me. No matter what happens, you'll never leave."

She frowns. "I'm not going anywhere."

I could never hear those words enough.

ASHLYN

I wanted to have sex in the ocean. After the way he looked up at me, I was totally ready to take the chance of getting sand in my pussy and let him take me right then and there, but we didn't have the time. We had to get back to the house and shower and get ready for the wedding.

I find it odd that his cousin's wedding is on a Friday night, but I guess that was the only available date for the venue they wanted. Ryder informed me that she would have got married at noon on a Monday if that was her only option. I understood the translation. The venue was very popular, and it is July fourth.

I stand in the bathroom of the mansion that reminds me more of a luxurious resort than a house. It has over twelve bedrooms, and I don't even know how many bathrooms.

The cabinets and drawers are a dark wood with gold knobs. The countertop is a cream marble. The tile white. An old clawfoot tub sits in front of a window overlooking the ocean. I could stand here and look at it all day, but time won't allow it.

I run my hands down the dress that I bought while Becca and I were out shopping earlier this week.

It's dark blue. The back is longer than my front, almost reaching my ankles, and the front stops right above my knees. It has a nude color thin belt high on my waist with thick shoulder straps. It's pretty yet comfortable. It's the slinky material so it moves really well.

I bend down, slipping on a pair of nude wedges, and pull my blond hair over my right shoulder. I put a few bobby pins in the back to keep it there.

I walk out of the bathroom to see that Ryder isn't in the bedroom. "Ryder?" I call out as I walk out of the bedroom and into the hallway.

I call his name out a few more times as I try to find him in this maze. Ryder said it needed some work, but I don't see where it needs anything done. It's a beautiful home. It is fully furnished, but all the furniture is covered with plastic with the exception of the bedroom where we are staying.

I enter the open kitchen and just happen to look out the windows. I smile when I see him standing outside on the beach.

I take my wedges off and make my way out the back door. I take a deep breath as I smell the ocean and the fresh air. I can see the waves rolling and hear them crashing into the shore.

"Ryder?" I ask as the wind blows my dress around. I try to hold my hair, afraid the wind will mess it up.

He turns around and smiles when he sees me. "I didn't know how much longer you would be," he says as he reaches his hand out to mine. He wears a pair of black slacks and a dark purple button up with a black skinny tie. His sleeves rolled up and his hair is spiked to perfection like always.

"I'm ready if we need to go," I tell him as I slip my hand in his. He looks around as if he's looking for someone. "Who are you looking for?"

"No one." His eyes are back on mine as a smile spreads across his face. "I have a gift for you."

I frown. "You know how I feel about gifts."

He chuckles. "I couldn't help myself, sweetheart." He digs into his pocket and pulls out an oversized square Tiffany box.

"Ryder ..." I say in warning even though my heart beats wildly in my chest. The box is too big to be a bracelet or a ring. Not that I expect a ring. Or anything for that matter.

"Open it," he orders softly.

I take it from him and take a deep breath before pushing it open. I gasp, placing my right hand over my mouth when I see what's inside. "Ryder," I breathe as the sun hits the gorgeous diamond and makes it sparkle.

"Do you like it?" he asks.

My eyes meet his, and he stares at me nervously. "Do I like it?" I ask as tears start to fill my eyes. "I love it," I say, lowering my hand from my mouth and running my finger over the large heart-shaped diamond that sits on a silver chain. "It's absolutely gorgeous."

"May I?" he asks, gesturing to the box.

"Please," I say, nodding my head, my throat closing at this beautiful and thoughtful gift. I turn, giving him my back, and pull my hair up as he fastens it.

I turn around to face him. "Perfect," he whispers, looking down at it, and then his eyes meet mine. "Just like you."

I look at him through watery eyes. "Thank you," I say softly.

He cups my cheek. "You're very welcome, gorgeous."

"I love it," I say, swallowing the lump in my throat. Why does he do this to me? "But you shouldn't have," I can't help but say. He's already done so much for me.

I let out a shaky breath. He leans in and kisses my forehead. "Let's get going."

• • •

We pull up to another mansion that is right on the beach about five miles from where we're staying. And we get out of the car as the valet gets in and drives it off. Ryder takes my hand, and I watch him smile and make small talk with people I've never seen before as we walk down a long hallway. He catches me staring and gives me a wink then goes back to his conversation with a gray-haired old man. And I think how did we get here? Almost two months ago, we were complete strangers ready to jump each other for a one-night stand, and now here we are. I can't help but imagine a future with him. I see us laughing while we roll around in bed. I see him rubbing my belly as he speaks to our unborn child, and I see us sitting on a rocking chair watching the waves crash on the beach. It terrifies me as much as it excites me.

He brings me to a stop in front of a white door. He knocks on it. "Knock, knock," he says, not even bothering to wait for someone to answer it.

We enter, and I see a woman sitting on a white loveseat in a white wedding dress. She sees him, and her eyes light up with surprise. "Ry," she says, jumping to her feet. Her black hair is up in a pretty updo, and her makeup is flawless. She has soft brown eyes and is smaller than I am, very petite.

He lets go of my hand and walks over to her. He pulls her in for a big hug, and I watch her smile and then sniff. "What are you doing here?" she asks, pulling away.

"You thought I would miss this day?"

"You never RSVP'd," she says, placing her hands on her hips.

He scratches the back of his neck. "Well, here I am." He looks over his shoulder and raises his hand. "Sweetheart," he says to me as he gestures for me to take his hand again.

I walk over to him and take it. "Melissa, this is Ashlyn. My girlfriend."

I can't help the smile that I wear. It's brighter than the woman who is about to get married.

She wraps her arms around me, surprising me, and Ryder chuckles. "It's great to meet you," she says as she pulls away. "Becca has told me so much about you."

My eyes widen in surprise. Becca never talks to me much about her family.

"Look at you." She looks at Ryder and punches him in the arm. "Finally growing up."

He laughs. "Well, I won't keep you," he says as if he's getting uncomfortable. "I just wanted to see you before the show got started and then you were too busy taking pictures or running off to catch your plane for your honeymoon."

She gives him one last hug and then gives me another. We walk out of the room and make our way to the back of the house. When we walk outside, I see seats lined up forever. "Wow!" I say wide-eyed as I look at the abundance of red roses that line the aisle. They're on either side and then wrapped around the white pillars underneath the awning. "This is a big wedding," I say quietly.

"I think she has four hundred coming."

My eyes widen. "I don't even know that many people."

He laughs as he places his hand on the small of my back. "They're mainly their fathers' friends. People like my father use opportunities like this to show off." I frown when I hear the tension in his voice. He hasn't mentioned his father in the past week. Not since we had the family meeting at Rosie's.

"What does your uncle do?" I ask. That's one thing we've never discussed. His family.

"He's in oil," he says.

He guides me down the ten steps off the porch and onto the red carpet that lines the aisle as well. "Why didn't he help your father with O'Kane Enterprises?" I wonder.

He reaches down and fiddles with his Rolex as if a nervous habit. "Because it wasn't left to him," he says curtly.

I nod my head and drop it. It's obviously a sore subject. "Come on; let's go find Becca and Jaycent," he says as a guy dressed in a white tuxedo walks by carrying a tray of flutes filled with bubbly. He grabs two and hands me one. I take a sip. Hmm. It's champagne.

"Where are your parents?" I ask, looking at the people standing around, but I don't see his mother or father anywhere. "Have you seen your dad?" I'm not all that excited to see his mom, but I have become quite fond of Timothy.

"No and I don't know."

I stop walking. "Are you okay?" He comes to a stop as well and turns to face me. His eyes look hard and his jaw sharp. "Did I say something to upset you?" He was fine not five minutes ago.

He stares down at me for a few long seconds, and he lifts his hand to my cheek. I place my hand on his, my charm bracelet dangling from it as the charms clink together. He looks at it, and then his eyes come back to mine. They soften, and he sighs. "Not at all. I just don't care to see my mother."

That's one thing I can agree on. But if I had to choose between her and Vicki, I'd choose her. But it's bound to happen. I know they're both here somewhere.

He leans in to whisper in my ear. "Have I told you that you look absolutely gorgeous tonight?"

"Yes," I say in a whisper, my chest rising and falling fast from his words. All I can think about is him and me in that large bed rolling around sweaty and panting.

He runs his hands up and down my arms, leaving goose bumps from his soft touch. "I can't wait until this wedding is over." He licks his lips as his dark green eyes fall to my chest. "I'm gonna play with you tonight."

Wetness pools between my legs, and I tighten them. "I have to go to the restroom," I say suddenly.

He smirks. "I'll show you the way, darling."

I step into a master bath and walk past the sink and mirror to the door over in the corner to see it separates the toilet from the rest of the bathroom.

I'm in the separate room when I hear the door open and then a woman's voice. "Did you see her?"

"Yes. I can't believe he brought her here," another woman answers.

I freeze as a sickening feeling hits me. Are they talking about Ryder bringing me? They can't be. Can they?

I hear the door open again, and then I hear a familiar voice. "Vicki. How have you been?"

It's Becca, and she just said Vicki. Just great! Once again, the door opens and closes as if the other woman who came in with Vicki left.

"Becca," she says coldly. "Surprised to see you here?"

"Why Vicki, I'm surprised *you're* here. You know after you made a fool of yourself on Ry's boat." I cover my mouth to keep from snickering.

"How is Ryder doing anyway?" she asks.

I roll my eyes. "He's great. Ashlyn and he just moved in together," she announces proudly.

"What?" Vicki squeals, and I place a hand over my mouth to keep from laughing. *Bitch!*

"Yep. He's in love."

"I don't think he's over me," Vicki snaps. "That's just my opinion, though," she adds.

"Well, fact and opinion are two very different things, Vicki. And your opinion holds no value."

Vicki gasps. "And how's your love life, Becca? You ever find out if your mother was paying Jaycent to fuck you like Conner?"

I unlock my door and shove it open. They both turn to face me. Becca's eyes are narrowed, and Vicki's are large in surprise. "I don't see how any part of Becca's life is any of your business," I say and make my way over to the sink to wash my hands, placing my drink on the countertop.

Vicki laughs, but it sounds more nervous than genuine. "Well, if it isn't the woman playing Cinderella," she says, placing her hands on her purple dress. Her eyes drop to my glass of champagne, and she sighs. "You shouldn't be drinking, honey."

I smile at her in the mirror. *Bitch!* And choose to ignore her comment about my drink. "So that would make you the ugly step sister?"

Becca laughs, and Vicki fists her hands down by her side. "Listen, bitch …"

"No, you listen," I say, taking a step toward her. "Stay the hell away from me and Becca," I warn her.

"Not gonna warn me to stay away from Ryder?" she asks, arching a dark brow.

"I don't need to warn you there. We all already know he won't let you get close." Then I walk past her and grab Becca's arm, reaching to open the door when she speaks. "And Bradley? What about him?"

I turn and narrow my eyes at her. "How do you know about him …?"

She gives me a smile and pushes her hip out crossing her arms over her chest with satisfaction. "I know more than you know, honey."

I grind my teeth and want to say more, but I know women like her. She could go on and on, and I don't want to make a scene here at their cousin's wedding. Instead, I hold my head up high and spin around, yanking Becca out of the bathroom.

"I need to pee, though," she whispers to me.

"Choose another bathroom. This mansion has like fifty," I snap.

• • •

The wedding went as I thought it would. It was beautiful, the bride cried, and the groom choked on his vows. It was like a storybook wedding with the red roses and sunset with the smell of the ocean and the crashing of the waves.

The wedding just ended, and now we sit under a large white tent as the sun continues to set. They kept the reception on location due to the firework show that will be happening soon. I know I'm exaggerating, but the tent looks the length of a football field. People pile underneath it at round tables with white tablecloths and eight red roses in a crystal vase. A soft white material covers the chairs, and a red ribbon is tied around them with a bow hanging off the back of each chair.

The bride and groom sit at the front of the tent with their wedding party. She has twenty bridesmaids, Vicki being one of them. I lean over to whisper in Becca's ear. "How do you have that many bridesmaids? I don't even like twenty people," I state.

She snorts, her white wine flying out of her mouth as she cups her chin, and I laugh. "Me either." She wipes her chin. "How would you do it?"

"My wedding?" She nods. "I would want something small. Secluded. Just me and my groom with our parents and closest friends." I smile. "I picture something on the beach with no shoes. Just our toes in the sand as the sun sets." I tilt my head to the side. "I guess that's kinda like this, just on a much smaller scale."

"It sounds beautiful," she says, smiling.

Ryder snorts from beside me. He lifts his glass and takes a big gulp of the amber liquid.

Becca taps my leg softly, and she gives me a smile. I look ahead and stare at nothing really. What the hell was that? I don't want him to think that that's what I do, sit around all day and picture us getting married.

"Here are my children," Ryder and Becca's mother says as she comes up to our table.

I feel Ryder's body stiffen beside me, and I watch as Becca cuddles up closer to Jaycent's side as if she's afraid of the woman.

I square my shoulders and lift my chin. I've only met her five times, and she looks as beautiful as I remember. Too bad she's a bitch.

She doesn't overdo it to where she looks plastic and fake. She looks more like a porcelain doll. Her makeup and hair perfect. She wears a white dress, and I frown; you're not supposed to wear white to a wedding unless you're the bride.

"Well, aren't you going to say hello?" she asks.

"Hello, Mother," Becca says timidly.

Ryder ignores her as he takes another drink. "Your father's looking for you," she tells him.

"I've been right here all night," he says flatly.

"Ashlyn, it's good to see you again." She looks at me and smiles. "Like New York?"

I almost swallow my tongue at her words. I'm not a fake person, but I can play if that's what she wants. "Yes."

Ryder leans back in his seat and places his right arm over my shoulders. I stiffen as his mother's eyes narrow just a bit. "Mother, Ashlyn and I moved in together," he states, and Jaycent is the one who chokes on his drink. Becca is quick to clean it up off his button up.

"What?" she asks, clearing her throat. To be honest, I'm surprised she didn't already know that.

He gives her a fuck you smile. "I asked her to move in with me, and she said yes."

Her blue eyes dart back and forth between us, and she opens her mouth and then closes it. "But I thought—"

"You thought wrong," he snaps, interrupting her.

She huffs, and her eyes move back and forth between me and Ryder. Then they settle on me. "So do you plan on marrying him or just gonna play house with my son?" She doesn't let me answer as she then looks at Ryder. "You'd better make her sign a prenup. Women like her are only after one thing."

"Excuse me?" I snap as I stand.

"Mother," Becca squeals as she also stands.

She narrows her eyes at me, and Ryder very slowly stands, stepping between us. "She's not the whore you are, Mother."

She gasps, placing her hand over her heart as if his words just stabbed her. "Julian …"

He rolls his eyes and throws back what's left of his drink. "Play the victim. Like always." He leans into her face, and she pulls back, eyes wide. "But we're not your friends, Mother. We're your children, and we know exactly what kind of piece of shit you are."

Her eyes narrow, and she opens her mouth. "Gwenda?"

We look over to see Vicki has joined us, a fuck you smile on her face as she stares at me for a second. "Let's go take some pictures," she says, offering her hand.

"Run along, Mother." He gestures to Vicki. "To your little pack of sheep."

Surprisingly, she takes Vicki's hand and walks off without

argument.

I place my hand on his shoulder and let out a long breath. "Ryder …"

He looks down at his empty drink and pulls away from me. "I need another drink," he states and then walks off.

CHAPTER TWENTY-TWO

RYDER

I make my way over to the open bar at the far side of the tent. I place my empty glass on the white tablecloth, and the female bartender smiles at me. "Ready for another already?"

I nod. "Make it a double."

She takes my glass and puts a scoop of ice in it followed by a shot of scotch. I reach up and undo my tie and yank it off, before stuffing it in my pocket. I feel like I'm suffocating. I only agreed to come to show off Ashlyn. She's my trophy that I wanted to wave in people's faces. Mainly my mother's. I wanted her to see that I finally found the one that was meant for me. But I got pissed the moment I saw Vicki here. I tried to prepare myself, but it wasn't enough.

"Ryder." My father says my name as he comes up next to me.

"Father," I say tightly.

He sighs. We haven't really spoken since he kicked me out of his office. "Son, I wish you'd understand where I'm coming from."

"I understand that you feel you have no other option." I turn to face him. "And I also feel that you are wrong."

"Tell me what to do," he growls. "Tell me how you would make the situation I'm in better?"

"I wouldn't give that bitch whatever she wants," I say and throw back another gulp.

"I have no choice," he snaps loudly, and people turn to face us.

I laugh it off. "You make it sound like you owe her your life. When we both know it's the other way around."

He sighs heavily.

I go to speak, but a hand softly touches my shoulder. I turn to see it's Ashlyn. "Would you like a drink?" I ask, giving her a tight smile.

She frowns as if my mood swings are scaring her. "Yes, please. A glass of white wine."

"Ashlyn," my father greets her. "How are you doing?"

"Good." She lies. We all know that she's lost her job. And that I'm being a fucking douche.

He nods. "That's good."

She places her hand on his shoulder. "How are you doing, sir?"

He looks at me as if I have an answer for him, but I look away at the bartender, asking for a glass of wine for her.

"Good," I hear him say, and I snort.

"You're both horrible liars," I say, pulling out a ten-dollar bill from my wallet for a tip. "Thank you," I tell the woman as she hands me the glass of wine.

I turn to give it to Ashlyn, and she's narrowed her eyes at me. She takes the drink from my hand and throws me a fuck you look before turning to my father. "It was good to see you, Mr. O'Kane." Then she walks off without another word.

"Ryder, I—"

"I don't wanna hear it," I interrupt him before I walk off. "I fucking hate weddings," I growl to myself, taking another drink. I just wanna go back to the house and bury myself between her legs.

ASHLYN

I sit at the table as I watch Ryder dance with a little girl. She looks about seven years old. She has bright blue eyes and long dark hair that cascades down her back in big waves. He holds her right hand above her head as she twirls around and around. Every now and then, she sways as if dizzy. She giggles, and he picks her up, spinning her around. Her purple flower girl dress floats in the air as they spin around like a spin-top. Those toys you used to play with as a kid.

He sets her down, and she clings to his leg, laughing as she tries not to fall over. He laughs, and I smile. He seems to be doing better. It's been an hour since the weird conversation with his father, and the sun has officially set. The fireworks should be starting any second.

"Ashlyn." I look up to see Ryder standing beside me with his hand out. "Dance with me."

"Are you gonna spin me around?"

"No. I'm pretty sure if I spin anymore, I'll be in the bushes." He laughs at himself, and I know he's drunk. He's had more drinks than I can count, but I didn't try to stop him. I'm his girlfriend, not his mother.

"Then yes." I place my hand in his, and he pulls me to stand. He raises his hand above my head, and I spin around under it as we walk to the dance floor. Now that the sun has set, little white strings of lights light up the tent.

He pulls me close to him, his right hand on my lower back and his left on my cheek. Both of my arms wrap around his firm body. He lowers his forehead to mine and releases a long sigh. I can smell the lingering scotch on his breath. "You're not supposed to do that."

"Do what?" I ask confused.

He smiles. A drunken half-smile. "Look better than the bride."

I chuckle, and he pulls me tighter. "I'm serious," he whispers. "You're the most beautiful woman here." He stops dancing, and I look up at him through my dark lashes. We stand in the middle of the dance floor, people all around us probably staring, but all I see is him. All I hear is him; the music has faded away, and I'm lost in his dark green eyes.

His hand leaves my back, and he cups the other cheek. "I'm so in love with you, Ashlyn."

I can never get enough of those words. "I'm in love with you too."

He smiles, and I feel like my world just turned upside down. My knees threaten to buckle, and I suck in a deep breath. He steps closer to me and lowers his lips to mine. He whispers, "I'm in love with you, Ashlyn, and I want the world to know that you're mine." Then his lips are on mine. He kisses me deeply. I kiss him back passionately. Showing him everything that I'm unable to say at the moment as I hear the first fireworks explode in the sky above us.

Chapter Twenty-Three

RYDER

"Get a room."

I open my eyes and pull away from Ashlyn to look at the woman who just walked by us. And I think I'm seeing things when I see who said it. "Yes, they're here…" She says into her phone. "Yep. They've moved in together." She rolls her eyes bitterly. "I don't know. She's drinking…" She snaps as her eyes look Ashlyn up and down. They linger on her belly for a second longer and then her eyes meet mine. "It's pathetic," she says and then hangs up.

"Vicki!" I slur her name. She must have been talking to her mother. I'm sure Debra has a lot to say about me and Ashlyn.

She then looks me up and down with disgust. I laugh. "Finally, we feel the same about one another."

"Ryder," Ashlyn says my name in warning and glares at me. "Please stop. She's not worth it." I giggle snort and she looks at me like I've lost my damn mind.

Vicki walks over to us and stops right in front of me. "You are pathetic," she spits in my face.

"And you're a bitch!" I say with a shrug. "What's new?" I ask swaying on my feet.

Vicki gasps, and Ashlyn places her hand on my chest and shoves me backwards. I stumble but manage to stay upright. "He's drunk," she informs Vicki as she stands between us. "Walk away, Vicki," she warns.

She gives Ashlyn an evil smile, then tosses her drink at her. Ashlyn takes a step back gasping in surprise, her arms out wide. The champagne runs down over her face and onto her blue dress. I should be pissed, but my first thought is I want to lick it off her chest.

Vicki simply says, "Don't worry, honey, shit floats."

Ashlyn wipes some of the excess drink off her and flings it down to her sides and lets out a laugh that makes Vicki raise her brows in question.

"Everything okay?" Becca asks as she and Jaycent join us. She looks at Ashlyn and gasps. "What the …?"

"Yes," Ashlyn answers, interrupting her. "We were just leaving," she adds, turning to face me, and grabs my upper arm. "Let's go."

"How does it feel to have my sloppy seconds?" Vicki shouts.

I come to an abrupt stop when Ashlyn yanks on my arm. She lets go of me and spins around. "What did you just say to me?" she demands.

"Not everything is about you, bitch," Vicki snaps.

Ashlyn fists her hands down by her sides. "You piece of—"

Jaycent grabs Ashlyn's arm as she takes a step toward Vicki. "As I said, not everything is about you," she interrupts her. Vicki looks over at Becca, and she licks her lips and gives her a big smile. Then her eyes land on Jaycent. "Give me a call when you're done with your little toy. I'd love another round …"

Becca gasps, and Ashlyn shoves Vicki back.

"What the fuck …?"

"Shut your mouth!" Ashlyn snaps at her.

Vicki just laughs at that. "What are you gonna do?" she asks with an arch of her brow. "Gonna make me? Maybe I should call Bradley …"

Ashlyn steps up to her, and I see her fist her right hand, but it's like in slow motion. She pulls it back and then swings, connecting with Vicki's jaw. Her head snaps back as I call out Ashlyn's name. I'm running for her when she hits her again.

I connect with Ashlyn's back, and I can't stop my momentum due to my drunkenness, and we go crashing to the ground.

"You fucking bitch!" Vicki screams as she gets up off her ass beside us. Ashlyn had hit her so hard it knocked her to the ground.

I try holding Ashlyn down.

"Ryder …" She snaps at me and then elbows me in the stomach, knocking the wind out of me, and I roll off her, feeling I may vomit due to alcohol and getting hit in the stomach. She's up on her feet the next moment and has a hold of Vicki's hair. She yanks it back as Vicki lets out a scream.

My father comes out of nowhere and rips them apart. He holds Vicki as Jaycent grabs Ashlyn.

"I'm gonna kill you!" Vicki yells at her.

"I'd like to see you try," Ashlyn growls back, trying to fight off Jaycent, but he has a good grip on her.

I manage to stand but sway on my feet. "What the hell is going on?" my father demands.

"This whore is attacking me!" Vicki cries.

Ashlyn throws her head back, laughing. "Whore? Honey, between the two of us, you're the one who has spread their legs for both Ryder and Jaycent."

"Is that true?" Becca asks, looking at Jaycent.

Vicki smiles, knowing exactly what she's done. Jaycent lets go of Ashlyn and turns to face Becca. "It was a long time ago—"

"Don't lie, baby," Vicki interrupts him. "It was right before Becca moved back …"

"Enough!" my father orders. He lets go of her and turns to face her. "Leave!" he orders Vicki.

"But …"

"Vicki, get out of here now!" he snaps.

Blood runs down her lip, and I can see her eyes already starting to swell. She takes a few deep breaths and then throws a "fuck you" look at Ashlyn before turning around and storming off.

My father turns to face us, taking in a deep breath himself. "I think it's time you all leave as well."

I reach out to Ashlyn, but she yanks her arm away from me before I can get a hold of it. And then she too storms off with Becca right behind her.

My father straightens his tie and turns to face me and Jaycent. "I hope you guys have learned a lesson."

"What would that be?" I can't help but laugh. They don't.

"To keep your fucking dicks in your pants!" he snaps.

ASHLYN

I sit on the floral-patterned couch back at the house. The plastic on the floor by my feet. Becca sits next to me, and Jaycent sits on the floor in front of us cross-legged.

"I'm sorry, Becca," he says for the millionth time.

She shrugs. "I can't really be mad at you. I was with Conner before I moved back."

"Yeah, but I should have told you." He sighs.

Becca looks over at me. "Do you think Ry is okay?"

I snort. "He's passed out cold. I put a trash can by the bed and made sure he was on his side just in case he pukes." I'm so pissed at him. His attitude tonight and how much he had to drink. What was he thinking?

"I know Vicki likes to talk a lot of shit, but why does she bring up Bradley?" Becca asks. "How would she even know his name?"

"I don't know," I say, fisting my right hand. It's sore, and I have a cut across my knuckles. I think a tooth got it. "Maybe your mom."

"How would she …?"

"She met him when she came down for your birthdays and for graduation. I mean, we were best friends. We were always hugging and … friendly. Maybe your mom thought we had a thing." I shrug.

"Maybe," she agrees.

Jaycent clears his throat, and we both look down at him sitting on the floor. He smiles at me. "I just wanna be the first to tell you that you hitting Vicki was awesome," he says, and we all laugh.

I tried so hard not to be that woman. The one who looks jealous or causes a scene. I couldn't care less what she said or does to me. She's just jealous that I got the guy. But she crossed the line when she threw Jaycent under the bus and hurt Becca. I will always take up for my friends. No matter what.

"It's late, and I'm tired," I say, looking outside the big floor-to-ceiling windows and see nothing but blackness. The fireworks stopped long ago.

We say our good nights, and I show them to a bedroom. As I walk back through the living room to the other side of the house where our bedroom is, I stop and walk outside. I overlook the back porch and swimming pool. I can't see the ocean, but I can hear it. I think about what Vicki said.

I hold my cell in my hand and pull up Bradley's number. He still randomly calls and texts me, but I quit responding a long time ago.

I decide to dial it, and after the second ring, it goes to voicemail. I smile, good for him for moving on. He deserves someone who loves him.

I walk into the bedroom and find Ryder in the same place that I put him. His mouth is open, and he snores. I get out of my dress and crawl into the king-size bed and turn my back to him, close my eyes, and let out a long sigh. Maybe tomorrow will be better.

Chapter Twenty-Four

RYDER

I wake with a pounding headache and find myself alone in the king-size bed.

I sit up and rub my temples. It's daylight, and I have to blink a few times to adjust my eyes.

I shove off the covers and swing my legs to the side of the bed. I wait a few seconds as I try to get my vision to stop spinning. Fuck, I drank too much last night.

I'm naked, so I dig through my bag to find a pair of boxers and sweatpants. I open the bedroom door and make my way through the house. I hear Ashlyn's voice before I see her coming from the kitchen.

I walk in, and she stops as she sees me. To my surprise, I see Jaycent and Becca also present. "Morning," I say but no one returns it.

Becca's eyes are red, and Jaycent's lips are thin. "Can you give us a moment?" Ashlyn asks.

They both nod and silently make their way out of the kitchen, and I turn to face her. She's looking at me like I did something wrong. Her eyes are narrowed, and her lips are thinned too.

"What's wrong?" I ask, walking around the bar.

She takes a step back shaking her head. "Ashlyn?"

"I have nothing to say to you," she finally says.

"What?" I ask. "You just told them to give us a second. So you had planned on saying something," I say.

"Well, I changed my mind," she snaps.

She walks past me, and I grab her upper arm, bringing her to a stop. She spins around, fisting her hands down by her side. "What's wrong?"

"You are what's wrong!"

"What did I do?" I ask, flinching from her tone. My head hurts so badly.

She yanks her arm free of my hold. "Do you even remember last night?"

"I had a lot to drink …" I trail off, running my hand through my hair.

"I'd say. You could barely stand," she snaps.

"I pissed you off," I say, nodding my head.

"Is it that obvious?" she demands.

I hang my head. Fuck, I need some Advil. "What do you want me to do?"

She shakes her head. "Unbelievable."

"Ashlyn, wait," I call out as she walks away.

"You know, I'm trying, Ryder. I'm trying to understand why you're being a prick to everyone. I get that you're busy with work and you have a lot going on, but what I can't understand is why you had to get so fucking hammered at your cousin's wedding that you don't remember me punching Vicki in the face after she admitted to sleeping with Jaycent in front of your sister," she snaps, pointing a finger at me. "You were too busy having to concentrate on standing rather than helping me out."

My eyes widen. "You punched Vicki?"

She lets out a growl and storms off.

ASHLYN

I ended up riding back with Jaycent and Becca. I was so pissed that I didn't want to be around Ryder. And to be honest, I was more pissed at myself than I was at him. It wasn't his fault that I got out of hand. And it wasn't his fault that Vicki had opened her mouth. I was just so pissed and wanted to stick up for Becca. We all knew she wouldn't do it, so I ended up making an ass of myself.

I stand in front of the floor-to-ceiling windows with my head against the cool window. It's late, and Ryder still hasn't arrived home. I'm not sure when he will. I haven't spoken to him. We both needed to cool down.

My phone rings, and I pick it up off the coffee table and turn back to face the windows, looking over Manhattan.

It's a number not saved in my phone, and I frown. It's half past ten here on a Saturday night. "Hello?" I ask.

"Hey," comes the soft male voice, and I close my eyes as I feel my chest tighten.

"Bradley," I whisper his name.

"I won't keep you," he says in a rush. "I just … I just wanted to apologize. For everything." He pauses.

I sigh heavily. "You don't have to …"

"No, I do. I knew you didn't love me like I did you."

"Why do you have to say that?" I ask.

"Because I hid my feelings from you for so long that I don't know how to anymore," he says honestly.

"I'm with Ryder, Bradley," I admit.

After a few seconds of uncomfortable silence, he finally says, "I know. I heard you two moved in together. And I'm happy for you." His voice is rough, and he clears his throat. "I truly am. I hope he's everything that you deserve, princess."

"Bradley …" I pause, not really knowing what to say. I look over Manhattan and the lights that make the city glow and let out a sigh. "I miss you," I say honestly.

"I know," he says softly. "I miss you too. Take care, princess." Then he hangs up.

I remove my phone from my ear and turn around to place it back on the coffee table but come to a stop when I see Ryder standing in the living room staring at me with an unreadable look on his face.

I swallow nervously and feel like I've once again been caught doing something I wasn't supposed to. "That was—"

"Bradley," he interrupts me. "I heard."

I nod and brace myself for a fight when he sighs heavily. "I don't want to fight with you."

"I'm not trying to start one," I say honestly.

He runs a hand through his hair. "What am I supposed to do?" he asks. "Tell me what you want me to do, and I'll do it." He gestures to our apartment and then his hands fall to his sides. "You want me to admit that I'm in way over my head? Yes, I have come to terms that that is the case."

"No!" I say, shaking my head. "I want you to forgive your dad for something that is out of his control," I say truthfully. Not caring that he didn't help me with Vicki last night. She's the least of our problems.

"See, that is where we disagree. He has every opportunity to fix that. He chooses not to."

"Did you know that Rosie has left town?" I ask.

He frowns. "Left town? Like she went on a vacation?"

"No. This morning before you woke up, Becca told me that she spoke to her yesterday, and she, Maggie, and Ronald went out of town to hide from your mother. She's been calling her and threatening her to take Maggie back."

He drops his head. "No one told me."

"Did you really need to know that in order to know what your dad is doing, is right?" I ask. "You think everything is black and white, and that's not the case here."

"I don't know what to think anymore," he admits.

I take a step toward him. "I think you're mad, and that's okay, but you have to be mad at the right person."

He reaches out and touches my cheek with the back of his hand. "Are you still mad at me?"

"I can't stay angry with you. We both know that," I say softly.

CHAPTER TWENTY-FIVE

RYDER

Monday morning, I find myself sitting in the conference room with my father drinking a strong cup of coffee to try to wake myself up when the door opens and my sister walks in.

"What are you doing here?" I ask in surprise.

"I called her in," my father says in answer to my question.

She sits down next to me and looks over at him. "Is this a family meeting?" I ask. After what happened at the wedding, I wouldn't be surprised if he chewed our asses out. It came back to me last night, and I wished it hadn't. Not knowing what had happened was much better than remembering it.

"No, this is a business meeting."

Just as he says that, the door opens again, and Jaycent walks in. "I don't have a lot of time, so I'm gonna make this quick," my father says, getting to the point.

"Jaycent, do you have what I asked for?"

"Yes, sir," he tells him, pulling a USB drive out of his pocket. He hands it to my father who places it in the computer that sits in front of him. Then he spins it around to face all three of us.

"What is this?" I ask as a set of blue prints pop up.

"This is what I'm going to put in place of Hahn's restaurant."

"A clothing store?" I ask. I've seen enough blueprints to know what certain stores look like.

My father nods. "Becca's clothing store."

"What?" I ask, looking at her.

Her eyes are wide as she looks between Jaycent and our father. "What?" she repeats my question breathlessly.

My father speaks. "Jaycent and I have been working together on getting this done for you, Becca. It's a rough draft, and if you want to change anything, just let us know, and we can make it happen."

I lift my hand. "You're opening a clothing store?" I feel stupid for asking, but I don't like feeling lost.

"Yes," she says excitedly, nodding her head. "I want to open a clothing store. And for every article sold, we donate to a homeless shelter," she informs me as tears come to her eyes. "I can't believe you guys have been working on this."

I smile as Jaycent leans over and hugs her. I have never been prouder of my sister.

We finish up our meeting, and as I go to walk out, my father stops me. "Ryder?"

"I'll see you guys later," I call out to Jaycent and Becca as they continue. I turn to face my father. "Yes, sir?"

"We need to talk." He gestures to one of the empty seats at the conference table.

"So much for not having a family meeting," I mumble, but I know he heard me.

"This is about business," he says, clearing his throat.

Oh. "Carry on."

"I did some research on the Anderson file and spoke to the company who bought it."

"And?"

"They're willing to sell for the right price."

I smile, wanting that property, and say, "Give me their number."

• • •

I walk into the apartment and place my briefcase on the kitchen counter, listening to the silence. It's dark. I had to work late tonight, as usual, and I'm exhausted.

I remove my suit jacket and place it on the back of the chair at the dining table. I hear Harry meow as he comes down the hall.

I reach down and pick him up. He wears a shirt that says *friendly pussy* across his back, and I chuckle. The little rat is growing on me. Setting him down, I push the already cracked bedroom door open to find Ashlyn already asleep in bed. She's naked, tangled in the sheets. Her back faces me with her laptop open. I walk over to the bed and pick it up, placing it on my lap.

She has employment for the Manhattan area pulled up. They vary from waitress to businesses needing a receptionist.

I look over at her when she stirs, but she stays facing away from me. I go to her browser history and see where Talia's is selling all their current artwork due to closing. Running my hand through my hair, I sigh. Not sure what to do. I want her to do what she loves, but Ashlyn is also not the type of woman to sit around. She'll take a job anywhere, and I hate that. I've come close to telling her several times not to worry, that she doesn't even need a job, but she's not like my mother. She doesn't want to spend her days at the country club catching up on the latest gossip. She wants a job, a career. She wants to be independent. And although that won't be the case as long as she's with me, I can respect it.

I close the laptop and lie back, resting my head against the headboard. Closing my eyes, I run my hand down my face, letting out a frustrated sigh. My mother has literally pissed me off for the last time.

My eyes spring open when I feel a hand on my arm. Looking over, I see a set of very sleepy blue eyes staring up at me. "Hey," I say softly.

She closes them and yawns. "What time is it?"

"Almost eleven," I tell her.

She sighs heavily. I sit up and lean over, placing a soft kiss on her forehead. "Go back to sleep, baby." She's back to sleep before I even pull away.

The following morning, I was up and out of the apartment before Ashlyn was awake. I had an early meeting with Jaycent and a project manager on location. It ran an hour longer than it should have, and by the time I reached the office, I was in a pissed-off mood. My usual attitude lately. I should be getting used to it by now.

I sit in a board meeting, listening to these men discuss their golf game when my assistant comes barging through.

"Kelly?"

Her eyes are wide with fear. "Ashlyn has been in an accident …"

• • •

I rush into the hospital "Ryder?" I see my sister sitting in the waiting room.

"How is she?" I ask, my heart pounding when she stands, and I see tears in her eyes.

"They won't tell me anything. I'm not family …"

I turn to the nurses' station. "Ashlyn Whitaker?"

"Are you family?" she asks.

"Her husband," I lie.

She looks down at her screen. "Room 138 …"

I take off in a mad dash down the hallway, looking for her. I almost pass it in my haste. I yank the curtain back and let out a sigh of relief when I see her sitting up with her legs hanging over the side of the bed. Two police officers stand on the other side of her.

"Ryder?" she asks wide-eyed. "What are you doing here?"

A nurse writes something down on her tablet. "Do you still feel nauseous?" she asks.

"No. I'm better."

The nurse nods. "The Phenergan is working. I'll be back to check on you in a few minutes."

As she leaves, I make my way over to her. She looks up at me with her blue eyes, and I place my hands on her face. "Are you okay?"

"Yes. What are you doing here?" She licks her lips nervously.

"Why do you keep asking me that? Why wouldn't I be here?"

"I called Becca," she explains.

I frown. "Why didn't you call me?"

She sighs. "You were busy at work. I didn't wanna bother you."

My jaw tightens at the thought of her thinking that calling me at work would be a bother. Instead of telling her that, I ask, "What happened?"

She sighs heavily. "I was on my way to meet her for lunch when my cab was rear ended … A woman hit us—"

"Why didn't you call Milton to take you?" I interrupt her.

"Why would I call Milton?" she snaps then her face falls. "I'm sorry. It's just been …"

"I know. No need to apologize."

"Excuse me, miss, but we have everything that we need," the officer says, and she nods. "I have all your information and will contact you if I have any more questions."

They exit her room, and not long after, the nurse returns with the doctor, and I watch her stiffen as if he was going to give us bad news. But he told her everything checked out, and that she would be discharged in the next hour. I made some phone calls to Kelly and told her I wasn't going to be coming back in for the rest of the day and was taking the following day off as well. Even though he assured me she was fine, I still had a feeling she was hiding something. Either from me or the doctor, I didn't know.

ASHLYN

I lie in bed wide-eyed, staring up at the ceiling. My heart racing and my mind wandering. Ryder breathes deeply beside me, his body turned away from me.

Unable to fall asleep, I listen to the sound of silence. The curtains are pulled shut, and it's pitch black. My head is pounding, and I feel sick to my stomach. For more reasons than one.

I'm pregnant!

They told me today at the hospital when I arrived after the incident with the cab. They were taking me for X-rays and asked about the possibility of pregnancy. I started to say no when I realized I never had my period last month, and that wasn't like me. My body is always like clockwork. They took my urine sample and sure enough.

I had just finished my ultrasound when Ryder walked in. I panicked. I didn't know what to do or say. I prayed that the doctor didn't congratulate me because, in all honesty, I didn't know what to say to Ryder. How could I let this happen? We've had unprotected sex so many times. They said I was about eight weeks, yet I couldn't bring myself to tell him.

I just couldn't seem to put two and two together all day until I was in the back of the Escalade while Milton drove us home from the hospital, and Vicki popped in my mind. Suddenly, the words Vicki had said to me in the bathroom at the wedding started to make sense. Only they didn't. She had mentioned Bradley's name, not Ryder's ... And she kept mentioning me drinking and stared at my stomach. Did she know something?

There was only one way to find out, and I needed to know. Very slowly, I lean over Ryder, careful not to touch him, and grab his phone off the nightstand. I unplug his charger and the cord falls to the floor with a soft thud.

I slide it to the right, looking at him while quickly going through his recent messages. I pray I don't see they have been talking, but a part of me needs to know.

I see her name, and my heart stops. Opening it up, I let out a long breath. She's been texting him, but he hasn't been responding. Her messages all read the same.

I need to see you.
Please call me
I'm sorry, Ryder. Please talk to me.

Then the last one she was back to *I need to see you.*
I responded to it with a time and place.
I hold his phone to my chest as I wait for her response. This is gonna screw me in the long run, but I can't think that far ahead right now.

His phone dings, and I bite my lower lip nervously as I look over at him. Still no movement. Very slowly, I pull his phone away from my chest and open her message.

Vicki: *Can't wait to see you :)*

I hate how enthusiastic she is to see him. But then again, that's what I was hoping for.

• • •

Ryder spent two days at home with me, and although it was nice that he cared about me, it also put me on edge. His phone went off nonstop yesterday, and every time, I wondered if it was Vicki. Is she reminding him of their lunch date? Thankfully, she never text him back.

I could tell this morning when he left that he didn't want to. He thought about calling in again, and I had to assure him I was fine. But I really just wanted to run to the bathroom and puke. Morning sickness is a bitch.

Now I sit in a little coffee shop on the Upper West Side waiting for Vicki to show up. Ryder has been blowing up my phone all day to check on me, and although it's sweet, it's also annoying. I've needed silence to think about what I'm going to say, and with him messaging me, I'm not getting it.

I stand when I see her get out of the back of a black Town Car. She is dressed in a pair of skinny jeans, black silk blouse, and black pumps to match. It makes me sick how pretty she is. Too bad she's an evil person. Not wanting to make a scene inside the coffee shop, I meet her outside. She comes to a stop when she looks up and sees me.

"What are you ..." She trails off and then crosses her arms over her chest. "I should have known."

"I need to talk to you," I say sternly.

"I'm not doing this." She spins around and starts to walk back to her car.

"I'm pregnant," I call out.

She comes to a stop and turns back to face me, and a smile slowly spreads across her face in satisfaction. "You sound surprised."

"I am," I say honestly. "But you do not."

She flips her brown hair over her shoulder. "I expected as much."

It doesn't make sense. Why would she think I am pregnant? "And what would make you think that?" I ask with an arch of my brow.

She takes a step toward me. "Have you told Ryder yet?"

I say nothing.

She laughs. "Yeah. I'm guessing you wouldn't want to tell him. Since he's going to leave you the moment he finds out."

Shaking my head, I say, "Ryder isn't that type of guy."

"Oh, honey, you think he's gonna raise another man's child?" she asks still laughing happily.

I take a step closer to her. "Who said it isn't his?"

CHAPTER TWENTY-SIX

RYDER

I'm sitting behind my desk, my phone in my hands texting Ashlyn when she walks right in my door.

"Babe?" I stand, noticing that her cheeks are wet and her blue eyes red. "What's wrong?" I ask coming around my desk.

She sniffs. "I just spoke to Vicki …" Her chest heaves.

"What?" I ask, coming up to her.

"She said she knew …" She covers her mouth with her hand.

"What's wrong?" I ask, placing my hands on her upper arms. I can feel her body physically shaking. "Are you hurt?" She seemed fine yesterday from the accident. "Talk to me," I say, patting her down, looking for bruises and blood.

"She knew all along," she growls, removing her hands from her mouth. "She knew about the pregnancy."

"Vicki's pregnant?" I ask. Fuck, when was the last time I slept with her?

Shaking her head quickly, she then rambles on. "Vicki said Bradley did it."

"Bradley? What does he have to do with this?" She's not making any sense.

Her shoulders hunch forward as she lets out another sob, and then she slaps her hand over her mouth. I step to her, and she lifts her free hand, shoving me away before running to my adjoining bathroom.

I enter behind her as she kneels, vomiting into the toilet. "Jesus!" I hiss coming up behind her. I grab her hair and pull it back the best I can. Her body jerks as she does it again and again. I softly rub her back. "It's okay," I say although I'm freaking out. She was in a wreck just two days ago, and now, she's vomiting. Maybe she has a concussion. "We need to go to the hospital," I tell her, but she just shakes her head before getting sick again.

Five minutes later, she gets up from her knees, and I turn the sink on for her. She splashes her face with cold water before taking some little sips to rinse out her mouth.

"I'm sorry." Her voice is hoarse.

"Don't be sorry," I tell her, pressing my hand to her forehead. She doesn't really feel hot, but she is clammy. "Come sit down." I guide her back into my office and have her sit on the couch then run to get her a cold rag. "Here, hold this on your head."

She complies as she leans her head back against the couch and closes her eyes. "Now tell me again what is going on."

She opens her eyes to look at me, and they fill with tears again. "I got on your phone the other night and sent Vicki a message to come see you. It was the only way I knew she would show up."

Show up where? "I don't understand."

"I needed her to explain a few things she said to me at the wedding." I watch her swallow. "She told me that Bradley had been replacing my birth control pills with sugar pills. And I'm pregnant."

• • •

I pace back and forth in my office to the point I think I may fall through from putting a hole in the floor. Several minutes have gone by since she told me she was expecting. But it feels like hours. My girlfriend is pregnant, and I wish it to be mine, but it's her ex fuck-buddy.

"Say something." I can hear the fear in her voice, but I can't speak yet.

So I stay silent. Just continue to pace. Sugar pills? He tricked her. I knew the bastard was in love with her, but this? What kind of man is he? How could he do this to her?

"You have to believe me," she pleads. "I had no idea …"

"I do," I respond without hesitation.

"Then talk to me. Please," she begs.

I come to a stop and look over at her. Tears still stream down her face as she stares at me wide in fear matching her voice.

It breaks my heart to see her like this. Going over to her, I fall to my knees at her feet and grab her hips, pulling her ass to the edge of the couch. Then I rest my head on her lap and say the one thing I want her to know. "I don't care that it's his. I'll take care of you both." That's all there is to it. I love this woman, and I will love her child as if it's mine!

A sob wracks her body, and I look up to see her placing her hands over her mouth. She looks down at me and shakes her head quickly. "It's yours."

"What?" I ask, pulling away from her.

"The baby is yours." She manages to get out through another sob.

"But I thought …?"

"I'm only eight weeks." She reaches up and wipes the tears from her face. "The doctor checked me in the hospital, and I'm eight weeks. I had been sleeping with Bradley before I met you, yes, but it had been three weeks prior to meeting you in Panama."

My heart rate picks up with excitement. "What are you saying?"

"I'm saying I got pregnant with your baby while on your balcony in the pouring rain. On your birthday."

I watch her speechless. *It's my baby! We're having a baby!*

"I'm so sorry …" she cries.

The door to my office decides to open at that time, but I don't even look to see who it is. "Get out!"

"But, sir …" comes Kelly's voice.

"I said get out!" I snap. The door closes instantly.

I stand and sit down next to her. I take her face in my hands and turn her head to face me. "Don't be sorry. I'm not sorry, Ashlyn."

She closes her eyes and takes a deep breath. "I don't know what to do."

I place my hand on her belly, and I can't help but smile. She looks at me as if I've lost my mind, and maybe I have. This isn't how I planned on starting a family, but as long as it's with Ashlyn, I don't care. "We have a baby," I say simply.

She lets out a noise that sounds like a growl and stands. She turns to face me, her red eyes now narrowed at me. "How can you be so calm about this?" she demands. "How can you agree with what he did?"

I stand. "I don't condone what he did for one second. But I do know that it doesn't matter how it happened; we are going to have a baby."

She runs a hand through her hair, and I can see the emotion change all over her body. Her shoulders pull back, and her nostrils flare. "How could he do this to me?"

"I'm not taking his side, but Vicki is a manipulator. You can't trust everything she says." Her eyes shoot daggers at me. "And how would she find that out? She doesn't even know Bradley."

She places her arms over her chest and starts to pace like I was doing only moments ago. "She had this look of satisfaction on her face when she told me that you would leave me when you found out I was pregnant."

"I wouldn't—"

"And then I said Ryder's not that type of guy," she interrupts me, and I smile at how much this woman believes in us. "Then she said why would he raise another man's baby? I told her the baby was yours. And she got pissed." She shakes her head at herself as if she's replaying the moment in her head. "She just started vomiting at the mouth. Telling me how she was standing inside the lobby of Q's when I chased you out."

I frown. "I never saw her."

"She said she overheard the entire thing and guessed there must be another man. She said she had a choice to follow you and make her move or wait. She chose to wait. That it wasn't hard to pick out the man who was pissed off, and she stopped him in the lobby. They went and had some drinks, and he confessed to her how much he loved me and how he had been switching my pills for months. Fucking. Months," she shouts. "And that they both saw that as their way to get what they wanted. Vicki gets you, and Bradley gets me ..."

I step in front of her and place my hands on her shoulders, bringing her pacing to a stop. "Calm down. Take a breath."

She doesn't. "Ryder, I—"

"Need to rest," I interrupt her again. I gently guide her backwards and when her knees hit the couch she falls onto it. I kneel in front of her again.

She shakes her head. "It all makes sense now. The fact he won't go away. The fact he just won't accept I love you." Her eyes meet mine. "I told him I loved you. That I wanted you." I smile. "But he just kept lingering around." She swallows. "Vicki told me she suspected I was pregnant. So he must have been hanging around thinking I was but thought it was his."

I run a hand down my face and let out a sigh. Fucking bastard.

"That's why she looked at me funny when she saw I was drinking wine at the wedding …" Her words trail off, and her eyes widen. "I've been drinking."

"Baby?" I say, and her wild eyes meet mine. I gently rub her knee. "You said they checked you out at the hospital."

She nods. "Right before you walked in. They said everything looked fine."

"That's why you were so nervous," I state, and she nods as if I asked a question. "What were you so afraid of?"

She lowers her eyes to the floor. "I didn't want you to think I was trying to trap you."

I wrap my arms around her. "I would have never thought that."

She falls into my chest and whispers, "What are we going to do?"

"I already told you," I say, running my hand through her hair. "We're gonna have a baby."

My door opens, and she jerks away from me. My father was storming in, but comes to a stop when he sees Ashlyn wipe the tears from her face.

A silence follows as if no one really knows what to say. Finally, I stand and tell him. "Shut the door, please. We need to talk."

She stayed seated while I filled my dad in on everything that has happened up to this point since the wedding last weekend, and he seemed as calm and relaxed as I am. Ashlyn, on the other hand, was still a little panicked.

He comes to stand in front of me while she sits on the couch. "I need to speak to you privately," he whispers.

I go over to her and take her hand, asking her to stand, and walk her over to the door. "Kelly?" I snap, and she jumps from her desk, running over. "Will you get Ashlyn a water, please?" I ask her.

She nods quickly. "I need to talk to you …" Kelly spots my father behind me through my open door, and I watch him nod at her. She takes Ashlyn's hand and nods back at him.

"What was that?" I ask turning to face him.

"First, let me congratulate you on becoming a dad."

I want to smile at his words, but his tone tells me something very important is going on. "What is it?"

"I made a phone call to the sheriff's office."

I frown. "And?"

"I spoke to my friend, Detective Robert Mores, and he told me that the woman who hit Ashlyn didn't make it. And he also told me that I knew her."

"Who was she?"

"It was Jessica."

My eyes widen. "Are you sure?"

He nods. "And she was in a rental car. That was in your mother's name."

• • •

After talking to my father, I was all kinds of wound up. People were trying to fuck with what's mine, and I don't take kindly to that. But I can only deal with one at this time, so I brought Ashlyn back into my office.

She sits back down on my couch, and I stand in front of her. "Give me Bradley's number."

Her head snaps up and her eyes widen. She starts shaking her head quickly. "No, Ryder. Let it go …"

"Fuck no!" I snap.

She stands. "Don't do this. Please," she begs. "This is what he wants. To break us apart."

I cup her face in my hands and soften my voice. "Nothing is happening to us. I still love you. I still want you. And we're having a baby together. But he doesn't get to walk away after what he has done to you."

She opens her mouth, but I don't give her the chance to speak. "I'm calling him one way or the other. Either you give me his number or I call Vicki."

She narrows her eyes at the mention of her name. "Why would you call her?"

"Because they sound like they're best friends now. And I bet my ass that she has it."

She takes a step back and hangs her head. "She told me he's here in town."

"He's been here all this time?"

Shaking her head, she says, "I guess he has some business here and just comes and goes. But he's here until Friday."

I had called Milton and told him to come pick Ashlyn up. She protested the entire time, but she ended up going with him and back to our apartment while I took a cab ride to Brooklyn.

I should be nervous. I'm about to come face to face with a man who is also in love with her and has been her best friend for three years now. I mean, he does know her better than I do. He's had more time with her. But all I feel is hatred toward him.

I knock on the door, and it opens seconds later. The same man I saw half-dressed in her apartment weeks ago now stands in front of me, once again only half-dressed. A pair of jeans hangs on his hips, the button undone, no shirt, and a glass of something clear in his hand.

"Hello again."

He had been staring at me as if he recognized me but couldn't figure out from where. At the sound of my voice, his eyes narrowed with recognition.

"What the fuck …?"

I walk in, knocking my shoulder into his. He slams the door behind me. "Let me guess. You've come to kick my ass?" he asks with a chuckle as if that's impossible.

I spin around to face him. "No. I'm not gonna kick a dog when it's down."

He snorts. "Down? Listen, buddy, I don't know what Ashlyn's told you but …"

"She is pregnant," I say interrupting him.

I watch as his face turns from surprise to satisfaction. He even fucking smiles, and I have to fist my hands down by my side. I was telling the truth when I said I wasn't here to kick his ass. He's not worth that.

"So you came to tell me you gave up?" he asks with a smirk on his face. "You walked away again?"

"Why would I walk away from my child?" I'm not gonna tell him that I would have stayed with her even if it was his.

He takes a step toward me. "You're lying."

"I have nothing to lose." I place my hands out wide. "I have the girl after all."

"You fucking bastard," he snaps. "I'm not leaving her. I won't stop until I have her.""You think she wants you?" I ask with a laugh, and that just pisses him off more. "She knows that you switched her birth control pills." His eyes widen. "She knows you tried to trap her." I look him up and down with disgust. "You are a sorry excuse for a man."

I start to walk toward the door when his words stop me. "You don't know what it was like." I turn to face him. "Man after man," he growls. "To watch her come crawling back to me but not give me all of her." I hate that he makes it sound as if she needed him. "She fucking used me …""You sound like a fucking chick."

"I love her!" he shouts. "When she told me over Christmas break that she was going to move to New York after school, I didn't believe her. Thought she would change her mind, but as time went on, I realized I was gonna lose her. I needed a reason to make her stay. She just needed to believe we were meant to be together.""You're delusional."

"I needed to her to see that she had feelings for me," he snaps.I shake my head. "You were supposed to be her best friend. But you're nothing but a fraud."

"I don't expect you to understand. You walked away as if she meant nothing to you," he shouts.

"I made a mistake," I snap. "But I guarantee I won't make that mistake twice. If she told me today she wanted you, I would fight for her like a fucking man."

He takes a step toward me. "You think you have everyone fooled?"

"What is that supposed to mean?"

"When I refused to leave and went back to see her, your friend wouldn't let me enter the apartment. He told me that you loved her and that you just needed time to come around." *Jaycent said that about me?* "She believed it too. She fell so hard for all your bullshit. Then I met one who sees through all your lies. Vicki told me all about you and how you use women. How you need them to make you feel superior. How she's your true love, and you always run back to her ... And how you were going to marry her ..."

I throw my head back, letting out a laugh I can't keep in. "I've heard enough," I say, still laughing as his brown eyes shoot daggers at me. I slap him on the shoulder, and his body tenses. "I just wanted to say thanks for making me a dad with the woman who I plan on marrying."

"You son of a bitch!" he shouts.

I walk over to the door and open it. A brunette stands there with her right hand up as if she was about to knock on the door. "Vicki," I say with a smirk.

"Ryder?" She gasps. "What are you ...?"

I look over my shoulder at Bradley, and he still holds his glass in his right hand, eyes narrowed on me and nostrils flared. "Karma is a bitch, man," I say, referring to Vicki. He has no idea what he has gotten in to with that woman. Then I walk out, unable to contain my laughter.

ASHLYN

"You're kidding?" Becca gasps.

"No," I say with a giddy laugh. "We're having a baby." God, that sounds so crazy to say. I still can't believe it.

She jumps up from the couch and runs toward me, hugging me tightly.

Ryder and I spent all night last night going back and forth on whether we should tell anyone about the baby. I did some research on pregnancy while we laid in bed, and it said most miscarriages happen within the first twelve weeks. I told Ryder we should wait until we crossed that point just in case. He shut the laptop on me and said I had read enough. And then he brought up another good point. Vicki already knew, which meant his mom probably knew. And we had told his father yesterday when he came in and found me a bawling mess. And I wanted to be the one to tell Becca. She is my best friend, after all. So, not wanting to chance someone else beating me to it, we called them over tonight after Ryder got home and told them the good news.

"Congratulations, man," Jaycent says, hugging his friend and slapping him on the back.

Ryder pulls away smiling, and I can't help but stare at the way his green eyes light up. I think back to the way he danced with the little girl at the wedding and how natural he looked. He's gonna be a great father. He looks so proud. "I hope you plan on selling baby clothes in your store, Becca," Ryder tells her.

"Store?" I ask confused.

She bites her bottom lip nervously. "I'm opening up a store here in Manhattan."

I smile. "That's awesome."

Jaycent throws his arm over her shoulder and has that same smile Ryder wears. "She's being modest." He kisses her on the cheek. "For every article sold, she is going to donate one to a homeless shelter," he beams.

Tears come to my eyes, and my throat tightens. Becca's face falls. "I'm so sorry I didn't tell you ..."

I shake my head. "It's not that." Trying to finish, I take a deep breath, but the tears just come faster.

Ryder pulls me to his chest, and I can feel it vibrate against mine as he tries to hold in his laughter before he says, "Pregnancy hormones."

They all laugh, and I slap his arm. He just laughs harder and then kisses me on the head. "I think this is a good time," Ryder says excitedly.

I pull away, unable to contain my laughter. "I agree, babe."

Jaycent and Becca look at one another and then back at us. "Something else you guys wanna tell us?"

Ryder claps his hand and says, "We have a surprise for you."

"Go get it," I say, pushing on his arm. I'm so giddy.

Ryder leaves our living room, and they look at each other nervously. And I say, "You're gonna love it."

"Love what?" Becca asks just as Ryder reenters the living room.

He holds a big cage in his hands covered with a pink blanket. "What the hell is that?" Jaycent asks.

Ryder sets it down on the floor and takes a step back. "Well, open it."

They seem a little nervous, but after a long second, Becca reaches down and pulls off the pink blanket.

"SURPRISE!" Ryder and I both say.

"You have got to be kidding me." Jaycent says and then cracks up laughing.

"I don't understand." Becca looks back and forth between Ryder and Jaycent.

Jaycent leans down and opens the cage and then picks up the floppy eared bunny. "It's Nibbles!" I say.

"She's alive and well, and she's all yours," Ryder says, nodding his head at them, having way too much fun.

I laugh. "I gotta say, Jaycent, you put on a good show even though I was mad at the time."

They didn't stay long after that, leaving us alone in our apartment. We stand in the entryway after telling them bye, and I step to him. He places his arms around me and leans his head against my forehead, and I let out a long sigh. "We're having a baby." It's the first time I've said it out loud to him and not panicked.

"How do you feel about that?"

My heart pounds against his chest, and I know he can feel it. "Terrified," I admit.

"Don't be," he whispers. "I'm going to take care of you both."

I let out a shaky breath. "You're too good to me."

"I love you," he says, pressing his lips to mine.

• • •

"Shit!" I curse while I stand in the closet trying to find something to wear. Ryder's side looks well put together. He has his button ups hung in order by color. His jackets and slacks are mainly gray and black, also done by color.

My side looks like a disaster. I even have clothes on the floor. I decide on a black and white dress. Can't go wrong with black and white.

I hurry to dress and try to flat iron my curly hair, but it's no use. So instead of wearing it down, I put it up in a tight bun. Being pregnant has already changed my schedule, halting my life for about thirty minutes this morning while I hovered around the toilet. Ryder tried to help me out, but I ended up yelling at him to get the hell out and just go to work. Having the man you love watch you vomit isn't how you want him to see you first thing in the morning.

So I got a late start.

I just step out the front door of the Q's and see Milton opening the back door for me when my phone rings. "Hey, babe," I say, sliding in.

"Hey," he says softly.

"What's wrong?" I ask, knowing his tone is off.

He lets out a long sigh. "I've been thinking."

Panic rises. Has he changed his mind about the baby? "And?"

"You don't have to work."

I let out a breath. "Ryder—"

"Just hear me out," he interrupts me. "I don't want you to work."

My brows rise. "Are you saying I can't work?"

"No. That's not what I mean." He sighs. "I just …"

"Ryder, I want a career."

He's silent for a moment. "I know, it's just …" His work phone rings in the background, and he tells me he'll call me back.

My interview was shit! I sat in there talking to the older man about how I had worked at Talia's and my college degree. He didn't seem to care much about my potential. And I really didn't care. Ryder's words just kept bouncing around in my head.

He didn't want me to work.

It didn't take a scientist to know why. Nannies raised him and Becca. He doesn't want that for his children, and I understood that. I don't want them raised by nannies either. But women do it all the time—have children and a career—so why can't I?

When I arrived back at our apartment, I called the one person who could give me the only advice that mattered.

She answered on the first ring. "Hi, Mom."

"Hey, honey," she says excitedly. "How is your day going?"

Fucking pregnancy hormones have tears building in my eyes. Shit, I'm only eight weeks into it. How will I be by the time I'm eight months?

"Honey?" she asks, and her voice is now full of concern. "What's wrong?"

A dam breaks. "I'm pregnant." I couldn't stop. I told her about me and Ryder's breakup, and then how I got pregnant and what Bradley had done.

"Next time I see him, I'm gonna hit him with a shovel," she snaps, making me laugh. Then her tone changes. "How are you feeling?"

"I'm nauseated all the time. And I can't stop crying over everything,"

She gives a little laugh. "Oh, pregnancy takes over your body, and you're along for the ride." She makes a joke, and I laugh.

"Can I ask you a question?" "Of course."

"Did you ever want to quit your job and stay home with me?"

She's quiet for a long time, and I look at my phone to make sure she's still on the other end. Finally, she speaks. "I took six months off when I had you."

"You did?" I ask not knowing that.

"Yes. Your memaw was sick." My father's mother. "And we were paying for her in-home care. I had every intention of quitting when I got pregnant with you. After what had happened to Henry, I didn't want you out of my sight. But staying home just wasn't in the cards for us."

"Ryder wants me to stay home. But I've always seen myself as a woman who had a career and could also have a family."

"Honey, you don't have to have a career to be considered a hard-working woman. Being a parent is the hardest job in the world. And women who are stay-at-home mothers aren't any less of a woman than ones who have a career and children." She sighs. "Did you call to ask my opinion on the matter?"

"Yes."

"Put the career on hold. It will always be there, honey. That degree you got isn't going anywhere. But your child? I know nine months seems so far away, but it will be here before you know it. And then every year just goes by faster and faster. Then they're graduating college and moving far away from you." I hear her sniff. "My advice is to be a mother and a wife first. There will always be jobs available."

CHAPTER TWENTY-SEVEN

RYDER

I walk into the apartment, and this amazing smell of chicken and cheese hits my senses.

I look over at the kitchen table as Ashlyn places a dish in the center of it. She looks up at me and smiles. "How was your day, sweetie?"

"Good." I nod to the table. "What's up with this?"

She rubs her hands on my t-shirt that she wears. "I wanted to cook you dinner."

"Are we celebrating something? Other than the baby?" I ask, and she laughs.

"Something like that."

She comes up to me and wraps her arms around me. "You got the job?" I say the only other thing that comes to mind.

"Yes, they called me about an hour ago and told me it was mine if I wanted it."

I smile, but it's forced. Can she notice? I reach up and press a few loose blond strands behind her ear. "Congratulations, baby."

"I told them no."

"What?"

Her smile widens as she wraps her arms around my neck. "I told them no," she repeats. "I thought long and hard about it today, and dreams change."

I can't hide the smile on my face. "What is your dream now?"

"To be yours. To be here for you when you get home with dinner on the table and to be a mother to your children."

I arch a brow. "Children? We're having more?"

"As many as you want."

I reach down and grab her ass, lifting her off the ground. "We should get to working on that."

She throws her head back, laughing. "There's already one baby in there. We have to wait to make the next one."

"Practice makes perfect," I say, carrying her off to our bedroom.

• • •

I'm standing in the bathroom when I look out the open door and see her sitting on our bed on her laptop. I spit out my toothpaste. "What are you looking at?"

"Art," she says simply.

Placing my toothbrush in the holder, I walk out and fall onto the bed beside her. "What kind of art?"

"Talia's is having an auction this weekend. They are selling all the art left in the gallery."

"I bet their artists were pissed about them closing," I say.

She shrugs. "Not sure. I haven't spoken to any of them. But I can't say they would be happy." She scrolls down to the bottom of the page and clicks on a picture of what looks like to be a spider web but each piece of string is a different color. "This is my favorite."

As she begins to tell me about the differences in the colors, I realize I've never spoken to her about art. We were living together and expecting a baby, yet I never asked her about her true passion.

I sit back with my head against the headboard as she snuggles up next to me, showing me one picture at a time, and I just smile at her. I ask questions here and there, and her face lights up as she takes me through all the pictures. I realize I can't let her give up on her dreams. She was right when she said that dreams change, but that doesn't mean you have to give up on one for another.

She's selfless—giving up something she dreams of to make me happy. And I can't allow that.

"Yes," I tell the woman on the phone while I sit at my desk.

"Mr. O'Kane?" She confirms my name.

"Yes, ma'am."

"Okay. I have your information and will let you know when they're ready."

"Thank you," I say, hanging up just as the door opens to my office and my father steps in. "Good morning," I say with a big smile.

He looks at me as if I've lost my mind. I like to think I'm beyond that now. "What can I do for you this morning?" I ask.

He snorts and runs a hand through his hair. He tosses an envelope onto my desk, and I pick it up. "What's this?"

"Jackie just gave this to me. She said that you had her on a wild goose chase."

I nod, eying the envelope and getting a sinking feeling in the pit of my stomach. "Have you looked inside?"

"Yes," comes his clipped answer.

I look up to meet his eyes, and he nods his head once. "You were right, son. And I have already put things in motion."

I grind my teeth and pull the papers out to read over. My eyes scan over the words and figures. I find myself smiling even through the anger. "Well, looks like you're gonna get your divorce after all."

ASHLYN

"Where are we going?" I ask, reaching up to the blindfold.

"Don't," he says, grabbing my hand and pulling it away; he intertwines our fingers together so I can't remove it.

"Is this some new fetish of yours?" I ask with a laugh.

"Something like that," he answers with a laugh of his own. "Just a little longer."

I huff but smile. He's up to something. He's been this way for a month now. Anxious. I just figured it was work, but I realized it was more than that when I woke up this morning and he had a blindfold in his hands. I thought we were gonna have some kinky morning sex, but he obviously had something else in mind.

I feel Milton bring the Escalade to a stop, and Ryder helps me out of the SUV. "Just a few more steps," he says, and I can hear the smile in his voice. I think he's more excited about whatever it is than I am.

I walk up a few stairs and then hear a door open. Then my heels are clapping against the floor, and it echoes loudly. I frown. *Where has he brought me?*

I feel him standing behind me, and then his fingers are untying the knot to the blindfold. He removes it, and I open my eyes. It takes a second for them to adjust, and when I do, I frown. "I don't understand ..." *I say, turning to face him. He wears a sly smile on his beautiful face, and his green eyes shine. I'm confused.*

My mouth opens and then closes, looking around the inside of Talia's gallery. All the previous art still on the walls and the same crystal vase he sent me with red roses now sits on my old desk. But only this time, there are two vases with a dozen red roses in each.

I turn back to face him. "What are we doing here?" I ask.

He still wears that smile. "I wanna show you something." Taking my hand, he pulls me over to one of the white walls to look at a painting. I look over at it and notice it right away. It's the house where we stayed at in the Hamptons. It has the ocean behind it, and a sold sign out front ...

He steps up beside me. I look over at him. "You bought it to sell it?" I ask, wondering why he would tell me this way.

"Close," he says, smiling. "I bought it. For us."

My heart starts to pick up. He didn't. Did he ...? "We're keeping it?"

"You said you liked it."

"I loved it," I say, and tears sting my eyes.

He turns to face me, and I do the same. He grabs my hand and kneels on his right knee. My heart pounds as I gasp.

He just smiles up at me. "Ashlyn, you told me that dreams change. And I realized that mine changed the moment I met you. I didn't know I could love someone as much as I love you." He pulls a box from the inside pocket of his suit jacket, and my breath catches when I see the Tiffany box. "I will spend the rest of my life making all your dreams come true. I just ask that you make my dream come true by becoming my wife."

I can't speak from the knot in my throat and the pounding of my heart. He's nothing but a blurry mess before me, and I start nodding my head quickly. I feel him slip the ring on my finger, and then he stands, picking me up and spinning me around as a half-laugh, half-sob finally breaks free.

He sets me down, and I grab his face. "I can't believe you bought that house for us," I say still in awe.

He places his forehead on mine. "Baby, I bought this gallery for you too." I gasp. "It's all yours. I told you, every dream you've ever had I'm gonna make come true." Then his lips are on mine.

EPILOGUE

RYDER

Three months later

A shrill scream wakes me in the middle of the night. "Ashlyn?" I ask, blinking and trying to adjust my eyes to the darkness in our apartment. We still live here throughout the week. Only staying at the house in the Hamptons on the weekend.

"Ryder!" She gasps, and then she screams again.

I fumble to find the lamp on the nightstand and knock a few things to the floor before it comes on.

"Ashlyn?" I ask, turning to face her. Her eyes are closed and tears run down her face as she bends over the best she can with her pregnant belly. "Baby, what's wrong?" I ask, my panic rising and already grabbing for my phone that I had knocked to the floor.

She sits up, and I can see the sheets where she sits are soaked. Her blue eyes meet mine and tears run down her cheeks. "Something's wrong." She gasps.

I start shaking my head quickly. It can't be … It's too early … She throws her head back, letting out a cry so loud it makes my ears ring.

We crash through the hospital doors of the ER at Saint Meds. Milton runs to the nurses' station while I hold Ashlyn in my arms. She's pale and sweating as she cries in pain.

A nurse grabs a gurney, and I place her on it before they push her off into a room, telling me I have to wait out here. Moments later, my sister and Jaycent arrive followed by my father and his girlfriend. Her parents both rush through the door.

We sit out in the waiting room for I don't know how long when I see a doctor coming toward us. I jump up as he comes up to us.

"My wife, Ashlyn O'Kane ..." I stop, needing to swallow the lump in my throat as I twirl the wedding band on my finger.

He looks me in the eyes and sighs. "I'm sorry ... we did everything we could..." And I take off in a mad dash down the hallway to where I know she is.

Four months later

"You may kiss the bride."

The smile on her face as she looks at me makes my chest ache. The most beautiful woman in the world just said yes to me.

I place my hands in her blond hair that she wears down in big curls and pull her to me. She places her hands over mine and closes her eyes just as my lips touch hers.

A baby cries out, interrupting the dream I was having of our wedding on the beach behind our Hamptons home. I get out of bed and make my way across the hallway to her nursery to find my daughter wide awake in her crib, kicking her little feet and speaking in a language I haven't mastered yet.

"Hey, gorgeous," I say, picking her up and holding her to my bare chest as I move to the glider in the corner.

"Shh," I say, rubbing her back over her little pink onesie as she fusses. "How would you like to hear a story?" She cries louder, and I take that as a sign she wants to hear how I met her mommy. "One warm afternoon, I met a gorgeous blond on the beach," I say, and a smile spreads across my face as I remember those big blue eyes and feisty attitude. "And she was gorgeous," I say, closing my eyes as her cries start to quiet. "She had this look of pure beauty. So rare. She had these eyes that matched the ocean and this smile." I sigh. "It was blinding like the sun. When she looked at me, I knew right then and there that she was gonna get anything she asked for." I open my eyes and look down to see her little blue eyes closed and her little lips parted as her breathing evens out. "I just didn't know that she was gonna give me more than I could ever give her …"

"You gotta get a new love story."

I look up at the doorway and see my wife leaning up against it with a smile on her face, dressed in nothing but my t-shirt that she loves to wear. "Why? Ours is my favorite."

She laughs softly. "Why didn't you wake me?"

I stand, cradling her to my chest. "I don't mind getting up with her." I place her back in her crib as Ashlyn comes up beside me, leaning into me.

"She's so gorgeous."

I wrap my arms around her. "Just like her mommy."

She sighs and whispers. "It's after mid night. Happy birthday, Ryder."

ASHLYN

"Happy birthday, Ryder," I say for the fifth time today, leaning over to kiss him in the back seat of the Escalade while Milton drives us toward Fifth Avenue. I have a big surprise party planned for him tonight and I can't wait to see the look on his face when he sees who all want to share this special day with him.

"Thank you, my love," he says with a smile and then leans over to give me a chaste kiss.

Julianna, our daughter, makes a noise, and he leans down to kiss both her cheeks. It's crazy how one year ago today we stood outside his penthouse suite in Panama. And now he's my husband and we have a child.

Things have been going great. I have the gallery up and running. Between being a wife, mother, and business owner, life is hectic. But we got a routine down, and it is working for us. Ryder hasn't been at the office as late anymore. He even works from home one day a week now that his father doesn't have to step down to make his mother happy. She is in jail. Timothy's assistant, Jackie, had found checks written to a company that didn't exist, and after doing some research, she found out that Jessica and his assistants before her had been helping Gwenda embezzle from the company. So, needless to say, she went to prison, Timothy got his divorce, and somehow, he convinced Gwenda to sign away her parental rights to Maggie, so Rosie could make it official and adopt her. Mr. O'Kane took all the money that his ex-wife had embezzled and put it in a trust fund for Maggie to have when she turns twenty-one. That little girl is set for life. Ryder never came out and told me, but I know Gwenda was behind my car wreck. I overheard him talking to his father about it one night on the phone. I'm not sure what kind of charges she got for that, and I never cared to ask. She is out of our lives for good and can't hurt any of us anymore.

My mother and father quit their jobs in Seattle and moved here to New York while I was pregnant. Becca moved in with Jaycent, and since the apartment we had moved into was paid for, she sold it to my parents for a price they could afford. I love that they are so close to me and Ryder. My mother helps me run the gallery. My dad got a job at a practice here and spends most of his off time playing golf with Mr. O'Kane. Timothy is in a serious relationship. I actually set them up. She came into the gallery, and I couldn't help but think of how much they would hit it off. Her kids are also grown and live in California. She just seemed so lonely. Despite Ryder's objections, I set them up on a blind date. I'm pretty sure Mr. O'Kane fell immediately. I know he plans to propose in a few weeks when he takes her on vacation to Paris. She's always wanted to go there. I'm glad that after all these years he gets to have his happily ever after.

I never spoke to Bradley again even though he crosses my mind from time to time. I mean, me and Ryder have a little girl because of him, but I never have that desire to call him. Or talk to him. Becca told me that she heard he was seeing Vicki. And my first thought was God help this town—what those two are capable of—the city may catch fire. But I do wish them the best.

I had been pregnant with twins. It was just one more surprise we had. But only one survived. I lied there in the hospital bed while Ryder and I said our final goodbye to our son. The loss of one of our babies was the tragedy in our love story. It was hard on both of us. I cried for weeks, and Ryder still finds me crying at times. I don't think the pain of losing a child ever goes away. My mother and Becca both came and stayed with us at the apartment and helped me with our daughter, Julianna. I named her after Ryder's first name—Julian.

"We're here!" Milton announces as he pulls up to the curb.

Ryder gets our daughter out of her car seat as I look down at my phone. I have two messages. One from my mother telling me they are on their way. And the other is from Timothy letting me know they, too, will be here soon. Milton opens the door for me. We make our way up the steps to the grand opening of Becca's clothing store. A red ribbon drapes across the front, and I spot Becca along with a news crew over by Jaycent.

Ryder hands Julianna off to me as Becca spins around to see me. She rubs her growing belly and then heads for us. She too is expecting a little girl. I hope our daughters are as close as we are. Even if they are gonna be family. Just because you're family doesn't mean you'll be friends; the O'Kanes have taught me that.

"Hello, princess," she says, taking my daughter from my arms.

"This looks amazing, Becca," I say to her with a smile. The store was finished about two months ago, but it took time to pick an opening date and for her to get all the media here so she could show the world how big her heart is.

"I'm so nervous," she whispers.

"Don't be. It's gonna be awesome!"

"Can I get a picture?" a man asks as he comes up to us with a camera.

"One second. Let me get my husband and brother. Babe? Ry?" Becca calls out, and Jaycent comes running down the steps toward us followed by Ryder. All four of us stand side by side as Ryder takes our baby girl and smiles proudly at the camera. This reminds me of the picture I have sitting up in my office at the gallery. It was taken the day I opened it six months ago.

"Say cheese," he says.

Ryder wraps his free arm around my shoulders and pulls me to his side before kissing my hair. "I love you," he whispers.

I smile, looking down at my heart-shaped diamond wedding ring as the sun reflects off it and can't help but laugh. I always thought love was selfish, but Ryder has taught me that true love is selfless. He was also right about our love story; it is better than Romeo and Juliet because we choose to live for one another.

THE END

ACKNOWLEDGMENTS

First I would like to thank Kelly Tucker. The most organized person I have ever met. I drive her nuts, but she loves it and I love her too. She's the best assistant a girl could have and without her I would go insane.

I would like to thank Jenny Sims, my wonderful editor. I've been working with her for four years now and she's awesome!

To my cover designer, Tracie Douglas with Dark Water Covers. Thank you for making me another gorgeous cover!

I want to thank my lovely betas, Genice Cassidy, Stephanie Anderson-Cochran, Gemma Garcia, Jessica Lewis, Leslie Sims, Amy Cortez Rangel, Jackie Ashmead, Kayla Bartolet, and Kelly Tucker. Thank you so much for taking the time to read my book and your suggestions. Thank you so much for taking time to read my book and giving me your feedback.

I want to thank The Sinful Side for pimping and I love these bitches! This lovely group of ladies are awesome at pimping and making me laugh. It's amazing how you can become so close with someone when they live halfway around the world. These girls are my sisters, and I love them very much.

To all of my family who has spread the word about my books and shared my author page; I'm very lucky to have such a supportive family. I love them all.

And last but not least, my readers. Thank you for taking a chance and wanting to read my books. I hope that you all love them as much as I do.

ABOUT THE AUTHOR

Shantel is a Texas-born girl who now lives in Tulsa, Oklahoma with her high school sweetheart, who is a wonderful, supportive husband and their five-year-old little princess. She loves to spend time cuddled up on the couch with a good book.

She is the Amazon Bestselling author of the Undescribable series and is currently working on her fourth book Unforgettable, which is set to release September 23rd. She considers herself extremely lucky to get to be a stay at home wife and mother. Going to concerts and the movies are just a few of her favorite things to do. She hates coffee but loves wine. She and her husband are both huge football fans, college and NFL. And she has to feed her high heel addiction by shopping for shoes weekly.

Although she has a passion for writing, her family is most important to her. She loves spending evenings at home with her husband and daughter, along with their cat and dog.

For more information about the author and her books, visit:

To contact Shantel Tessier:
Email: ShantelTessierauthor@gmail.com
Website: shanteltessierauthor.com
Facebook: @ShantelTessierAuthor

Printed in Great Britain
by Amazon